Alastair Davie is a retired corporate publicist for leading US and Canadian corporations. He was born and educated in the UK and worked for the *Financial Times* and Reuters before moving to the United States in 1976.

He combines his fascination for modern history and his creative ability to weave an enthralling story so that the reader learns how historic events affected the ordinary person.

To my wife, Linda, who encouraged me throughout with her thoughtful suggestions and comments. Also, I dedicate this novel to my daughters, Leslie and Kathleen, and my grandchildren in the hope they will appreciate the sacrifice of thousands of people in World War II who made it possible for them to live in the peace and prosperity they enjoy today.

Alastair B. Davie

DESPERATE CONSPIRACY

AUSTIN MACAULEY
PUBLISHERS LTD.

A CIP catalogue record for this title is available from the British Library.

ISBN 9781786129840 (Paperback)
ISBN 9781786129857 (Hardback)
ISBN 9781786129864 (E-Book)
www.austinmacauley.com

First Published (2016)
Austin Macauley Publishers Ltd.
25 Canada Square
Canary Wharf
London
E14 5LQ

Prologue

Englefield Green, UK, August 1992

When I look back at what could have been, I shudder. My feelings are a mixture of relief and anger at the remembrance of what could have happened to change the course of world history some fifty years ago. My recollections are tinged also with bitterness towards those who would undermine the integrity of the British government in a time of the greatest danger the country has ever faced since the invasion of William the Conqueror in 1066. In many cases the attitude of the people involved was arrogance, fanaticism and narcissism born of privilege.

To me, and other men and women of my age, the Second World War was the defining moment of our young lives. But all would have been for naught if a desperate conspiracy had succeeded. It would have invalidated the sacrifices that countless people in Europe had endured and cost so many their lives.

These thoughts come to mind every time I make a pilgrimage to the Royal Air Force Memorial, which is set west of London on a hill that overlooks Runneymede and the River Thames. I like to sit on one of the benches in the garden and look down at Windsor to the left with its castle and bustling Egham to my right. I go there to remember those who I once knew and who are no more. Many might accuse me of nostalgia for what was, but it truly is a deep, innate sadness for the loss of the potential that these men and women had. Their hopes for the future were snuffed out. You'd think, as the years have passed, I would be over his melancholy. After all, I have a wife I worship, two wonderful children who have been successful in their chosen careers and a grandson whom I adore. You'd think I would put all this behind me, but the conspiracy has stuck in my craw despite the passage of time.

I am Dr. Roger Lawson, an eighty year old retired doctor. I became a general practitioner in the village of Englefield Green in 1947 after being demobbed from the Royal Air Force. My practice covered that village of eleven thousand and some patients came also from nearby towns such as Egham, Ascot and Virginia Water. My wife, Helen, is a registered nurse and had worked for a time at the King Edward VII hospital in Windsor until she retired as a ward sister in 1955 to look after our two children, Douglas and Rachel. Douglas is now in his mid-thirties and is a managing director of a computer firm. He is not married, although he has had many girlfriends and a fiancée at one time. Rachel is two years older and is a headmistress at a girls' school in Ascot. She is married to a professor at Royal Holloway in nearby Egham, which is a college of University of London, and they have a son, Michael.

Helen and I have lived in our eighteenth century cottage for over forty years. It is about half a mile from the RAF Memorial. As retirees, we go for walks, visit the theatre in Windsor, read a lot, travel and fiddle around in our garden. The heavy work in the garden, though, is done by Bert our gardener who I brought into the world some forty years previously. It's strange that by the end of my career I was delivering babies of mothers who I had delivered twenty or so years previously as well as their grandparents.

I am really astonished how time speeds along at a seemingly faster pace when you get older. When you're young, life seems to go at such a slow march. At middle age it turns into a quick march and when you retire it breaks into a run.

The ordinariness of our lives now belies our past and the traumas that underlie our story. Hidden away in our past is a story that might surprise and fascinate you. Like many of our generation, we don't talk about what we did in the Second World War and, like the Bletchley code breakers, we now need to tell our story before it is too late.

The events during the war had gnawed at me over the years, but I still wrestled with indecision about revealing what I knew. My self-absorbed behaviour had affected my relationship with Helen as I had become extremely introspective. She had pressed me to work through these nightmares and to focus on the future, but I couldn't, try as I might. I knew in my heart it was about time I got over the unspeakable traumas we had experienced. Helen had but I hadn't. Then events forced me to face up to my dreads and move on as my family put pressure on me to change.

My thoughts on this day were rudely interrupted as I was brought back to the present by the noise of the jet engines of an airplane as it flew low towards Heathrow Airport, which is about four miles away to the east. I started to walk back home along Cooper's Hill Lane with my mongrel dog Annie, who always accompanied me on these jaunts. We make this walk at least once a week and we are often accompanied by Helen, my companion now for almost fifty years.

I enjoyed my walk in the August sun and I worked up quite an appetite for afternoon tea. I like the weather at this time of year. It is warm and rain seems to keep away. In another month the weather will change with rains and winds as winter approaches.

As I walked towards the cottage, I saw Rachel's car parked in the driveway and I was hopeful that she had brought my grandson, Michael, with her for afternoon tea. Michael was a young man of sixteen who was at Charterhouse, one of the leading public schools in England. He had grown like a weed in the past two years and now stood at six feet. But he was gangly with a mop of brown hair and his face showed the after effects of acne, which he had a terrible bout of when he was fourteen and fifteen. Socially he was very quiet until you got him talking about his favourite subject, which was history, particularly medieval history. He had been on a number of digs of old battlefields and came back talking enthusiastically about what he had found. He was very bright and his teachers expected him to go to either the University of Cambridge or Oxford.

Annie and I went to the back door of the cottage where I took off my walking shoes in the mud room and I wiped her paws and tummy. We walked through the kitchen to the living room and Annie pounced on Michael who made a big fuss of her.

"Well this a pleasant surprise to see you both," I said, as Helen handed me a cup of tea. "To what do we owe this visit?"

"Roger, they don't need a reason to come and see us!" Helen chided me.

"That's true," I said, but I remember the last time Rachel had visited us she had asked for a loan for Michael's school fees. We gladly said we would pay these, but it had made me suspicious in case there was an ulterior motive to this visit. I was known for my suspicious mind, which had served me well in the past.

"So what are you doing this term at school, Michael?" I asked.

"French has become harder and science is worse. I think I want to study history at university; it fascinates me. For example, we are learning about the World Wars One and Two in history. We are studying their causes and some of the awful things that went on."

"Yes, they were bad times alright, weren't they Helen?" I said.

"All of us were affected by the hardship war causes," Helen responded. "We had rationing in this country until 1950 and many people here had lost their homes and everything they had. This country was broke but, thanks to the Americans and their Marshall Plan, we were able to pull through."

"Were you in the war, Granddad?" Michael asked.

"Well, yes, in a minor way. I was a doctor in the RAF here in England and then in the Bahamas," I replied.

"Roger, tell the boy about your medal," chimed in Helen.

"I didn't know Dad had a medal," said a surprised Rachel.

"He doesn't tell anyone but he won an OBE for gallantry. Go on Roger, tell them!"

"It was nothing really. I helped pull some airmen out of a burning plane that was all," I responded between my clenched teeth, as I was loathe to talk about this.

"You did it by yourself and got badly burnt as a result. You see the scars on his neck and face, and have you always wondered about his limp. Roger, you saved those men's lives. You shouldn't keep this to yourself.

Your family has a right to know! Why don't you show them the medal?"

"Please Granddad," Michael pleaded.

"What I did and went through had nothing on the sacrifices many made in that wretched war. It's not something I want to talk about."

After more pleadings from my family, I got out the medal and showed it to them. When they had all seen it, I put it in my pocket and said angrily, "Now can we change the subject?"

At this, the silence in the room was palpable. No one said anything and then Rachel began 'happy' talk about what was going on with the governors at her school and she told some amusing stories about her staff. This cut through the ice-cold atmosphere.

When Michael and Rachel had left, Helen started to give me a hard time when we were washing the dishes in the kitchen.

"I know you too well Roger. Ever since you retired you've had time on your hands and your past is festering. You are bad-tempered and getting more so. Talk about post-traumatic stress, you're certainly a candidate for that. You need to get it out of your system. You can't go on reliving the past!" she said angrily.

"Rubbish. You don't know what you are talking about."

"You've got to do something about it. Otherwise it will only get worse. You're a really grumpy old man these days!"

"Well I'm not going to a shrink!"

"I don't know why not. It might help."

Silence.

"Why don't you write it all down? No one is going to see it," she suggested after a while. I just grunted in response.

We planned to have dinner with the Johnsons that evening. Derek was a rear gunner in Lancaster Bombers during the war and I had met him at a RAF reunion dinner twenty or so years before. We got on well and we had been seeing him and his wife, Laura, for many years. Derek was my best friend and we had become closer when I had helped him in a professional capacity after he had developed lung cancer some years back.

After dinner in a local restaurant, the four of us drove back to our cottage for a nightcap. While the women were in the living room talking, Derek and I settled down in the study with a couple of brandies.

"I couldn't help feeling a chilly breeze in the restaurant tonight blowing between you and Helen. Is everything alright?" he asked. "Tell me to mind my own business if you like, but we have been friends for a long time and if I can help you know I will."

"Thanks Derek. I am sorry we ruined your evening, but Helen and I had a row this afternoon." Then I told him about it, including her suggestion about writing everything down.

Derek thought about this for a minute or two and took a sip from his brandy.

"Perhaps Helen has a point. Many former RAF men I have known who had great traumas in their war have written books about their experiences and I think it was cathartic for them. Anyway, I'd like to hear about what you did in the Bahamas."

"Hmm. I suppose it won't hurt put a few notes down, but I can't write book because I haven't got the skills to do so."

"I've got an idea, Roger. A young friend of mine is a World War II history buff and a darn good writer, he might be interested in working with you to develop your story. He's more interested in the effects the war had on individuals rather than campaigns or geopolitical strategies.

"I tell you what, here's his name, address and telephone number," Derek said as he wrote down the information on a piece of paper. "Why don't you write to him and at least talk to him on the phone about it?"

"Oh I don't know. It's not a very interesting story anyway."

I was still hesitant, believing that nobody in this day and age would be interested in hearing about what happened so long ago.

The next morning after breakfast, I went into my study and switched on the computer Douglas had given me for Christmas last year. He had given me some lessons and I had used it for writing letters. I sat looking at the screen. I was hesitant because I was still not sure that this was a good idea.

I sat there continuing to look at the screen and nothing was coming to mind. I then opened the bottom draw of my desk and took out my medal. I stared down at it for many minutes and thoughts came tumbling into my mind. Right, I was going to tell it all, warts and all!

I began the letter to Alfred Marks: "If you are interested, I can tell you what happened to Helen and myself before and during the Second World War. The recollections in my story are factually correct. I have been able to piece together the events I didn't witness from conversations I had with many of the participants. I was prevented from talking about these events because I had signed the Official Secrets Act, which stopped me disclosing the information until now. The war ended some fifty years ago and it's about time to reveal one of its many secrets. This is a story is about privilege, arrogance, and treasonable acts, which could have seriously affected the outcome of the war. Let's start with before the war…"

Helen's Story

Chapter 1

August 13th 1932, Binz, Northern Germany

Fourteen-year old Helen Masters dived into the surf followed by her German cousin Albrecht Bader who was two years older. His mother was Helen's English Aunt Cynthia who had married Alexander Bader. They had met when he was a student at University of Cambridge and she was a German language teacher at a school in the town.

Cynthia had lived in Germany during the First World War and she struggled to hide her feelings from people in a country that was at war with her own. Fortunately, Alexander's parents, who treated her as if she was their daughter, owned a large house near Freiberg in the Black Forest where she lived in seclusion until 1919. Her husband was in the German artillery and saw action in Belgium. In her mind, there was a constant tussle of loyalty to her countrymen, who were being slaughtered in the trenches, and to her beloved German husband, wishing he would survive and come home to her. Fortunately, her German was by that point excellent and if someone detected a slight accent they assumed she was from either Austria or Switzerland.

The only joyous thing that happened at that time was the birth of Albrecht in 1916. His birth gave new meaning to her life and she soon put the war in the back of her mind as she embraced with enthusiasm her new role as a mother.

The end of the war brought blessed relief to Cynthia as she was then able to emerge from her exile. However, she found that people she had contact with were at first wary and resentful of her. The appalling strictures of the 1919 Versailles Treaty forced on Germany by the victorious allies hampered the country's recovery and had led to massive unemployment. The reparations demanded by the treaty were unrealistic and the country was unable to pay its debts. In 1923, France and Belgium occupied the Ruhr, Germany's industrial heartland, in order to take from the Germans such valuable commodities as coal and steel. This was another nail in the country's coffin, which was later exasperated by the worldwide depression beginning in 1929.

After the war, Alexander joined the German Imperial Railway Company first of all in Essen and then he became a senior manager of the railway in Hamburg. Alexander was now a tall, handsome forty-five year old who sported a large moustache which was topped off by his long sideburns. He bore no resentment towards the British, although he had little time for the French. He saw the First World War as an imperialistic conflict caused by two overbearing men – Tsar Nicholas II of Russia and Germany's Kaiser Wilhelm II – who dragged their countries and their allies into one of most devastating struggles known to mankind.

Helen's mother Jean had married Gordon Masters who was totally different from his friend, Alexander.

Gordon was short but he made up for his size by his ebullient personality. He had served in the Royal Navy in the First World War on board a destroyer and was now managing director of a small freight shipping company in Plymouth, England.

Both families were at the German resort town of Binz, which is on the island of Rügen on the Baltic Sea. They were staying at the Kurhaus, which was a magnificent hotel with a sandy beach. The Masters and Bader families holidayed together alternating between Germany and Britain.

This was the fourth day of their holiday. Helen and Albrecht wallowed around in the water and played at splashing each other. Albrecht's English was very good, but Helen spoke no German. The four parents watched the children as they sat in beach chairs soaking up the sunshine and relaxing.

Finally, Alexander and Gordon got up from their deck chairs and announce that they were going for a walk along the beach.

When the men were out of earshot, Cynthia turned to her younger sister Jean: "The children seem to enjoy each other's company."

"They have done so for years. Albrecht is becoming quite grown up now," she replied. "Has he got any girlfriends yet?"

"Good lord no. He's only a child!"

"I don't think so any more, Cynthia. What does he do in his spare time?"

"Apart from his studies, he plays a lot of football and he is in a bike club. His friend Kurt joined the Hitler Youth, which is for adolescent boys. He tried to get Albrecht to join but he said he wasn't interested in politics. I think there was a lot of peer pressure by his friends at school to join and he told them he wasn't interested. Alexander and I warned him to be careful what he said to these people as they seem to start a lot of fights and cause riots. It's a very wild time here in Germany.

"Talk about growing up, your Helen is turning out to be quite a lady. She's starting to become shapelier and more buxom as the years pass. What does she want to do with her life?" asked Cynthia.

"It's really too early to say. Once she sits her School Certificate and then later the Higher School Certificate, we'll have to see."

The two men lit their pipes as they walked along the beach and joked about the young women they saw in swimming costumes. Gordon turned to Alexander and said to him: "So tell me how are things in Germany? We see so many newspaper reports of rioting and of the economy getting worse, if that's possible."

"I'm really worried where this country is going," replied a worried Alexander. "We have a useless government which is facing two extreme parties – the Nazis and their right-wing agenda and, on the left, the communists. Hitler's Nazis won big in July's elections for the Reichstag but they didn't achieve a majority to become the government so it looks like we'll have another ineffectual coalition government under Franz von Papen," commented Alexander morosely. "We also have a real problem of unemployment here. It has reached about six million people. Politicians like Hitler and his communist counterpart, Ernst Thälmann, are promising wonderful-sounding strategies to get the country out of this mess, but this is just fool's gold.

"Every other western country is suffering from this terrible depression and here in Germany it has been made worse by the Versailles Treaty reparations we still have to pay. Although reparations have been reduced by the Dawes Plan, we are still suffering from high inflation. No wonder people are attracted to the extreme parties because they don't see any way out of this mess.

"How's business in Britain at the moment, Gordon?" asked Alexander.

"We're hurting with something like three million unemployed mainly in coal mining and industrial production. This has affected my business in a big way and I've had to lay off half my staff. We certainly haven't had it as bad as Germany and we are beginning see some light at the end of the tunnel but it's a long way off. We'll have to see how things pan out."

Back at their end of the beach, Helen and Albrecht ran out of the sea and began to towel themselves down. The water was cold even in August and they couldn't stay in the sea long. They lay on the beach and let the hot sun dry them off. After a while, they put on some shorts and tops on over their damp bathing costumes.

"Let's go and catch some crabs in the rocks," suggested Albrecht. They put their sandals on picked up their fishnets and ran off in the direction of the rocks which were north of the beach. Overlooking the rocks was a cliff face and on top of this was a small wood.

"Be back by six. We have dinner at eight and you both need baths," Cynthia called after them.

They found a pool that looked promising and began use their nets to stir up the sand at the bottom so that any crabs there would be exposed and would scurry away to hide anew. There were a number of small crabs but nothing big enough to warrant their attention so they moved on to another pool. They were so busy that they didn't notice three older boys walking towards them who had come around the cliff promontory.

The boys, who were seventeen or eighteen, were dressed in Hitler Youth uniforms of a brown shirt, grey knee-length socks, black shorts, which were held up by a black belt. The belt had a large silver buckle and in the middle of this was a swastika. Around their necks were scarves on which was a leather toggle rather like that of a boy scout and they had khaki caps on their heads. When Helen looked up she thought they were German Boy Scouts but she realised they were different because of the swastika arm band they wore on their left arms and they were older.

The Hitler Youth was junior version of the SA or Brownshirt thugs who had become a law-unto-themselves and had helped in Hitler's rise to power by sowing hatred for Jews and communists. They brutalised anyone who got in their way and very often started riots at an opposing party's meetings or rallies.

Two of the boys were tall, blond and muscular and they came from working-class families. They were the product of their brutal and unsophisticated upbringing in the cruel coal and iron towns of the Ruhr, such as Essen, Dortmund and Burg. Both boys enjoyed their new roles as enforcers of the Nazi party which had given them the freedom to bully those who showed any disinclination to believe in Nazism. They were both veterans of the recent disruptive riots at communist election meetings in May and June.

The third boy was the opposite of the other two. He was fat and wore thick-lensed glasses. He came from a family of intellectuals, but didn't share their love of philosophy and literature. Despite this, he was intelligent but in a pragmatic way and was not cerebral as they were or his siblings. He had many arguments with his parents who had become very judgemental of him and, finally, they had washed their hands of their recalcitrant son, telling him he wouldn't amount to anything. In truth, he despised his family and their sarcastic words about his worth and so was easily drawn to the Hitler Youth because they admired his organising prowess and didn't question his abilities. He learnt about the deprivations on working Germans from the many friends he had made and detested what he saw as his family's too comfortable existence.

He had one problem, as he saw it, and that was that he was still a virgin. He wanted to be so much like the other boys who were able to attract girls, particularly those from the League of German Girls, the female section of the Hitler Youth. However, his appearance and demeanour hadn't attracted anyone and as a result he was determined to do something about it when the opportunity presented itself.

The three boys looked down unpleasantly at Helen and Albrecht as they walked up to them. They each had a small bottle of schnapps and it was evident from their demeanour they were a little drunk.

"What are you both doing?" asked the leader of the group in German, a boy called Franz.

"What does it look like?" replied an irritated Albrecht, without looking up from what he was doing. "We're trying to catch some crabs, if you must know."

"Stand up when you talk to me!" was the leader's angry response.

Albrecht looked up at them for the first time.

"Why?"

"Because I'm your superior, asshole!"

"No you're not. You are just a jumped-up upstart with an overbearing attitude in a uniform."

The leader moved angrily towards Albrecht but stopped when he saw his size and decided he couldn't take him on physically by himself.

Helen asked Albrecht in English who the boys were and he explained.

"So she's a foreigner. Where's she from?" the leader demanded.

"My cousin is from England," Albrecht responded.

"So she's from a country that wants to crush the glorious German people."

"No."

"Is she Jewish? She certainly looks like one with that big nose. They are vermin that need eliminating!"

"She looks very sexy to me with her big boobs," leered the fat boy wearing the glasses. "Maybe we can have some fun with her and show her how German men screw women."

Albrecht began to realise that the situation was getting out of hand and that he needed to calm the boys' seeming sexual interest in Helen. It was pointless having a rational discussion with these people because the only thing they understood was force.

"Helen, I think you have to leave now. Just pick up your net and walk away," Albrecht said calmly in English.

"What about you?"

"I'll entertain these delinquents while you leave."

Helen stood up and began to turn around. In doing this, it was like a traffic signal turning green to the three boys. Two of them started to attack Albrecht and the fat one advanced on Helen.

"Run Helen, run as fast as you can!" Albrecht yelled as he wrestled with his two assailants.

Helen began to run but felt the hand of the fat boy grab her arm and stop her progress. She was surprised how fast he was considering his size. She turned around and with her fingernails she clawed at his face. The boy bellowed like a wounded bull and let her go. She ran as fast as she could towards the beach where her parents had been sitting. She turned around and could see the fat boy sitting on the ground holding his bloody face. The other two boys were busy pummelling Albrecht.

She knew she had to reach her parents as fast as she could so that they could rescue Albrecht. She somehow found strength to run but running in sand, as anyone who had done so knows, is very draining. Your energy begins to sap and your muscles quickly feel like putty and useless. Something inside her made her push and she finally climbed over a sandbank and saw her parents.

As she ran towards them, she thought her lungs would burst as her exertion began to take its toll on her body and her breath was laboured. She waved her arms in the air but they weren't looking in her direction. She stopped and screamed at the top of her voice and they turned to look in her direction. Then both fathers started to run towards her. Everything she saw happening was now in slow motion and it seemed a long time before they reached her, but it was only a few seconds.

When the men eventually reached her she said: "They're beating Albrecht! I'll be alright. Help him!"

Both men ran off in the direction she had come from and Helen lay exhausted on the ground. When the two mothers reached her, she began to sob uncontrollably.

Both fathers saw in the distance that two of the boys were kicking the motionless body of Albrecht. The fat boy had found a piece of driftwood on the beach and was using it as a bat to hit the prone figure. Alexander shouted at them and, when they turned and saw the approaching adults, they turned tail and ran.

When Alexander and Gordon reached Albrecht he was unconscious and bleeding profusely from a gnash on his head. Alexander picked him up in his arms and started to march back towards the hotel.

"I'll run ahead and warn the nurse at the hotel," said Gordon as he headed of as fast his small frame could go.

Gordon rushed into the reception area at the hotel and shouted in German for the nurse. By the time an exhausted Alexander reached the hotel carrying the unconscious body of Albrecht, the nurse was there with a hospital trolley and she wheeled him into her examination room and started to examine him.

After a few moments she said to the anxious group of parents: "We need to get him to the hospital in Bergen. He's has a broken arm, a broken leg and probably some broken ribs and they'll need to X-ray his head to make sure there are no skull fractures. I'll call for an ambulance right away." She disappeared into her inner office and they could hear her on the telephone. Cynthia began to sob as she looked at the unconscious figure of her usually vibrant son. Alexander put his arm around her to comfort her.

Albrecht then began to groan as he came around and Cynthia rushed to his side, kissed him on his forehead and held his hand.

The ambulance came thirty minutes later and Cynthia and Alexander climbed in beside Albrecht.

"Alexander, please call sometime to let us know how he's doing. Do you want me to call the police?"

"No. Don't do that. I'll explain why later," he replied as the doors of the ambulance closed.

Gordon watched them go and a feeling of uselessness came over him. He just stood there watching the ambulance disappear down the hotel driveway and wondered what he should do. Then he was woken from his daze when Jean and Helen walked up to him. Jean had kept Helen away from the nurse's office but once the ambulance left she joined her husband.

"How is Albrecht?" asked Helen.

"He's alive but I'm afraid he's in a bad way and I'm just praying he'll be alright. Helen, what exactly happened?" Between sobs, she explained how they had been crabbing and were approached by the three boys who had some sharp words with Albrecht, which she didn't understand. The boys then attacked them.

That evening they had a very miserable dinner with nobody saying anything. Jean and Helen went to bed and Gordon sat in the hotel lounge drinking a brandy, still wondering what to do. Then a page called out his name and when he went to the concierge he was told there was a telephone call for him.

On the telephone was a very sombre Alexander: "They had to operate on Albrecht to relieve some of the pressure on his brain. He's awake and making progress. He keeps asking whether Helen was alright. We have assured him she was but we don't know whether he believes us. Could you bring her to the hospital tomorrow so he can see her and put his mind to rest?"

"Of course. We'll be there."

"Thanks. Cynthia and I will be staying here for the night so we'll see you in the morning."

"Alexander, should I talk to the police about the attack?"

"Please don't. If you do, we'll have the SA on our backs and that won't be a great experience. They guard members of the Hitler Youth acquisitively because they are their future recruits. The police are either afraid of them or sympathise with their cause and so it will be a complete waste of time. Once you rile these people, the situation would likely escalate to the SA in Hamburg and that could affect my work."

"I don't believe this. What has happened to the rule of law?" questioned an astonished Gordon.

"It doesn't really exist. That's Germany today, I'm afraid," replied his friend.

When Gordon returned to his seat in the lounge, he could hear raucous laughter coming from the bar and bawdy singing from about ten or so men in SA uniforms. Other guests were leaving the bar and some of the women were pawed as they left. Then a fight broke out with one of the men who was leaving and he was thrown out of the bar a bloodied mess. The SA men returned to their boisterous singing and this time it was the Horst Wessel Song, which was the anthem of the Nazi Party.

Gordon left the lounge and went to bed. He had decided what he would do and he would talk it over with Jean in the morning.

The next morning Gordon, Jean and Helen took a taxi to the Bergen hospital. In the waiting room they sat on hard chairs as they waited to be taken to the ward Albrecht was on.

"Your mother and I have talked this morning and we decided to leave tomorrow to go back to England," Gordon told Helen. "We have only a few days to go and Uncle Alexander and Aunty Cynthia will want to take Albrecht home as soon as possible so he can get better."

Helen burst into tears and pleaded with her parents to change their minds, but they firmly told her that their minds were made up.

A nurse came into the waiting room and took them into a ward that had at least twenty beds which were arranged with ten on each side of the large room. Alexander and Cynthia were sitting by Albrecht's bed and the sisters greeted each other with hugs and kisses. Alexander was unshaven and looked quite tired.

Helen rushed to Albrecht's side and kissed him on the cheek. His head was bandaged and one of his legs was suspended in a cast. "You're a sight for sore eyes," he mumbled very tiredly. "Are you alright now? Did they do anything to you?"

"No they didn't. Fatty was too slow and I scratched his face. Thanks for saving me from those roughnecks. You were extremely brave to do so and I will always be in your debt."

They had said their teary farewells to their Bader relatives early next morning and caught a train from Binz to Hamburg then one to Rotterdam in Holland. From there they caught a ferry that took them to Harwich in the Britain. During the trip Helen was exceptionally sullen worrying how her cousin was doing. Alexander and Cynthia were planning to take Albrecht home in another day or two so he could recuperate in comfort.

Chapter 2

The Germans invaded Poland in the September 1939 and, although Britain declared war then, no further action was seen until May 1940. Then the Germans invaded Norway followed by the low countries of Holland and Belgium and then France.

Winston Churchill had become prime minister on May 10th, 1940 after ten years in the political wilderness, which was when he wasn't a government minister. His appointment followed the disastrous campaign to stop the Germans from invading Norway. The country, with its rich reserves of iron ore as well as its strategic position in the North Sea, was important part in Germany's plan to dominate Europe. The British, French and Polish forces sent to protect Norway were forced to retreat and in so doing they lost many important warships and many men.

The British Parliament held the then prime minister, Neville Chamberlain, responsible, and, after a vote of no confidence, he resigned. Winston Churchill scrambled to put together a cabinet of national unity, which was made up of the leaders of all the country's political parties. He was also busy appointing key positions such as Lord Beaverbrook, the newspaper magnate, who became minister of aircraft production and Brendan Bracken who was Churchill's parliamentary private secretary and then minister of information. A key appointment was General Hastings Lionel 'Pug'" Ismay as his chief military assistant who served as the principal link between Churchill and the British defence chiefs of staff.

In his first important speech in the British Parliament on May 13th 1940, Churchill set the stage for British resistance to Nazism. In it, he outlined his strategy:

"I would say to the house, as I said to those who have joined the government, I have nothing to offer but blood, toil, tears and sweat. We have before us an ordeal of the most grievous kind. We have before us many, many long months of struggle and of suffering. You ask, what is our policy? I will say: It is to wage war, by sea, land and air, with all our might and with all the strength that God can give us; to wage war against a monstrous tyranny, never surpassed in the dark and lamentable catalogue of human crime."

Great Britain was now on a proper war footing with a man whose time for leadership abilities and greatness had come. His first major task was to mobilise the rescue of the British Expeditionary force trapped at the port of Dunkirk in Northern France.

The British Expeditionary force and its French allies that were sent to prevent further German incursions were defeated. They were pushed back to the town of Dunkirk and a desperate effort was made to rescue them. An armada of some 800 small ships, fishing boats, cabin cruisers and yachts, owned and captained by civilians, crossed the English Channel to help evacuate the men. By the end of the operation on June 4th the small ships had miraculously saved close to 339,000 men. A further 220,000 Allied troops were rescued by British ships from other southern French ports bringing the total of Allied troops evacuated to 559,000.

On this momentous day, Helen Masters was sitting in a train as it wended its way from London heading south west towards Plymouth and she was excited about going home. She loved seeing again the lush, green fields of the English countryside which was such a huge contrast to the drab, dirty and dingy streets of south London that she had known for the past four years. She was overjoyed when the train left the town of Ivybridge and she could see the rugged expanse of Dartmoor to her north with its rocky hill features called Tors. She had enjoyed hiking on this wild and treacherous moor with her friends but they all had had a healthy respect for the moorland. Dartmoor has its own climate which is known to change quite suddenly from sunny to a thick, dangerous mist or heavy, unrelenting rain with high winds.

It had been over a year since Helen had seen her parents and she couldn't wait to tell them about her just completed midwifery course. She had spent three years in nurse's training at St. Thomas' Hospital in London, first becoming a State Registered Nurse and then a further year of study and practical experience to pass her midwifery exams. She was looking forward to starting work at the Prince of Wales Hospital in Greenbank, a neighbourhood in east Plymouth. She had chosen to apply to that particular hospital as it was one of the largest in the area and would give her the breadth of nursing experience she wanted.

Helen knew at sixteen that she wanted to be a nurse because at school she excelled in biology and she had a fascination for how disease was overcome and managed. She had joined the local chapter of the St. John Ambulance Brigade as a cadet, which gave her another insight into healing and the dreadful realities of death.

When she graduated from the Plymouth High School for Girls passing both her School Certificate and Higher School Certificate by eighteen years of age, she had already decided that nursing would be her calling. Her father, Gordon, advised her that the best training was at one of the teaching hospitals in London and after some research and a number of interviews she was accepted by St. Thomas' Hospital. This hospital was on the south bank of the river Thames and served the poor and destitute people of such neighbourhoods as Lambeth, Vauxhall, Newington and Southwark.

Helen had lived for two years in the hospital's nurses' home at Riddell House on the Lambeth Palace Road. The home was operated like a fortress by an assistant matron who kept the unwelcome attention of potential male suitors at bay, although visitors were allowed in a very drab lounge on the ground floor once a week. The nurses had strict rules to follow and there were stringent ten o'clock curfews that had to be obeyed. To Helen and the other trainee nurses life was like living in a nunnery, but they put up with it because of their drive to become qualified. Finally, in her third year she became a staff nurse and was able to share a flat in Lambeth with two other nurses, which was financially subsidised by her parents.

Helen had grown into a lithe, shapely woman and had shed her early teenage puppy fat. Standing naked at a mirror she would see her plump pointed breasts, a lean, muscular body and flowing auburn hair, which hung down onto her shoulders. Her hair was often admired by both her male friends and other women for its natural colour and fullness, but it was a devil to put up on her head under her nurse's cap each day. Her legs were muscular but not too muscular and were like those of a professional dancer at the Palladium Theatre in London's West End. She had a visceral attitude towards fitness and, when she could, liked to exercise each day at a local public swimming pool.

When she first arrived at the hospital to start her training, she attracted a gaggle of male admirers who were mainly medical students or junior doctors. She was very wary of these admirers and made sure she was always in a group of other nurses when she went out to the local pubs. She knew that their interest in her was purely sexual and a few nurses who fell for their insincere compliments found out how wrong they were the following morning when they woke up, naked, in some stranger's bed. What was worse were those nurses that found they were pregnant and were dismissed from training. Their so-called lovers were no longer interested in them and could not be contacted. The unfortunate former nurse was on her own, friendless, pregnant and out of work.

Helen had been on one or two dates but found that the men she dated were too self-centred or too self-absorbed in their medical training to be interesting. It wasn't as if she didn't have an interest in men, she just didn't find any of those she had come across as very attractive. Some were entertaining and even funny, but they were often shallow or very immature to be of interest to her.

One medical student she liked a lot for a while was Peter Riley who treated her well and they had often gone to the theatre and concerts together. One evening after a visit to a country pub in Dulwich Village, he pulled his car into a wooded area and started to kiss her. She responded but before long his hand was up her skirt and on her inner thigh. Frightened about what would happen next, she pulled his hand away and demanded to be taken back to the nurses' home. After that, Peter never asked her out again and she had seen him with some other women. After this, she lost interest in developing a relationship and turned further admirers down. She found out that word had gotten out about her and that she had the nickname of 'Miss Iceberg.' This had, at first, annoyed her but then she realised that this name and reputation would protect her from unwanted attention.

Helen stopped her dreamy reminisces as the train pulled into Plymouth North Road Station, shuddered to a halt and the engine let out a belch of steam. The passengers climbed down from the carriages and walked with their suitcases towards the exit. As Helen walked along the platform, her father waded against the tide of departing passengers towards her.

"Helen!" Gordon shouted to attract his daughter's attention. When they drew close to each other, he hugged and kissed her on the cheek. "It is so good to see you. You're looking well." But she could see something was troubling this always ebullient man.

"I'm glad to be home dad. Where's Mum?"

Gordon stopped walking and looked into her face: "Aw, she has had a rather disturbing letter from Aunt Cynthia. Look, let's get a cup of tea and I'll tell you all about it before we go home."

They left the station, crossed the road and went in to a small café. They ordered tea and sat down in a quiet corner.

Gordon continued telling Helen about her Aunt Cynthia: "We'd been getting letters occasionally from Cynthia and Alexander but we could tell by their tone everything was not right. The Nazis had been censoring mail, especially those letters that went abroad, so they had to be careful what they said. But when you read them you had a feeling that there was something wrong. Of course we wrote back with news but we could not get any response to our pointed questions. It turns out that answering any of those questions could have had severe consequences. They were living in fear. And when war was declared we didn't hear from them again."

"Oh my God, Dad! How did you find out the truth?"

"You remember in 1938 there was a major culling in Germany of Jews and their businesses called Kristallnacht?"

"Of course," replied Helen. "How could anyone forget such a nightmare?"

"Well, as a result of this, the emigration of Jews from Germany almost doubled overnight and one family, who knew Cynthia and Alexander very well, smuggled out a long letter of some ten pages from Cynthia to give to us. They didn't know how to reach us other than we lived in Plymouth. They went to Sweden at first and when Norway was invaded in April they feared neutral Sweden would be next so they decided to come to Britain. We received the two-year old letter yesterday and since then your mother has been beside herself with grief.

"That letter it is quite troubling. Alexander was forced to join the Nazi Party in order to keep his job. Then a disgruntled employee of his denounced him as anti-Nazi and accused him of saying negative things about Hitler. Despite vehemently denying this, he was interrogated by the Gestapo for several days and thrown into prison in Hamburg. His accuser was a leading member of the SA and they believed him rather than Alexander. Aunt Cynthia doesn't know for sure where he is, although she heard he had been taken to Fuhlsbüttel prison, which is north of Hamburg and is now a concentration camp.

"She has been living in absolute fear and their house has had bricks thrown through its windows. The streets have been taken over by SA thugs who look for any excuse to indiscriminately beat people up. They loot known communist or Jewish sympathisers or anyone who they suspect of being so. She eventually gave up living in Hamburg and left to stay with Alexander's parents in Freiberg. Their house in Hamburg has been taken over by a Sturmhauptführer in the SA, that's like the rank of captain."

"What about Albrecht? Do we know anything about him?" Helen asked.

"I'm afraid that boy has gone completely off the rails. I don't know whether it was the effects of his beating in Binz or not, but he is now part of the tragedy which this deplorable Nazi system has caused. A year after we last saw them in 1932, Albrecht was pressured by the local SA organiser in their neighbourhood in Hamburg to join the Hitler Youth, which his shocked parents only agreed to reluctantly. They saw the way the country was going and had advised him to go along with whatever the managers of the Hitler Youth wanted and to keep his head down, although he was reluctant to do this. Cynthia and Alexander thought he would be better off towing the line.

"However, in just a year they noticed a difference in him. He was beginning to accept as truth the propaganda he was being fed and would often mouth the words and slogans as if he truly believed them. He then started to tell his parents how to organise their household better and was very critical of the way they ran their lives. He started to have long arguments with his parents and would throw tantrums if he could not get his way. He picked upon the fact that his mother was English and someone that would undermine the new Germany. Their previously loving son had become a stranger to them.

"Also what was troubling was that they heard stories of some Hitler Youth members denouncing their parents because they had expressed anti-Nazis opinions and some had been thrown in jail so they decided not to say anything negative in front of him or argue with him. They had become afraid of their own son!"

Helen began to cry and between her sobs she lamented the loss of her cousin and his family to the unstable and tragic country that was Germany at this time.

"What is he doing now?"

"He left home for good three years ago and joined the Luftwaffe and has become a bomber pilot. Cynthia has lost touch with him and doesn't know where he is. He never contacts them and is unaware of his father's and mother's current predicament or, if he does, he doesn't want to know them. Alexander's father made some discreet enquiries and heard that he was in Spain with his squadron taking part in the Spanish Civil War. But that's all they know."

"Why doesn't Aunt Cynthia come home to England? She would at least be safe here."

"We are at war with Germany and she would be arrested if she tried to come here. I think she holds out hope that Alexander will come home."

They left the café without saying another word. They found the car and drove a short distance to their home in Leigham Street. The Victorian house at the back looked onto Plymouth Hoe, an open space of parkland that looks out towards Plymouth Sound and the Atlantic Ocean. The Hoe was made famous in 1588 by Sir Francis Drake who played his famous game of bowls there while awaiting the tide to turn so he could take on the Spanish Armada. In 1940, Plymouth was to become one of the focal points of Britain's resistance to yet another invasion.

They found Helen's mother Jean at the kitchen table still pouring over the letter from Cynthia. Her eyes were red from crying and she was still in her pyjamas and dressing gown although it was four o'clock in the afternoon.

She then saw Helen: "Oh, my love, I'm so happy to see you. Has your father told you our terrible news?"

"Yes Mum. I can't believe what has happened." Helen hugged her mother hard and they sat in each other's embrace for many minutes.

"Have you slept at all?" Helen eventually asked her mother.

"Well not really, dear. I tried to sleep last night but I just lay there thinking about Cynthia."

"I'll call Dr. Madden and see if he will give you a sleeping draft. You've got to keep your strength up while we work out what to do. I bet you haven't eaten. I'll make some dinner."

After the doctor had left and they had eaten, Helen took her mother upstairs to bed and made sure she took her sleeping pill.

Helen went downstairs to the lounge and sat with her father in front of a roaring fire. He had a large scotch whisky in his hand.

"What are we going to do?" she asked him.

"I have no idea," he said. "There is very little we can do. I'm at a loss to think of anything. We're at war with Germany so we can't go there. We can't telephone or write. No, I'm afraid we'll just have to try and bear with the awful fact that we can't do anything."

"You're right I suppose, but there's always hope that something will turn up."

"I hate the word hope," her frustrated and angry father said. "Hope is something you cling to when all else has failed," he paused. "But that's what we're doing, I suppose. It's such a superficial word that is born only out of desperation."

Helen said nothing because she didn't want to add further to his despondent mood. Unfortunately, the news from her relatives in Germany was just the start of the tragedy that would befall her family.

Chapter 3

The next morning Helen left home early for her eight o'clock meeting with the matron of Prince of Wales Hospital, a Miss Kinnear. She sat outside matron's office for more than an hour before matron came walking down the corridor with a nursing sister in tow.

"Ah, Staff Nurse Masters, come in and don't dawdle!" she ordered as she entered her inner sanctum.

Matron was a heavy set woman in her late fifties and was smartly dressed in a navy blue uniform with her heavily starched white, frilly cap which denoted her rank. She had a no nonsense approach to her work and everyone who crossed her got a tongue lashing they would never forget. Even the senior administrators, doctors and nurses went out of their way to avoid her. However orderly and well run a hospital ward was, she would always find fault with something. The nursing staff lived in fear of her and quietly resented her autocratic management style.

Matron was a bitter woman who begrudged the young, enthusiastic nurses under her command who had their whole futures in front of them compared with her career which was near its end. Her vocation had started well enough. She had made ward sister by her late twenties and then the First World War intervened to destroy her future. She had fallen deeply in love with an officer of the Devonshire Regiment but he was killed in The Battle of the Somme in 1916. She was devastated at the news of his death and was an emotional mess. She had to take time off from her work to recover and as a result she lost seniority and was passed over for a number of promotions. As a consequence, she became a harsh and sour woman who was determined to show the world she could run an efficient hospital regardless of the resentment and outright hatred by colleagues she left in her wake.

She sat behind her desk, which was organised in an orderly and efficient way. Her inbox was on her right and an outbox to her left. The files in each were neatly stacked. Her pens were in front of her lined up in order in a brass pen holder. The nursing sister stood behind her and Helen stood in front of her desk with her arms to her side.

Matron took out a file from one of desk draws and read it. She looked up at Helen: "Why would you want to work at this hospital and not continue at St. Thomas's in London?"

"Plymouth is my home and I want to do my nursing here," Helen replied.

"Why didn't you do your training here instead of going to a London hospital?"

"I was able to receive a broader training in many specialist areas."

Matron gave Helen a withering stare: "Let me tell you something, Missy, I resent an outsider coming here to teach us yokels how to be proper nurses." Her animosity toward Helen was obvious. "I won't have it. I only agreed to your appointment because we have a shortage of nurses and we have to get what we can even if they come from London.

"You will go with Sister Frank here and start work on the geriatric ward."

"But my appointment letter said that I would be working as a midwife, matron."

"You'll go where I tell you to go, Nurse. Good day."

With that she was dismissed.

As Helen walked down the corridor behind Sister Frank, she realised her appointment to the geriatric ward was some sort of punishment or was it a sign to her of matron's need to show dominance over her. Did she feel threatened by Helen? Either way, she dreaded the work. Few nurses really liked working on a geriatric ward where they were faced by incontinent, older patients and their dementia-related tantrums. The ward had sad aura of the finality to it as these patients, often deserted by their families, faced the end to their lives. At this time, these geriatric wards were often just dumping grounds for families that didn't want to care for their old relatives. There was very little attempt to rehabilitate them so they could go back to their loved ones and the very few nursing homes that there were only really catered to wealthy families.

Sensing Helen's dread, Sister Frank turned to her: "Bear with matron's ire. We all have to and it's no good trying to fight back. What's important is helping our patients, which can be difficult most of the time." This seemed to be a very passive-aggressive attitude and perhaps matron wanted yes-people like this sister who she could bully.

The next three months were very exacting for Helen who tried her best to accept her fate. The other nurses and the unqualified nurses' aides on the ward were not exactly bright and often made elementary mistakes which Helen corrected before Sister Frank found out. There was a great turnover of nurses on the ward as many resigned rather than continue trying to serve the difficult and demanding patients, but Helen was determined to not let matron win in her blatant attempt to squash any attempt of dissent. She was really puzzled about why the woman was so aggressive towards her.

Every month, a meeting was held with the doctors who ran geriatric department and the senior nursing staff to which Helen as the staff nurse, Sister Frank and matron attended. The head of geriatric department was a Dr. Ronald Inchcape and the meetings were usually held in his office. He was about forty years old and had been appointed to his position a year before. They all sat around a meeting table and spent time discussing each patient's care. At the end of the meeting Dr. Inchcape asked whether they had any suggestions for improving care.

Helen put her hand up, but before she could be called upon matron intervened.

"Staff Nurse Masters has not been with us long so she hasn't got anything to suggest." Matron was angry that staff were being asked to make suggestions. It was never heard of in nursing. They just did what they were told.

But Dr. Inchcape was made of sterner stuff than matron had imagined and he knew her for what she was: "Nevertheless I would like to hear what she has to say."

"That won't be necessary. Nurse Masters, leave the room," Matron ordered.

"Matron that will be enough!" shouted Dr. Inchcape as he angrily slammed his fist on the table. "This is my department and I will listen to what she has to say."

Matron turned red but said nothing.

"We doctors are tired of your bully tactics. These might have been the way medicine was run thirty or forty years ago but it has absolutely no place in modern medicine. And let me remind you that if I hear of any retribution carried out on Nurse Masters I will bring the subject up with this hospital's board. Now, Nurse, what do you suggest?" he said in a kindly tone.

Helen thought, to hell with matron, and began: "I believe that one of our important goals should be to discharge as many patients to their families whenever possible. And to do this we need to do more physiotherapy work and consult with families about care at home. Also, it would improve their mental health if they were helped by a psychologist who has had experience dealing with elderly patients. I've seen it succeed, although I know that it won't work with everyone."

"I think that's a very thoughtful suggestion," said Dr. Inchcape. "Where have you seen this before?"

"At St. Thomas's in London, sir."

When the meeting broke up, a distraught matron didn't say a word but headed for her office and locked the door. It wasn't until later that Helen found out that on her way home matron had deliberately crashed her car into a wall and smelt strongly of gin. However, she survived her suicide attempt and had been taken to Freedom Fields Hospital to recover.

The hospital's assistant matron, Ann Chalmers, was made interim matron and started to reorganise the staffing structure. She was a fairly strict disciplinarian somewhat in the mould of her predecessor but had a kinder personality and was at least approachable. Helen was appointed to the causality department, first of all on night duty, which she didn't mind because this was the type of nursing she preferred. There was the usual casualty work with people involved in mishaps at home or in the cars and with some industrial accidents.

The first German air raid on Plymouth had happened on July 6th, long before Helen was with the department, when three people were killed, but it was a very small taste of what was to come. The Germans were targeting the royal dockyards at Devonport which was north-west of the Plymouth city centre and was an important industrial suburb of the city. After this raid, there was none for a further eight months as the Germans were focussing their air power on winning the Battle of Britain by bombing RAF airfields and strategic targets such aircraft manufacturing and such cities as London, Portsmouth, Birmingham and Liverpool.

Living had become more difficult for everyone in Britain. Rationing of food and clothing was a challenge for every family and the blackout restrictions at night were onerous but necessary. Fear of a gas attack in the early days of the war had led the government to issue gas masks to everyone. Not everyone carried them and the police and air raid wardens tried to enforce the law without much success. The newspapers constantly reported the bombing of London and other major cities so there was a fear you could feel in people that was quite palpable.

Public air raid shelters had been built in the city of Plymouth at various strategic points and many families, Helen's included, had built Anderson shelters in their back yards which were buried four feet deep with a soil covering on the roof. This covering was some twenty inches deep and families planted vegetable on top of their shelter as well in the remainder of their gardens to supplement their meagre rations.

Helen's mother Jean's demeanour had improved a little and she had been helped by some pills the doctor had prescribed. She had accepted that there was nothing they could do to help her sister and she had found solace in her church which she visited every day. Helen's father Gordon's business had not been good but he had built up savings over the years which he called his 'rainy-day fund' and he was able to keep his essential staff on and carry out a limited operation.

As Christmas approached they heard from one of Jean's school friends, Vivian Thomas, who wanted to see her before she left for New Providence, an island in the Bahamas, and retirement. Her husband, Brian, who was already on this Caribbean island, had had a very successful engineering business in Manchester which he sold in 1938. Vivian was planning to join him after she had tied up some loose ends in Britain. She planned to fly with British Overseas Airways Corporation flying boat from Poole, Dorset, to Lisbon in Portugal and from there board an American ship to New York.

Three days before Christmas, Helen was at the main railway station to meet Vivian Thomas who was travelling from Manchester.

"Cooee Helen, I'm over here!" Vivian called out.

Helen waved and walked over to her on the platform where Vivian was surrounded by suitcases.

"Hello sweetheart," Vivian said as he hugged and kissed Helen. "My you've grown into a beautiful woman. I remember the last time I saw you must have been ten and you were quite a tomboy. You were always climbing trees and coming home with scrapes and bruises. Now tell me, how is your dear mother?"

"She is doing better Aunt Vivian, but she is still very worried about Aunt Cynthia and Uncle Alexander. We got a smuggled letter from them which really makes us worry."

"Now Helen I want you to call me Vivian. You're old enough now," she said and then continued: "Your mother should be worried about Cynthia, but she was able to survive the last war in Germany so hopefully she'll survive this one."

"It's completely different. This Nazi regime is so vicious and cruel and they have made the ordinary people paranoid with fear and they have become informers to curry favour with the regime. If your neighbours don't like you they will report you for whatever reason and then you're in big trouble. The Nazis turn on anyone who is not what they call Aryan and imprison them in concentration camps."

"How do you know such things?"

"We learnt this from some Jewish people who brought the letter to Mother and who had escaped from Germany. Now, how have you been? How is Manchester?"

"I'm afraid we had two air raids this summer and I wouldn't be surprised if we get more. I'm glad to be out of there and I feel sorry for the poor people that can't move. Did anything happen here?"

"We had a small air raid in July but it didn't amount to much. Being so close to the naval dockyards in Devonport makes us a natural target.

"Now Vivian, we have to walk to our house from here. Because of petrol rationing, I couldn't bring the car. Dad said he'd meet us here to help. Oh, there he is."

After dinner that night Vivian and Helen were sitting by a fire in the living room. Gordon was going around the house to check on the blackout and Jean had gone to bed.

"How's nursing, Helen?"

"It's going quite well now. It was a bit bumpy when I first started here but now I'm working in the casualty department." She then explained her problems with the hospital's matron.

"I suppose some people are stuck in their ways, although it seems as if she had mental problems. Sounds like you ran into a buzz saw.

"You know when Brian and I visited Nassau before we decided to move there, we were shown the large hospital by an oily estate agent called Harold Christie and we were quite impressed by it. The Bahamas is a delightful spot with wonderful beaches, ocean sailing and a fantastic social life. It's cheap to live there with no taxes and the climate is warm all year, although it can be very hot and humid in the summer. It couldn't be better for us. Why don't you think about coming out there away from the day-to-day stress of surviving here?"

"It sounds great, but I couldn't leave my parents. Also, my country needs me and young people like me to fight this Nazi threat. I can't desert them now so I'm afraid I stuck here."

"Well if you ever change your mind, you will always have a home to stay in there."

On Christmas Eve, the newspapers and the radio broadcasts were full of reports of massive air raids in Manchester and the surrounding area on the nights of December 22nd and 23rd. The raids left almost nine hundred dead and over three thousand people injured. The loss of people's homes was devastating and it was a Christmas that would be remembered for decades to come as Mancunians began to put back their lives.

The Masters family and their guest, Vivian Thomas, had a desultory Christmas dinner. Gordon had somehow managed to find two scrawny ducks which they ate with potatoes and broccoli from their Victory Garden and washed their meal down with some home-made wine. No one spoke as the air raid news weighed on everyone's mind.

The celebrations, if you can call them that, were held after a church service where the vicar had made an impassioned call for his congregation to remain steadfast in their determination to defeat the barbaric Nazi enemy.

He urged them to donate any clothing they had so that it could be sent to the Salvation Army in London and Manchester.

The steadfast theme was repeated by King George VI in his Christmas message on the radio later that afternoon. The King wanted to emphasise the need for everyone to help each other.

He said: "Time and again during these last few months I have seen for myself the battered towns and cities of England, and I have seen the British people facing their ordeal. I can say to them that they may be justly proud of their race and nation. On every side I have seen a new and splendid spirit of good fellowship springing up in adversity, a real desire to share burdens and resources alike. Out of all this suffering there is a growing harmony which we must carry forward into the days to come when we have endured to the end and ours is the victory."

The King's words were inspirational when he said them, but facing the reality of life with its hardships put people's optimism was at a low ebb.

Vivian Thomas left for the Bahamas at the beginning of January and everyone in the Masters household resumed their desultory lives not knowing what the future held. This glum outlook was repeated in just about every household in the country.

For Helen the one bright spot was the appointment of a senior houseman to the casualty department, a Dr. Eric Moore. To say that he was very handsome was putting it mildly and all the nurses developed immediate crushes on him. They took it in turns to flirt with him during the many down periods when no accident patients were in need of attention and he did nothing to discourage them. Helen thought he was full of himself and seemed to have a big ego, but she was amused at how the other nurses tried to outdo each other for his attention. Finally, one of the nurses, Pat Egan, was asked out by him and an affair began, much to the chagrin of the others, but to Helen's amusement.

However, as the weeks passed she grew to appreciate his skill as a doctor, not only in diagnosing problems and dealing with them but his bedside manner with patients was positive and friendly.

Then a major road accident occurred in Plymouth, which changed Helen's opinion of Dr. Moore. A car didn't stop at a junction and crashed into a single-decker bus full of people returning home from work. The old man who was driving the car died in the collision and the later post mortem determined that he had had a heart attack. There were four passengers who were seriously hurt in the bus and all were brought into the hospital's casualty department.

Dr. Moore and a junior doctor had a quick look at each patient and determined who they would prioritise and then went to work. Helen was helping middle-aged Madeline Wilson who had a mangled arm. The ambulance crew had put a tourniquet on her arm to stop the bleeding but she had lost a lot of blood and her pallor was a deathly grey. Helen set up the equipment for a plasma transfusion, then inserted the large needle into the vein of her good arm and started the flow of plasma from the glass bottle hung up beside the bed. She then took a sample of the semi-conscious woman's blood and sent it for screening to determine her blood type.

The badly injured woman was then transported to the casualty ward and Dr. Moore called in the duty house surgeon. After the patient was thoroughly examined, the surgeon decided that her right arm needed to be amputated just above the elbow. He determined that amputation was necessary because her arm had been mangled beyond repair and there was a serious chance of infection leading to gangrene.

Helen went looking in the waiting room for the Madeline Wilson's husband who had been brought to the hospital by the police. She took him into a small office where the surgeon and Dr. Moore explained what they wanted to do. The man was very upset and at first refused to agree to allow the emergency procedure to occur. Eventually, he relented when it was explained that it was only way to save her life.

Meanwhile, the injured woman began to regain consciousness as the transfusion she had received began to take effect. When she realised where she was and Helen had explained that her hand and lower arm had been crushed, she began to cry inconsolably. Dr. Moore and the woman's husband came to her bedside and the doctor very gently explained the situation she was facing.

"I'm very frightened, Doctor," she sobbed. "What if it goes wrong? I don't want to die!" she cried.

Dr. Moore took her good hand and squeezed it.

"It will be fine Madeline. I will be there all the time. And let me tell you something; Mr. Davis, the surgeon, is the best there is and if I was in your shoes I would not hesitate to call on him to operate on me. Now get some rest and I'll see you later."

The operation took three hours and when Madeline Wilson came round from the anaesthetic, Dr. Moore was there to assure her and her husband all went well.

Helen's view of Dr. Moore changed from being professionally impressed to being personally attracted to him. She always thought about him when she lay in her bed at night but disabused herself of such thoughts, dismissing them by rationalising that he was just a work colleague and, anyway, he had a girlfriend.

One night, Helen was leaving the hospital after her shift when a figure appeared in front of her from the shadows of the building. Because of the blackout she couldn't see who it was but when he spoke she knew it was Dr. Moore.

"Helen, I wonder if you would like to go for a drink?"

Helen was taken by surprise, but agreed. And so began a torrid affair.

Chapter 4

Plymouth, March 20th, 1941

Helen woke up and turned over in bed, but Eric wasn't there. She knew he only stayed for an hour and had gone back to work. Since their affair had started, she had often come to his small flat in the late afternoon before she had later gone on her night shift. That day was no different.

She lay there naked thinking about Dr. Eric Moore and his unspeakably beautiful body that was so muscular and she wondered how he stayed in shape. She was a virgin before she went out with him, but now she didn't care about that any more since he was able to bring her to such spasms of pure ecstasy in their love making. She longed to see him again.

Helen was at first reluctant to go out with him, but had convinced herself there wasn't any harm. Although he had been charming and solicitous of her, she still heard a small voice inside her that told her to beware. However, she threw caution to the wind by letting him make love to her for the first time and the effect allowed her to ascend into another dimension of sheer bliss which she had never experienced before. By now she was addicted to him and was lost in her lust for him.

She looked at the clock on the bedside table.

"Oh damn!" she exclaimed as she realised it was four fifteen and she had to be at the hospital at five. She quickly started to dress and then went into the bathroom to put on her make-up.

Then there was a knock at the door and a female voice said: "Eric darling, I know you're in there. How about a quickie before I have to go? You were so good to me the last time, I want to come all over again," she purred.

Shocked, Helen finished dressing and was ready to go. She sat down on the edge of the bed and a coolness came over her. She laughed to herself as she thought I've been had by a smooth operator, a modern Casanova (the famous Italian 18th century womaniser). She realised she had been a challenge to him because she would not flirt or pay any attention to him. He had conquered her and she realised that his perceived sexual ego was now fully satisfied. She had been duped by a master into thinking maybe he was really interested in her. God, that's a foolish girl, she said to herself.

She didn't cry but instead was now white with anger. This was a life lesson. How could I have fallen into the trap of actually adoring him? Well it was good while it lasted, but I'm not going to become one of his harem. Or am I now one anyway? Nope. Goodbye Dr. Casanova Moore.

She left the keys he had given her on the kitchen table and opened the front door of the flat and standing there was Nurse Pat Egan.

"You!" Nurse Egan cried. "So, miss goody-two-shoes was going out with my Eric behind my back!"

She went to claw Helen's face with her nails. Helen was too quick for her and punched her in her solar plexus. She collapsed on the floor in pain.

"He's all yours Pat! You deserve each other."

Between gasps for breath, she shouted after Helen who was going down the stairs: "I'll get you for this!"

Helen rushed to the hospital and quickly went to the casualty department.

"You're late, Nurse!" cried an angry Sister Jacobs. "There's some bedpans in the sluice that need to be washed." This job was usually left to trainee nurses but this was sister's punishment.

There wasn't much going on so the medical staff were looking for small jobs to do. Helen ignored Dr. Moore who was in his little office and busied herself with little tasks. As she walked down a corridor an arm grabbed her by the wrists and pulled her into a linen closet. It was dark in there but she could smell Dr. Moore's cologne. His free hand started to fondle her breasts.

"Stop it, you bastard!"

He took no notice and began to put his hand up her uniform skirt.

"I know you like it rough, Helen, so here goes you little minx."

But instead of submitting she kneed him very hard in his groin. He let out a bellow and released her. He collapsed on the floor holding his wounded crotch.

Helen opened the door to the closet and said: "Now hear this, I was a fool to ever get involved with you but I have now come to my senses. I don't want to see you ever again so go and seduce the other nurses but leave me alone." She slammed the door.

After completing some other small tasks, she went to the cafeteria for something to eat and was just eating a sandwich when, at nine, the air-raid sirens started to wail. Although Helen didn't know it at the time, this was the start of Plymouth's devastating blitz, although there had been a small raid in July. By the end of the war in

1945, there were fifty-nine separate air raids on the city and, as a result, there was hardly a building standing. Over one thousand people had lost their lives and some four thousand people were injured. The shear destruction that the raids caused gave Plymouth the dubious title of the most devastated city in Britain.

Helen and the other medical staff grabbed their steel helmets and went down into the hospital basement where shelters had been constructed. Some fifteen minutes later they heard the drone of aircraft engines overhead followed by the whiz of the bombs as they fell and then heard the large explosions. The Germans dropped mainly incendiary bombs, which were firebombs whose purpose was to set buildings ablaze and as a result, many casualties were badly burnt.

As they cowered frightened in the shelters the bombs kept falling. Some of the nurses screamed as the cacophony of sound continued and they jammed their hands against their ears to keep out the noise. And then there was silence. The first wave of bombers had passed.

Half an hour passed and a voice yelled: "Is there anyone there? We need medical help!"

Helen and the others rushed upstairs to the casualty department and were met by an ambulance driver and air raid warden who very officiously said: "There's no time to hide. These people need attention!" And he marched off.

There were some six patients in first intake of casualties. Some had broken bones and lacerations on the faces but many suffered severe burns. Two of the patients died before they could be helped and were taken to the mortuary. And still the casualties kept coming. The trickle of patients soon became a torrent and medical staff worked mechanically as they provided help to the wounded and dying.

Chaos reigned in the overflowing department as wounded people came in some screaming in sheer terror for help and lay anywhere they could. The bedlam of noise was only matched by the unsanitary flow of blood on the floors, which made the department look like an abattoir, and the putrid smell of vomit as well as other human waste hung in the air. The frazzled medical staff in teams of two moved quickly from one patient to another tending to their wounds, which included broken bones, serious lacerations on faces and bodies, burns and, in the worst cases, lost limbs.

Then the medical staff heard the second wave of bombers coming. They all stopped what they were doing but didn't move. As the bombs fell they just continued to work on patients. The lights flickered and went out but the hospital porters lit hurricane lamps and their gruesome work continued. They hardly noticed the third wave.

The hospital's casualty department was so overwhelmed with people needing help that some of the patients had to lie in the corridors. The same situation happened in the city's five other large hospitals. By dawn the exhausted staff sat outside the hospital on a low wall. Some lit up cigarettes and those who didn't smoke lit up as well. They didn't talk because they were too tired but just stared into space not believing what they had been though.

A shattered Helen walked to her parent's house on Leigham Street. The walk usually took about twenty minutes but it took over an hour that day. The devastation was all around on the streets she walked on. The destruction on some streets was so complete she had to climb over piles of rubble that lay strewn about. People were collecting their belongings as best they could from these destroyed houses and some were planning to stay at relatives in the country.

Helen quickened her pace because seeing all this desolation made her wonder about her parents and their home and whether it had been hit. She was relieved when she rounded the corner of her street to see her house still standing. She rushed in to the kitchen to find her mother at the sink washing dishes.

"Where's Dad, Mum?"

"Oh, he's gone to work. The docks at Devonport took a real beating last night and your father went there to help out. Want a cup of tea, dear? You look awful."

"We had a very rough night. There were so many casualties it was quite unbelievable and we didn't finish helping them until six this morning. What did you and Dad do last night?"

"We spent the night in the Anderson shelter. Now take your things off and go and wash up; I'll make some breakfast for you."

Helen gratefully sunk into her bed after breakfast. She slept solidly for about three hours but eventually her sleep was disturbed by her dreams of the carnage she had seen the night before. Try as she might, she was unable to shake those images of the devastated casualties she saw that night from her mind and eventually she got up at midday.

Helen and the rest of the medical team reported again for duty at five that evening. And that night was a repeat of the grisly night before. This time there were many more burn patients than before, an indication that the Luftwaffe planned to set the city alight with their incendiary bombs. What broke the hearts of so many of the nurses were the number of children who they had to help. After this raid, many families packed their children off to live with relatives in such country towns as Newton Abbot, Totness and Launceston.

Then for the next four weeks there was a lull in the bombing. Most people were relieved and began to think there wouldn't be any more. The docks at Devonport began to operate again but not at full capacity because of the previous damage, but at least ships were being repaired and Gordon Masters' business had a few contracts to work on.

Easter came and went and people picnicked on the Hoe to celebrate Bank Holiday Monday on April 14th. The weather was dull and cold although temperatures in the afternoon reached sixty-five degrees Fahrenheit. The Royal Marines Band played in the afternoon and people were able to relax a little.

Then on April 21st events changed for the worse as Luftwaffe air raids began again and the same scenario was followed at the hospital. The same devastation happened the following night and this time the central part of Plymouth was hit. To reach their target of the navy yards on the west side of Plymouth, the German bombers had to cross the city from the east and unload their bombs as they went.

Helen was just cleaning up the causality department early the next morning when a young policeman came into the department asking for her.

"Excuse me, Miss, are you Helen Masters?"

"Yes. What can I do for you, Officer?"

The nervous policeman continued: "I'm sorry to have to tell you, but both your parents were killed in the raid last night."

Helen's heart was seized by fear: "How? Where were they?" she asked incredulously. Her eyes widened as she erupted in uncontrollable tears.

"They had taken cover in the Portland Square communal air-raid shelter, which took a direct hit. There were a lot of people killed."

Helen felt faint and was caught by the policeman just as she began to fall and someone brought a chair for her to sit on. Sister Jacobs came in wondering what the fuss was, but when she found out from the other people there what had happened she said: "God Helen, this is appalling news. Have you got anyone else we should contact for you?"

Helen took a deep breath: "No, Sister. My English aunt is trapped in Germany and my father's relatives are all dead. I'm on my own now, it seems."

"Miss, we need you to identify their bodies, I'm afraid," said the policeman timidly.

"Oh, can't that wait man?" said an angry Sister Jacobs.

"Its fine sister, I'll do it." And then she got up and walked as if in a trance out the department with the policeman.

Helen's parents had been walking back home from visiting some friends in James Place in the centre of Plymouth when the air raid sirens sounded. They knew about the air raid shelter in Portland Square and went there to await the all clear. However, the direct hit from a bomb killed them and seventy other people.

When Helen returned home from the city mortuary that afternoon she closed the front door of the house and went into the living room. She sat in her father's chair, which she thought smelt of him and his pipe tobacco, and began to sob uncontrollably: "Why-oh-why did this happen! I can't cope. This is all too much! Mum, Dad, why?"

There was a knock at the front door and when she opened it there was Reverend James Beasley standing there, the elderly vicar of the church they attended.

"Would you mind if I come in?"

"Of course not vicar. I would welcome some company."

Helen made some tea and they sat in the living room.

"So, how are you coping with your terrible loss, Helen? Can we talk about it?"

"In a sense, the fact that they have gone has hit me with the first salvo, but I expect in the coming months or even years, I will have moments of utter despondency and the feeling of hopelessness. I just can't believe that I will never be able to see or speak to them again. The best thing I think I can do is to focus my life around my work so that their untimely deaths would be in the back of my mind."

"I would caution you about becoming too engrossed in your work as a panacea for your grief. What about your friends? Or perhaps a boyfriend? Or relatives?"

"I have none. I suppose some of the women at work are friends, but I have no close friends. As for boyfriends, I stopped seeing a doctor from the hospital some months ago. How's that for timing!" said Helen and she began to sob. "And my only aunt is stuck in Germany."

"Now, now Helen," said the kindly old vicar as he put his arm around her to comfort her. "You and I will have to sort things out together. I want you to know that I'll be here to help you go through this the most difficult period in your life. Now let's start with the practical side of things and discuss what funeral arrangements you want."

A few days later, Helen and a small group of her parents' friends attended their funeral service conducted by the Reverend Beasley. Also there were her father's business manager, Brian Sargent, and his solicitor, Stanley Casement. The funeral service was held at the chapel at the Weston Mill Cemetery near Devonport and her parents were buried together. After the ceremony, she accompanied Stanley Casement back to his office for a reading of their wills.

"Their wills are very straight-forward. The money they left you is not substantial but enough to live on. Your father's firm was going through a bad patch because of the war and I expect business will pick up once the war is over."

"Mr. Casement, I would be grateful if you would draw up papers for me to sign handing over my father's business to Mr. Sargent for the nominal sum of, say, five pounds. I have no intention of going into business myself and Mr. Sargent has worked faithfully for my father these past twenty-five years and deserves to run the business. My father always spoke very highly of him."

"Are you sure this is wise?"

"Absolutely."

True to his word, Reverend Beasley arranged for some women from the parish to come and clear the house of her parents' clothes which were donated to the needy and victims of the air raids. Helen gathered all her family's most important papers and small belongings such as her mother's jewellery and her father's coin collection and other knick-knacks. Always the pragmatist, she opened a deposit box at a bank in nearby Tavistock, which was safe from the air raids in Plymouth. She would not see these items again until after the war was long over.

Helen continued to live in her parents' house and she realised that she might come back home one morning to find that it had been bombed. That was the risk she took because she planned to work at night when the need for her services was more urgent. She recognised that, even if the house was bombed, the land on which it stood would be of value after the war and she advised Mr. Casement of her wishes should this happen.

Helen returned to work the day after the funeral. Much to her regret, her nemesis Nurse Pat Egan was working the same shift. They were coldly polite to each other but studiously avoided talking. One result of the devastating air raids was that the nerves of the nursing staff were raw and small problems were magnified as if they were major crises. Psychologically everyone was suffering from the sheer trauma of the work they had to do. Tempers were frayed so that arguments were frequent and tetchily.

On April 29th, another German air raid occurred and the ambulance drivers brought in many casualties. One patient turned out to be a German pilot whose bomber had been shot down. A member of the Home Guard stood watch at the end of his bed. He was in a bad way with burns to most of his body and was clearly dying. The doctors could do nothing for him as it was only a matter of time before he died but they gave him some morphine to ease the pain.

"I wouldn't waste good morphine on that bastard, Doctor," Nurse Egan remonstrated angrily with one of the young doctors. "Save it for one of our people, not that Nazi killer!"

"He's a human being nurse who is in great pain," the doctor replied.

"He's no more of a human being than Adolf Hitler. He's a killer who has to be left to die!" she screamed.

Nurse Egan's outburst brought other members of the medical staff to the man's bedside, including Helen who looked at the patient for the first time.

"That's enough, Nurse!" cried Sister Jacobs. "Go to my office at once!"

"Oh my God, Albrecht! That's my cousin Albrecht!" Helen cried out all at once.

"So, you're a German as well, Masters!" bellowed a triumphant Pat Egan. Her words were full of vituperation. "I knew there was something strange about you. What have you been doing, spying for the Germans to tell them where to bomb in Plymouth!?"

Everyone stopped talking and looked confused. Helen ignored them. She hurried to Albrecht's bedside and took his hand.

"Albrecht, its Helen!" she cried.

He opened his eyes slowly, then smiled a faint smile when he saw her and died. Helen cried.

"Nurse Masters, I think you'd better go home. The army will take care of his body."

Reluctantly, Helen left the ward and slowly gathered her things together watched by other members of the staff, who, all of a sudden, seemed very suspicious of her and she could sense their hatred. She left the hospital for the last time.

When she got home at about two that morning she crawled into bed but couldn't sleep. She kept on seeing the image of Albrecht lying in a hospital bed almost burnt to a cinder. Here was the boy who had protected her from those Hitler Youth louts all those years ago. She remembered that they had such a fun time together then, swimming and crabbing at the beach. Why had he changed so much? She didn't know why only that another member of her family had been killed by the war. She longed to get as far away from the war as possible as it had brought her such heartache.

The next morning there was a knock at her front door as she was eating breakfast in her dressing gown. When she opened it there was a police officer in plainclothes and a uniformed policewoman standing there.

"I'm Detective Sergeant Alexander and this is Constable Murdoch," said the man in plainclothes as he showed her a warrant card. "Are you Helen Masters?"

"Yes."

"We would like you to come with us."

"Why?" asked a surprised Helen.

"We are arresting you on suspicion of spying for the Germans."

Helen burst out laughing: "You've got to be joking. Is this some joke? I bet Pat Egan sent you."

"No, Miss, I'm not joking. Now Murdoch here will go upstairs with you so you can get dressed."

When Helen was dressed, she was handcuffed and taken out to a waiting car. A crowd of onlookers were gathered on the pavement outside curious to know why Helen had been arrested. She was driven to the nearest police station and neither police officer answered her questions. She was taken into an interview room and sat at a table. The policewoman who had arrested her stood by the door saying nothing.

About thirty minutes later, a well-dressed man in his late forties came into the room. Chief Inspector Harold Channing was from Special Branch, the police department that was responsible for national security. The department works very closely with MI5, the domestic spy agency.

Chief Inspector Channing was a native of Cornwall and had joined Scotland Yard as a constable some twenty years previously. He had climbed the ranks at the yard transferring to Special Branch five years before. He was a small man with a rugged complexion, a bachelor and career driven. He had a hair-trigger temper and didn't appreciate the fools the police force recruited those days.

He was happy about his appointment to head up operations in Plymouth because the assignment was near to his beloved Cornwall. To him, Plymouth was a natural target for German spies because of the Royal Navy Dockyards in Devonport as well as other military facilities. He had been successful in catching a few spies already but this nurse didn't fit the mould and he had a feeling that this investigation wouldn't lead anywhere.

He introduced himself to Helen and in a friendly tone asked her: "Do you know an Albrecht Bader?"

"Yes. He was my German cousin. My Aunt Cynthia married a German student in 1912 and he was their son."

"When did you last see your cousin?"

"Uh? It must have been in 1938 when we went on holiday with my aunt and uncle at Binz in Germany. I've lost touch with the family and with the war on we haven't heard from them. I know my mother, before she died, was very concerned about their safety. I hadn't seen him until last night in the hospital."

"Do you speak German?"

"No. Would please tell me what this is all about?" said Helen getting a little annoyed with questions.

"You have been accused of spying and having Nazi tendencies."

"I'm not surprised that Pat Egan says these things about me. It's wasting your time and mine when we both have other things to do which are more important than questioning me."

"Why has she accused you so publicly?"

"Well, I stole a boyfriend from her and she threatened revenge. My cousin appearing out of the blue was golden opportunity for her. Can I go home now?"

"Not just yet. We are searching your house to make sure and we have to look into your family's background."

He got up and left. Helen was put in a cell and spent the night there. Apart from being woken at midnight by two drunken sailors being thrown into a cell next to hers, she slept well because she was so tired.

The next morning, she was led into the same interview room and Detective Chief Inspector Channing came in.

"I apologise for putting you through this, but we thought we were acting on reliable information at the time," he explained. "I'm satisfied this was malicious prank and Miss Egan will be charged with wasting our time."

When Helen got home, she was shocked to see a broken window and when she entered the house she found a brick on the living room floor with a note attached to it. The words on the paper were cut out from a newspaper and read: "Get out Nazi lover. This is your final warning before you die."

There was knock on the front door and when she answered it she found a postman on the doorstep holding a registered letter. She signed for it and went back into the house. She saw from the envelope that it was from the hospital. When she opened it and read she couldn't believe what she was reading. The letter was signed by the hospital's secretary saying that her services were no longer needed as the hospital was cutting back on its expenses. She knew that this explanation was just a cover to get rid of her because of her German connection, even how tenuous this was.

The next day she went to the shops with her ration card to buy some groceries and people in the street who would always greet her turned away as she approached. When she tried to buy some meat from the butcher she was told that they had no more although she noticed that women who came in after her were able to buy some meat.

Then one bold women, who had the reputation in the neighbourhood of being excruciatingly frank, shouted at Helen: "You're not wanted here. Why don't you go back to Germany where you belong, you evil Nazi." The other women in the street started chanting: "Nazi lover, go home." Helen just ran back to her house, slammed the front door behind her and collapsed crying on the sofa in the living room.

She had never been the subject of such venom. Why? Someone must have wound them up by telling lies about her. The situation was making it impossible to live there anymore. But where should she go and won't be followed be such hatred? She knew that it was very unlikely that any hospital in Britain would hire her without a positive reference. Also, the personnel departments at hospitals had an informal network to unofficially check with others about a candidate for a job and they would soon find out about her history in Plymouth.

Helen knew that she couldn't remain in Plymouth if this was the treatment she would be subjected to in the coming months or years. Maybe she should go abroad and return home once the war was over and start again. She remembered what Vivian Thomas had said about the Bahamas. Maybe this was temporary move she should make. In the next few days, she thought about the options she had and then decided to take Vivian's suggestion and move to the Bahamas. She knew Vivian would know the hospital's management so that would help her find a job. The next big question was how to get there and then she remembered Brian Sargent, who now owned her father's business.

The next morning she reported early to the offices of Masters Trading Company Limited near to the Devonport docks and was ushered in to Brian's office.

Once the pleasantries were over, she told him what she wanted: "Brian, I need a favour. I've decided to move to the Bahamas to be with my Aunt Vivian now that I have no longer any relatives here or a job. I need to go across the Atlantic by boat and then get another one to New Providence in the Bahamas. Could you arrange this for me?"

"Helen going across the Atlantic is a very dangerous business because German U-boats are on the prowl and sink ships even in closely watched convoys. I suspect that the best way for you would be to take a ship from a neutral country such as the United States or Ireland. Look, come back in a week's time and I'll tell what I've found out. Have you got a current passport?"

"Yes. Daddy, Mummy and I went to Bordeaux on holiday about three years ago and we had to get passports."

"Good. The delay in getting one would be horrendous because of the war. I'll see you next week then."

The week between the meetings with Brian Sargent were filled with bank visits to arrange the transfer of cash that she would need and briefing her solicitor, Mr. Casement, on her new needs as far as her parents' house, which would be boarded up. Time was also spent packing two large suitcases of clothes and other belonging she would want for her new life. She sent a cable to Vivian Thomas about her decision to take up her offer of help in the Bahamas. Several days later she received a positive response from Vivian, who told her about a job opening at the Bahamas General Hospital.

Helen visited Brian Sargent a week later. He looked up from his desk and smiled: "A lot of people owe your father many favours for his support of them over the years and they have lined up to help you, so to speak. You will have to take the BOAC clipper (British Overseas Airways Corporation) to Lisbon from Poole, Dorset, where you will be met by our agent there a Mr. Alfonso Da Cunha. Here are the tickets and your Portuguese visa. While in Lisbon you have to visit the American Embassy and receive your US visa. Now, Alfonso has arranged a hotel room for you and he will take care of your expenses while you are there.

"You'll like Portugal, it's a beautiful country but beware it's a hotbed of espionage right now because of its neutrality. Don't get mixed up with anyone there as they will likely have an ulterior motive and can't be trusted. For example, accept no parcels, gifts or envelopes to be taken to New York because that could land you in a heap of trouble with the authorities.

"Now, your passage to New York has been booked on the *SS Exeter* owned by American Export Lines, which leaves Lisbon on May 31st. Funny enough her sister ship, the *SS Excalibur*, took the Duke and Duchess of Windsor from Lisbon to Bermuda in August last year and then they went on to the Bahamas where he is now the Governor General.

"I digress. When you reach New York you will be met by Michael Creighton, an old time friend of your father's. He will put you up in a hotel and then you will catch a train to Miami. It's a two-day trip but you'll see many cities on the east coast of America. Michael has arranged passage for you from Miami directly to Nassau, the capital of the Bahamas."

When Brian had finished, Helen was stunned by the elaborate arrangements he had made.

"I don't know what to say Brian, I'm left so speechless by the wonderful plans you have made for me. I will always be grateful to you for your help."

"Like everyone else here, we were very fond of Gordon. He was a great mentor to me and I will always cherish his memory, so anything I can do for his daughter I will. Now I hear that you have had some problems because your cousin was in the Luftwaffe and I can understand peoples' anger because of the bombing we've suffered, but I don't think the rumours I've heard about you are true. I think you're doing the right thing in leaving because it will take people a long time to forget."

Brian got up, came around his desk and shook her hand. Helen kissed him on both cheeks and said, "Thank you, thank you."

Two days later as the BOAC flying boat took off with a roar from the estuary at Poole, she looked out of the window for the last time at a part of Britain she wanted to forget.

Roger's Story

Chapter 5

At about the same time Helen became a state registered nurse in 1940, Roger Lawson qualified as a doctor at Guys Hospital in London at the ripe old age of twenty-six. After a year as a houseman at the same hospital, he volunteered for the Royal Air Force and was assigned to an RAF bomber command base as its medical officer in Brookbery, Lincolnshire. And that is where his adventures began.

***

Over the North Sea, May 31st, 1942

Flight Lieutenant Jeffrey Jackson fought with the controls of his crippled Wellington bomber as he headed back to England after a bombing raid on the railroad yards near the city of Cologne, Germany. It was two in the morning.

He and his crew had unloaded their bombs, escaped the attention of the German night fighters and headed home. They had seen at least two Wellingtons go down after being hit by anti-aircraft fire and two Sterling bombers had collided over the city.

The British had bombed military and industrial sites in Belgium and France since 1940 and by 1942, the bombing raids drove deeper into Germany's industrial heartland. This Cologne operation was the first British one-thousand aircraft raid inflicted on a German city and its transportation infrastructure. Many other raids of this size were carried out after this by the RAF and the United States Air Force until the end of the war.

The raid Flight Lieutenant Jackson and his crew were involved in that night was codenamed 'Operation Millennium.' The operation was composed of a mesh-mash of seven different types of bombers drawn from units all over England and the crews were made up of experienced airmen as well trainees. The first target for the raid had been Hamburg, but it was bathed in fog so the alternative target of Cologne was selected. The damage to the city as a result of the raid was minimal, but the propaganda effect was substantial in Great Britain where it was hailed by the government as evidence of how the country was now hitting back in a big way at Germany. It was an important morale booster for a people devastated by the onslaught of Nazi Germany during the blitz in the previous two years.

As they headed home, Jackson's twin engine Wellington bomber was hit by anti-aircraft flak over the Dutch coast. He quickly pulled his control stick back and the aircraft climbed into the clouds to sixteen thousand feet to avoid further flak. However, the starboard engine began to lose power. The oil pressure indicator for that engine started to fall and it soon burst into flames

Twenty-three year old Flight Lieutenant Jackson was a born pilot. Before the war he had been a Pilot Officer in the RAF Volunteer Reserve at the age of eighteen and received his wings at nineteen. So far he had completed twenty operations and he had ten more to go before he was 'rested'. He would then be transferred as an instructor to a training unit for aircrew and after six months he would have to complete twenty more operations.

Dr. Roger Lawson had been the medical officer at RAF Brooksbery for about a year by time this operation took place. The airfield was in Lincolnshire on the windy east coast of England facing the North Sea.

The base had opened a year earlier and was one of the first with a concrete runway. Its runway layout was typical of most of Bomber Commands bases in that it was triangular so that take offs and landings could be undertaken from six different directions depending on the prevailing wind.

Roger's experience at RAF Brooksbery had been a busy, harrowing one because of the tremendous casualty rate of its aircrews, which was typical in Bomber Command in general. In this short time, the carnage he saw among the crews had matured him as an emergency doctor and as a human being. He lost many aircrew members in his meagre emergency facilities. Normally he would send cases to local hospitals in the area but some of these men were too badly wounded to move. He could only stop the bleeding, sew up the wounds, give them morphine and comfort them before they died.

Many of the men he knew and socialised with were dead and, despite the cost, the young faces kept coming only to be lost after a few raids. The most poignant event for him was seeing the base adjutant after a raid emptying the personal lockers of those men who were not coming back.

An estimated forty-four percent of RAF Bomber Command crews were killed by the end of the war in 1945 and many were captured or badly wounded when their aircraft crashed. It was expected that some five percent of aircraft would be lost during each raid and sometimes this figure was even greater. It has been said that a crew member had a worse chance of survival than an infantry officer in the trenches in the First World War.

After many months of this distressing, stressful existence, Roger determined that the best way he could mentally handle the human suffering he saw without becoming a casualty himself was not to become too close to or socialise with anyone from an aircrew. This might seem callous he knew, but it was the only way he could survive the almost daily trauma of seeing so many damaged, dead or dying men.

Flight Lieutenant Jackson, or JJ as he was known, was one of the longest surviving pilots in his Air Group and had been an exception to Roger's rule. He was easy to like and his boyish charm lit up the local pub where they would often go. He wasn't that much older than the rest of the lads, but Roger Lawson was regarded as the 'old man' of the group. So when JJ told him he was going to get married, he was guardedly enthusiastic, but inwardly shocked at the news. JJ seemed to have no thought about the frailty of his life and the real possibility that he wouldn't survive. On the other hand these boys, who had no foreseeable future, lived from moment to moment and it was their way of coping with the dangers known to all of them. And who was Roger to deny them their fleeting chance of happiness.

Roger met JJ's fiancée, Maureen, who seemed to understand the mess she might be in when, and if, he were lost. It turned out that they had been romantically involved for some time before the war. The daughter of a solicitor, she was a pragmatic woman who knew what she wanted from life. She was a member of an anti-aircraft team in her home town of Sheffield. It was evident that they were very much in love and Roger began to understand why they wanted to be as normal as possible while hiding that monster death in the basement of their minds. Two months later they were married and, after a brief few days of leave, JJ was back at the station and flying again.

The night of 'Operation Millennium,' Roger was in the control tower as usual waiting for the return of planes when the station wireless received JJ's emergency message and everybody knew he was in big trouble. Roger went out to the Austin K2 ambulance and told his medical assistants Flight Sergeant Cameron and Aircraftsman Harding what was happening. The medical staff just sat there in silence and waited. Some of the aircraft in the flight were beginning to return but there was no sign of JJ and his crew. After half an hour Roger was really worried that maybe they had ditched in the North Sea. What was he going to tell Maureen?

Meanwhile, JJ's Wellington had made it across the North Sea and was just south of Hull. The city was lit up by fires as result of a German bombing raid and, as the aircraft approached, the city's anti-aircraft fire from its guns lit up the sky, but the bursting shells were too far away to cause any damage to the aircraft. As he turned the Wellington south, the aircraft began to lose height and JJ started looking for an airfield to put his wounded aircraft down.

JJ's wireless operator was able to raise the tower at Brooksbery again and inform them of their position. The controllers at the airfield warned the wireless operator of other aircraft in the area which were trying to land. Then his navigator was able to give JJ the headings for Brooksbery and soon they were able to spot the flares and the landing lights at the airfield. As they flew over the village of Brooksbery, JJ ordered his five-man crew to move into the crash position, which was in the middle of the fuselage between the wings because it was the strongest part of the aircraft.

As the Wellington approached the runway another aircraft appeared in front of them and JJ pulled the stick back and throttled up the only engine and just made a turn to come in again. This time he was able to lower the undercarriage but the indicator on his panel showed that only one wheel was down. At this stage he was committed to landing and he knew he couldn't go around again. As the aircraft hit the hard runway, it turned in a vicious circle and then the good undercarriage completely collapsed. The bomber ended up in the grass strip on the side of the runway and immediately burst into flames and ammunition from its guns began to explode.

As soon as the aircraft came to a standstill Flight Sergeant Cameron drove the ambulance as close as possible to the stricken aircraft. Five men came flying out of the escape hatch. Some were badly burnt and, as the medical crew helped them into the ambulance, they said that JJ was still in the cockpit.

The loss of his friend and the probable devastation it would cause his wife flashed through Roger's mind. He knew he would never forgive himself if he didn't try and rescue the incapacitated pilot. He grabbed a fire axe from the fire tender, which was dousing the aircraft with water and foam, and ran towards the cockpit ignoring the warnings of the airmen that the plane's oxygen tanks might explode. The heat was tremendous and his uniform started to catch fire.

He saw JJ still strapped in his seat and it looked like he was unconscious. He started hacking at the Perspex windscreen of cockpit. He didn't know where he got the maniacal strength from but he persevered despite the painful burns to his hands and face. Suddenly he was joined by Flight Sergeant Cameron who came with another fire axe and helped him smash through the windscreen so they could reach JJ.

In order to free him from his harness Roger had to climb down into the well of the cockpit. He wrestled with his harness which would not come free. Flight Sergeant Cameron handed him a big knife and he was able to cut the straps. He then started to lift JJ from his seat but he had difficulty because the flying suit he was wearing was bulky. Eventually he pushed JJ up over the side of the hole they had made enough for the sergeant and two other airmen to pull him to safety.

Just as he started to clamber out of the cockpit there was loud explosion as one of the oxygen tanks blew up. The force of the explosion threw him out of the plane and Roger staggered towards many helping hands and then collapsed, unconscious.

In the next two days Roger was in and out of consciousness. He was kept very much sedated so he didn't know what was happening. He couldn't feel anything and he tried to speak but words would not come out of his mouth. When he tried to talk, he heard voices telling him to stay calm and then he drifted off again. Sometimes he would dream one of those nonsensical dreams of a train crash when everyone was killed except for a young man, who was badly hurt, and himself. He helped him out of the wreck and they were staggering up an embankment when there was a large explosion and the young man disappeared.

In one of his more lucid moments, he was aware of travelling in the back of what must have been an ambulance. In fact, the doctors at the local hospital in Peterborough, where he had been taken, had agreed to let him be transferred to the burns unit at Queen Victoria

Hospital near East Grinstead, which is about thirty miles south of London. To get there he was loaded onto a hospital train and sent to Kings Cross Station in London and from there he went by ambulance to East Grinstead.

This hospital's burns unit helped many disfigured airmen throughout the war as it developed new techniques in the treatment of burns. Doctors had found that aircrew with burns who had been rescued out of the sea healed faster than others. They developed a system where patients were treated with saline baths or with saline dressings and the results were outstanding. In addition to the physical injuries there was an emphasis on helping patients with the psychological scars which their trauma had caused.

When Roger began to wake from his drug-induced sleep after arriving at the hospital, he began to feel a pain which was at first dull and then it grew more intense. As he became more aware of his surroundings, he noticed his right leg was heavily bandaged with wooden splints attached to it. It was elevated in a sling which was attached to the bed.

A doctor came to see him and introduced himself as Dr. Archibald McIndoe. He was the famous burns doctor who had revolutionised the treatment of burns victims.

"Dr. Lawson, you have burns on your face, neck, hands and legs which, fortunately for you, are not too severe. We plan to treat these with saline baths, we have found that helps to rejuvenate the skin," he told him in his hard New Zealand accent. "We'll get you out of here as soon as possible."

Then the other shoe dropped. "You will be scarred for life I'm afraid, but you're a darn sight luckier than many of the poor devils here. Just look around you and you will see what I mean. The orthopaedic surgeons at the hospital in Peterborough operated on your right kneecap. They repaired some of the damage, but I'm afraid you have to use a cane indefinitely to help you walk," he said in his frank, no-nonsense manner.

"Will I be able to use my hands after the treatments so that I can operate?"

"Some of your dexterity will return, but not at the same level. However, you will get a general feeling back in them. I understand you had planned to become a surgeon. I'm afraid that won't be possible now with the injuries you sustained."

After Dr. McIndoe left, Roger just lay in bed with tears welling up in his eyes. This news hit him very hard and he forgot how lucky he was to be alive.

"Come on old chap it's not as bad as all that," said an enthusiastic voice of someone at the end of his bed.

"How the bloody hell would you know?" he replied angrily, lashing out at someone who did not know what he was going through.

"Well you look a lot better than I do."

Roger looked up and there before him was a man without a face. He was shocked beyond belief. This man had slits for eyes and a large opening for a mouth. The nostrils of his nose were visible as just two holes. He was so scarred it was as if his face had melted under an intense heat just as wax does if you hold it too close to a flame. He wore striped pyjamas, a RAF cravat and across his shoulders was his uniform jacket and Roger could see he was a squadron leader.

"I'm Iain Mackintosh formally of his majesty's Royal Air Force. They won't let me fly again so when I'm finished here they are going to pack me off home," said the cheerful Scot. "I'll probably join my dad's engineering firm in Paisley. I'm due for my next operation tomorrow which will mean I can join the Guinea Pig Club."

"What's that?" Roger asked.

"A few of the lads decided to form a drinking club to help us burn victims cope with our new looks. Dr. McIndoe has been doing great experimental work on grafting skin onto burnt areas giving us some semblance of our former looks. You can only become a member of the club if you have at least ten operations. Because what he does is experimental, we feel like guinea pigs. Hence the name of the club."

"How do you cope with the fact you will never look the same as you did before? It must upset and depress you."

"What alternative have I got? I could spend the rest of my life feeling sorry for myself. What good would that do? No, I'm going to go back to university and get my engineering degree and join my dad's firm."

Roger began a firm friendship with Iain as time went on. As he was still bed bound, they played chess on his bed and he would bring him a beer from the barrel in the ward. The patients had concerts laid on by the local community which always ended in a noisy sing along aided by the beer. It was surprising how morale was very upbeat and positive.

As the weeks passed, Roger continued treatment by dipping his hands and arms into a bath of saline solution for twenty minutes twice a day and his face and neck were treated with saline soaks. At first when they took off the dressings each day a large amount of dead skin came away with the bandage, but this gradually lessened. He slowly began to heal, although he still had little motion in his hands, which came back somewhat with physiotherapy and exercises.

After eight weeks his cast was taken off his leg and he began to walk again with aid of crutches. It was painful at first but he was now mobile and focussed on getting stronger with the physical exercise. Eventually, he lost the crutches and was able to walk with the aid of a cane.

This change in his recovery had stopped him brooding, but from time to time he suffered from bouts of morose and selfish feelings. As the storm clouds gathered in his mind, the waves of self-pity and anger began to wash over him. Selfish, evil thoughts invaded his mind from to time, such as why didn't he let the poor bugger fry and then he wouldn't be in this predicament! Despite the help he received from the hospital's psychologist and bolstered by Iain's positive attitude, he still bitterly resented his disfigurement and his permanent leg injury.

From the day he had gained consciousness, he had asked constantly for any news of Flight Lieutenant Jackson. No one knew or, if they did, they weren't going to tell him. When he regained some of dexterity in his hands he wrote a letter in a shaky hand to Maureen at her home address. Two weeks later he received a letter from Maureen's father telling him that JJ had died of the wounds he had received on that fateful night and that Maureen had been killed during an air raid. He was so angry that no one had told him about their deaths and, needless to say, he was devastated by the news.

It was this tragic news that woke him up to reality and stopped his self-pity in its tracks. Who was he to act like a self-indulgent degenerate? JJ and Maureen, with all the danger they were facing, had been determined to live life to the full. They had had that brief moment of happiness.

Roger had his whole life before him and he resolved then and there that he would follow their example and not let them down.

Old Friend and New Horizons

Chapter 6

September 20th, 1942

Roger was finally released from hospital on a rainy and cold day in late September. He was heading to his parents' home in Godalming, Surrey, and had been given two weeks leave.

He sat in the crowded waiting room at East Grinstead's railway station suffering from one of the biggest hangovers he had ever had. The night before his fellow patients threw a farewell party for him and someone had produced two bottles of Scotch whiskey, which everyone had guzzled down. Roger suspect this rare treat was provided by Dr. McIndoe who appeared halfway through the party and stayed for only thirty minutes.

Because of air raid damage, train timetables were virtually non-existent. When trains arrived they were always crowded and chances were you had to stand in the corridors. He was in luck when a train pulled in an hour after he had arrived at the station. He was one of the last people to get into the train and he had difficulty climbing up the steps with his case and walking stick. As he was wrestling with this problem, two strong arms grabbed him from behind and lifted him and his case into the train.

"There you go, sir," said a sailor who had seen his difficulties and helped him. He thanked him and hobbled along the corridor looking for a seat. There was none so he leaned against the side of the carriage and resigned himself to standing. He wanted to take as much weight off his right leg as possible so he put most of it on his left leg. Despite this his right knee still throbbed.

Then the compartment door nearest to him opened and out came a middle-aged woman.

"Take my seat, luv. You shouldn't have to stand while us able-bodied types lounge around. You served our country and, by the look of you, you got wounded doing so."

"Thank you. I just got out of hospital today and I'm not too good on my pins yet," he said.

Roger sat in her seat by the window and was conscious of everybody looking him over. When he looked up, everyone looked down. So this is how it's going to be, he thought to himself. People's natural curiosity will want them to know how he was wounded. Their British reserve stopped them, although he knew they were dying to hear his story. Then a child, as only a child would, said: "Hey, Mister, how did you get that way?"

A woman on whose lap he was sitting hushed him and apologised for his rudeness and was very embarrassed.

"I don't mind," Roger said. "What's your name, son?"

"Tommy."

"Well Tommy, I am an RAF doctor and I was trying to rescue a pilot from a crashed Wellington bomber when it blew up."

"Wow! You got burnt?"

"I'm afraid so."

Finally the train started to pull out of the station and made its way slowly, stopping many times. He fell asleep for what must have been an hour and he woke up as the train shuddered to a stop at a station. He looked out of the window and saw that we were just getting in to south London. He had never seen such devastation before, with street upon street of rubble where houses had been and others standing there incredibly unscathed. And this was not the worst hit area of the city. This doubtful honour belonged to the East End where the London docks were located. The people there bore the brunt of the blitz when German bombers had rained death on the city for fifty-seven consecutive nights.

When Roger got off the train at Clapham Junction, he climbed down stairs painfully and walked through the subway to the north side of the station from where his train for Godalming would leave. This simple act of walking from one platform to another was exhausting. He eventually made it to the right platform and again sat in the waiting room. Finally, when the train came, he was able to find a seat and again dozed off.

Roger got off the train at Godalming and started to walk towards his parents' house on Ockford Road. Rain was coming down hard as he made his way and he had to stop to rest several times. Finally, the house came into sight and he was grateful for the shelter the porch offered as he rang the doorbell. While he waited for someone to answer, he saw an army staff car parked in front of the house.

His eighteen-year old sister Elaine answered the door. At first she hesitated and then she recognised him and burst into tears. Tears rolled down her freckled face as she threw her arms around him.

"Oh, Roger, it is so good to see you! But your face is so scarred. What have they done to you!?"

"It's so good to be home, sis. I think I'm more handsome now," he said, trying to make light of it and she started crying again.

Elaine was always on the slightly heavy side and she constantly had trouble controlling her weight. But since rationing had begun, she had lost some pounds and he thought she had become remarkably attractive. She was dressed in the uniform of the Auxiliary Territorial Service or ATS and told him she chauffeured for some senior army officers at nearby Blackdown Barracks.

Just then, his mother came out of the kitchen and he had another round of hugs and tears about his appearance.

"Come on into the kitchen and sit yourself down. I've just made a cup of tea," she said.

"Mum, I must go. I've got to pick the colonel up at three. Let's talk some more Roger," Elaine said a few minutes later as she got up and put on her army great coat. Then she was gone.

"She's quite grown up now. She isn't the same flighty girl you remember I am sure. Joining the ATS has been really good for her and her confidence. It has really matured her a lot. She is billeted at the Blackdown Barracks and pops in to see us when she's nearby. When did you last see her?" Mother asked.

"It's at least two years, Mum. Are you sure she's alright living in the barracks with all those soldiers? You know what they're like."

"She's fine and she has made many new girlfriends. They look after each other. You've no need to be protective of her. I remember you were cutting up dead bodies in medical school at her age."

"That's different."

"No it's not."

Changing the subject, Roger asked her how his father was.

"Dad is very angry because he has not been called in to assist in the war effort. He's gone down to the library to read the newspapers and he'll be back for supper at five," she said with a sigh.

Roger's father was in military intelligence in the First World War and was one of the team that uncovered a German spy ring in Portsmouth, a vital naval port. He was seventy now and Roger believed it was unrealistic to think that anyone from MI5 would call him in to help. He retired from MI5 in 1928 and had worked for a bank until he was sixty-five. He had married Roger's mother in 1911 when she was only twenty and he was born a year later. His parents had been trying again to have a second child but they weren't able to until his sister came along in 1924, much to everyone's surprise.

Roger went up to his old room, which hadn't changed a bit since he had last been there. It still had that same damp and musty smell he remembered and it was cold. He changed out of his uniform, got into the bed. He was so tired after the strenuous journey that day and he was glad to close his eyes and fall asleep. When he woke up it was dark and he got out of bed, dressed as quickly as he could and went downstairs.

His mother and father were in the kitchen eating their dinner.

"Come in, Roger, and sit down," his mother said. She got up from the table and helped him to some stew and potatoes.

"Hello, Father," he said shaking his outstretched hand. His father was not one for showing any sentiment. He had always seemed gruff, but underneath it all he was a caring, pragmatic man. You could always go to him with any problem and he would give you an honest answer or opinion.

"I see you banged yourself up pretty badly. How did this happen?" he asked.

Roger then told him what had happened and about his time in hospital. He had asked his parents not to visit him because of the long journey to East Grinstead and he wanted them to see him more or less healed not the mess he was in at first. Also, they would have been shocked at seeing his fellow patients who were in far worse shape.

Both of them listened intently and peppered him with a lot of questions. His father then asked him what he was going to do.

"Well I've got two weeks' leave and then I have to report to the Air Ministry for my next assignment. With these damaged hands I can't become a surgeon so after this war is over I'll probably become a general practitioner somewhere. What are you doing with yourself since you retired, dad?"

"I expected to be called in to the ministry when war was declared. I know I am still a good analyst. I've called some people I knew and I've been given the brush off. This war is almost over and I haven't done a God damn thing except yell at stupid people who haven't closed their blackout blinds properly when I'm on duty as an air raid warden."

Roger listened and sympathised with him, but there was nothing he could say or do to help him out. He had never seen him so frustrated.

The first week he was back at home Roger spent his time reading medical journals to catch up with the latest developments. He was fascinated by the work that was being done on a wonder drug called Penicillin. It was in limited supply, but it had already helped cure infections caused by many battlefield wounds. He went on long walks since he was determined that he would get back in to some sort of shape and he had worked out a fairly rigorous schedule to achieve this.

Roger's mother said she was concerned about him moping around the house, as she put it. She suggested that he go out and see some friends at the local pub rather than stay home. Most of his friends were away in the services but there were one or two older men he knew. He wasn't sure whether his mother's suggestion was a good idea or not, but he decided to take the plunge.

The Richmond Arms pub was about half a mile away from home and it took him quite a bit of time to walk it to the door of the saloon bar. He heard the familiar hub-bub of conversations. The pub was full and when he entered he saw several familiar faces. There was Brian McDougal, a local solicitor, and Frank Case, a teacher at a local school. They were regulars at the pub. Brian was in his mid-forties and was rather rotund but he had a very sharp mind that belittled his appearance. Frank, on the other hand, was about same age but in contrast stood over six feet and was as thin as a rake. He was a scholar of English literature and had got his degree from Oxford University. Both men were talking to three women who were in Women's Auxiliary Air Force uniforms or

WAAFs as they were called. Behind the bar was the landlord Jim Thorpe.

When he entered the pub everyone there fell silent and stared at him, he thought with some distaste, or was it his imagination? He thought this wasn't such a good idea after all. As he slowly and painfully hobbled towards the bar, Brian McDougal started clapping and everyone in the pub joined in.

"Roger, let me buy you a drink, old man."

"No you don't Brian, his drinks are on the house tonight," declared Jim Thorpe.

The others greeted him and shook his hand lightly when they saw his injuries. The three women in the group were a little nervous of him. They seemed to back away and did not look at him directly. As the evening wore on they became friendlier although they were still wary.

Roger caught up with the news of his friends and much of it was not good. His boyhood friend, James Robertson, was shot down in his Spitfire over the channel. His body was recovered and he was buried in the churchyard at Busbridge Church there in Godalming.

It was about nine when the door to the bar opened and Patricia Jones walked in. She was dressed in slacks and a printed shirt and had on an anorak and sou'wester hat that were wet with the rain. Patricia was a very curvaceous thirty-two year old redhead who always caused a wave of desire from men as she entered a room. Many who saw her appreciated her obvious physical attributes but few knew of her business intellect as a leading young accountant in the City of London, the financial district of the city.

Patricia and Roger had been on-and-off lovers for many years and he had been meaning to look her up during his leave. In all honesty, he was reluctant to do

94

this because he believed she would have been sickened by his appearance. They had lost touch since he had joined the RAF and she had gone off to London to work for a big insurance company in the city.

She rushed up to him and kissed him on the cheek.

"Your mother told me you were here, Rog. How nice to see you again. Why didn't you call me, you old reprobate?"

"I didn't think you wanted to see me like this."

"Rubbish. You don't feel sorry for yourself do you?"

"No, but I feel embarrassed."

"Well you don't have to be with me. If anything it's an improvement."

Everyone around them laughed at her joke. They found an empty table in a quiet corner of the bar and talked for over an hour about what each of them had been doing since they last saw each other. Then she dropped a bombshell on him. She told him she was getting married to a forty-year-old banker from the city.

"I thought it was about time I settled down and it won't be long before my biological clock runs out for having children. I want to enjoy them when I'm young and I can't wait. All the young men of my age are in this war and it's a sort of here today and gone tomorrow existence with them and me."

"Do you love him?"

"No, not really. I respect him for his business acumen and he will make a great father for my children."

Roger thought that this was typical pragmatic Patricia. In all the years they had been on and off lovers they had enjoyed making love but they were never in love. They just enjoyed each other.

"So when is the big day?"

"Sometime this coming spring."

Jim Thorpe, the landlord, called time. As they were leaving the pub, Jim slipped Roger a bottle of Scotch whisky.

"That's a little something of a thank you for your service," he said. Roger thanked him as he went out into the rain-swept street with Patricia.

"Would you like to come in for a night cap? My flat is just around the corner," she asked Roger.

"You bet."

They walked slowly towards a large, four-story building which was a new block of flats that had been built just before the war. Patricia's flat was on the third floor and thank goodness there was a lift Roger could use.

They sat in her living room drinking the scotch Jim had given Roger. It wasn't long before they moved into her bedroom, took each other's clothes off and stood there naked looking at each other.

"God, Rog, I didn't know how badly burnt you were, you poor darling. Does it still work?"

"That's for you to find out," he said with a laugh.

His short affair with Patricia was a boost to his battered ego. She had rescued him from the depths of depression that came with the wounded man he was both physically and psychologically. He would always be grateful to her for that. When his leave was over they parted as firm friends.

On his last week on leave, apart from passing some of the evenings with Patricia, he spent time fishing on the Wey River and he began to relax as the peaceful river flowed past. Some days his father joined him and they enjoyed the time in each other's company. Despite appreciating the respite with his family, he really wanted to get back to practising medicine.

On a rainy Monday morning the next week, Roger got off the underground train at the Temple station in London and he walked slowly to the Air Ministry building at Adastral House on the corner of Kingsway and Aldwych. He had estimated that it would take him almost three times longer to do things and he factored that into his routine. He arrived at the building well ahead of his appointment at ten with a Group Captain Richard Rogerson, the RAF's chief medical officer, to learn what his new assignment was. He was puzzled why he was meeting the group captain because usually orders were sent out by mail, especially for such a junior officer.

The receptionist took his name and told him to sit in the reception area, which was a room next to the main desk. There were other officers waiting and they were all picked up by WAAF staff and taken to their various meetings. He was left on his own and, half an hour later, a WAAF sergeant came in and asked him to follow her. He did so very slowly and soon she was quite a few steps ahead. She turned around, saw him struggling and smiled.

"Let's take the lift, sir."

They went up to the third floor and she guided him through a warren of different offices until they reached one that had the group captain's name on it. They walked into the outer office where other WAAFs were pounding away on typewriters. The sergeant knocked on the door to the Group Captain's office door and entered.

"Flight Lieutenant Lawson, Sir"

"Come in, Roger," said a tall, wiry looking man with ginger hair and a moustache to match.

Roger stood to attention and saluted.

"Here, take your coat and cap off and take a pew on one of those seats," he said as he pointed to the chairs in front of his desk.

After asking how Roger was recovering, he said: "I have two pieces of good news for you. First, we are sending you to the Bahamas as part of the medical team there. The RAF has set up an operational training unit on the main island to train our pilots on Liberator and Mitchell bombers. It's also a staging place for ferrying these planes to Europe, the Middle East and Asia after they have been built in the States. There will be about three thousand RAF personnel eventually on the island when we open operations there early next year so we need to expand the medical team we have there. You will report to Wing Commander Meyer Rassin. Sergeant James will give you the details of your travel plans. Any questions?"

"Unfortunately, I can't use a scalpel anymore, so what will my duties be, sir?"

"We need a good diagnostician and someone who can deal with those tasks that don't need a surgeon.

"Now, I left the really good news until last. His majesty the King has graciously agreed to make you a Member of the Order of the British Empire for gallantry in recognition of your rescue of the crew of that Wellington bomber. Congratulations!"

Roger was stunned at this news.

"I'm grateful sir, but those boys who fly into danger night after night are the real heroes. They should be the ones to get the medals."

"That has been taken care of. Flight Lieutenant Jackson has been awarded a Distinguished Fly Cross posthumously and his father will be at the Palace with you next week to accept it on his behalf."

On the way home, Roger thought about the consequences of his not accepting the medal. Deep down he knew he didn't deserve it and he hated the fuss that was going to be made. He reasoned that he was really a very quiet and unassuming person who liked to keep his head down and just get on with his work. On the other hand, he realised he had a duty to his medical team at RAF Brooksbery, and medical staff like them in every RAF station. They needed recognition for the work they did to save aircrew lives every day after each sortie. He decided reluctantly that he had to accept the medal on their behalf.

Needless to say, his family was overjoyed by the news of his OBE. The next week they all trooped off to Buckingham Palace for the presentation. Obviously, Roger wasn't the only recipient of an award as there were about twenty other recipients gathered in the throne room for the ceremony. One of the King's equerries briefed them on what was expected of them and the agenda for the ceremony. When it came time for the medal to be presented to Roger, the King pinned it on his uniform and talked to him for a few minutes.

As they left the palace, there were a number of newspaper photographers taking photographs of the recipients. Roger tried to duck away but he was forced to stand there and show off his medal. The next morning, the *Times* newspaper had pictures of him under the headline 'The Reluctant Hero.' That summed up his feelings precisely.

A week later he began his journey to the Bahamas via the blustery and cold town of Greenock, which is northwest of Glasgow in Scotland. During the Second World War, Greenock, with its deep anchorage in the Firth of Clyde, was the base for the Royal Navy's Home

Fleet as well as the main assembly point for Atlantic convoys.

After two days of a gruelling train journey from London to Glasgow and then a local train to Greenock, Roger, and about one hundred airmen of different nationalities, were taken to the nearby town of Gourock. There they boarded a large tender which took them into the foggy Firth of Clyde. It was a very eerie journey because they couldn't see where they were going and where they had come from. Then suddenly they came upon a very large grey ship — the *Queen Mary* nicknamed 'The Grey Lady.'

This beautiful liner and her sister ship the *Queen Elizabeth* were being used as troop carriers first of all from Commonwealth countries to Great Britain then to and from the United States. They had both been painted in the Royal Navy grey which gave them an ominous appearance, especially in the fog. At a maximum speed of twenty-eight knots they could easily outrun the U-boats in the Atlantic and didn't need Royal Navy escorts, not that many could keep up with them. All the finery of a luxury liner had been taken away and the ships had been refitted to carry thousands of men and equipment. Anti-aircraft guns were set up on their decks for protection.

When they had settled in, they were all given tasks for their five-day journey to New York. Roger was assigned to the sick bay while others were given such jobs as passing ammunition when needed to the anti-aircraft gunners, cleaning the accommodations and galley duties.

No sooner had they boarded, when the ship began its journey as it slipped out of the Firth Clyde into the Irish Sea.

A Challenging New Role

Chapter 7

New York, December 27th, 1942

The journey to New York had been remarkably uneventful except for one night when the 'action stations' alarm was sounded at about three in the morning. Someone on the bridge had thought they had picked up a sonar echo from a submarine. After half an hour of waiting everyone was told to stand down.

Roger had made friends with the ship's doctor, sixty-seven year old Dr. Robert Gaskell. This extraordinary man was a retired general practitioner from Gateshead in England and had volunteered for service when the war broke out. He was too old for the armed services but he was accepted by Cunard. The sum total of their work on the trip to New York was one broken arm, an airman with boils and another with a high fever, which turned out to be flu. The mundaneness of the work didn't seem to bother Dr. Gaskell, who told Roger that he was glad to play a small part in the war effort.

In the evenings, Dr. Gaskell and Roger would play chess and drink his illicit store of scotch whisky, which he had picked up on one of his trips to New York. They would talk about some of the new operating techniques and drugs that were being developed. He was a wise, highly-intelligent man and he imparted some of his wisdom to Roger. This had been gained from his forty years of medical experience and he communicated this knowledge through sometimes amusing stories that were really allegories. Importantly for Roger, they had many discussions about his future and Dr. Gaskell emphasised that there was much more to medicine than being a surgeon. To him, being a good diagnostician and mending the minds of patients was extremely important.

He said that with his years of experience as a general practitioner he could tell the hypochondriacs among his patients. In his dispensary, he would make up bottles of coloured water – red, green or yellow – and give them a bottle to cure what was ailing them. Before long they would be back saying: "Doc, that green medicine you gave me did the trick. Can I have some more?" Although Roger laughed at the story, Dr. Gaskell's point about healing the mind as well as the body was well taken.

They had celebrated Christmas that year in the middle of the Atlantic Ocean and the navy cooks laid on a wonderfully gourmet meal, at least they thought it was gourmet compared with the meagre rations they were used to. It turned out the supplies of turkey and trimmings were picked up on the previous trip to New York.

Roger was sorry that his time with Dr. Gaskell had come to an end when the ship docked in New York.

The night before the ship reached port, they were told at a meeting that there would be lorries on the quayside which would take them to Camp Kilmer, a US army base near Edison in New Jersey. After spending twenty-four hours there, they were going to catch a train to Miami and then board a ship to the Bahamas. Roger thought it was a shame that they were not going to get a chance to see the sights of New York and explore the city.

Roger was on the open deck of the *Queen Mary* when she slinked into the New York harbour at seven in the morning and, with help of tugboats, docked at one of the Chelsea Piers, which were in the heart of city. It was still dark at this time although the city's skyscrapers were lit up like proverbial Christmas trees and there was no sign of any attempt to maintain a blackout. The war that he knew was thousands of miles away with its darkened cities and bombing raids.

Looking out over the sheds that housed customs and freight terminals onto the quay and beyond, Roger saw, as far as the eye could see, a very large contingent of about a thousand American soldiers and their equipment. They were ready to board the ship for the return journey to Britain once the incoming troops had disembarked.

An hour after the ship had docked the incoming servicemen began to disembark. As Roger went down the gangplank from the ship to the quay, he saw two plain clothes men at the bottom. As he reached the quay one of them asked: "Are you Dr. Roger Lawson, sir?"

"Yes. Who are you?"

"My name is Cummings and I work for the British Foreign Office," he said as he showed Roger his identification. "We would like you to come with us, sir"

"But, I've already received my orders. I'm to go with the other RAF officers to the Bahamas," he said, puzzled at this request.

"We know sir. It has been arranged that you will go there in a few days. Our boss wants to have a word with you first," said Cummings as he picked up Roger's case.

"Boss? Who is your boss?"

"Simon Cookson, sir."

"Simon?"

"Yes, sir."

That took Roger by surprise. Simon and he went to school together at Wellington College and he had lost touch with him when they left school. He went to Oxford and then, he thought, into the Foreign Office. He was an all-round good athlete and brainy too. Roger was intrigued by his interest in him after all these years.

"We've booked you into the Plaza, sir," said Cummings. "Our car is just over there."

On the car journey to the hotel, Roger stared out of the window at the enormity of cavernous streets with buildings stretching up to the sky. The sun was just beginning to peak through in the eastern sky and hundreds of people were scurrying around, probably on their way to work. He had never seen a sight quite like this. What struck him most was the seeming prosperity of the people who all appeared well-nourished and well-dressed compared with their much poorer equivalents in Britain.

They arrived at the Plaza Hotel and his companions left, wishing him a good stay. When he had been shown to his room on the ninth floor, he was astonished at its lushness with a double bed and modern furniture. There was a separate bathroom with a shower! He had never had a shower in his life and this was going to be a new experience for him. He took off his uniform and jumped under the shower. He stayed in it for a good half an hour luxuriating in the warmth and the pure luxury of the moment.

As he towelled himself off, he looked out of the window of his room onto the panorama of Central Park and the tall buildings surrounding it and marvelled at the scene before him. He was astonished at the seeming richness of life here in America compared with the harshness of life in Britain. He switched on the radio, which was on the desk, and he listened to a report by someone called Eric Sevareid from London who was reporting on a British commando raid on shipping in Bordeaux harbour. He thought to himself that most Americans probably have no idea what was happening in Europe. They hear these reports but he wondered how much they understand of Britain's plight.

Then the telephone rang as he was listening to the report. Simon Cookson was on the other end.

"Roger, how are you? Bet you were surprised at being whisked off to a posh hotel instead of grubbing around in an army barracks?"

"I was completely astonished, Simon. How did you know I was in town?"

"I read about your medal in the *Times* and the fact you were going to the Bahamas. I made a few enquiries and found out where and when you'd be here. I need to talk to you about this posting to the Bahamas. Let me take you to lunch for the best steak in New York. I'll pick you up at noon. See you then." And then he hung up.

Roger was in the lobby area of the hotel five minutes before Simon was to meet him so he could look around at the hotel shops. The concierge gave him a street map of the area and, surprisingly, warned him about going into Central Park after dusk. He said there had been a spate of robberies there and it was too dangerous.

Simon arrived promptly at noon and they climbed into a cab which took them to Gallagher's on West 52nd Street. They settled in a booth at the far end of the restaurant and ordered drinks and their meal. They started by discussing old friends from school and what they were doing now.

After these pleasantries, Simon looked seriously at him: "What I am about to tell you is very secret and must never be mentioned to anyone."

"I understand."

"I work for William Stephenson, head of our Secret Intelligence Service operations in New York, which is known as the British Security Coordination office. He is responsible for counter espionage in the Western hemisphere which includes the Caribbean.

"As you know, the Duke of Windsor is the Governor of the Bahamas. He was sent there by Winston Churchill to get him out of the way as the Royal Family didn't want him in Britain. Also, Churchill didn't want him to end up in any neutral European country because of the danger he might be kidnapped and used as a pawn by Hitler. He, and particularly his wife, have pro-Nazi sympathies and in Spain and Portugal in 1940 he nearly went over to the Nazi side. If it hadn't been for Winston offering him a job in the Bahamas and telling him he must accept it, he might well have gone to a neutral country or Vichy France and thus would have fallen into the hands of the Nazis.

"A German propaganda coup would have meant serious consequences for our war effort, particularly as we were in terrible straits at that time. It was only thanks to fighter command we survived as a country. We believed that the Germans, if they had succeeded in invading Britain, would have been put him back on the throne as a puppet king."

Roger was shocked at this information which was news to him. The former king had not been featured much in the newspapers in Britain in the last few years and certainly was not on the minds of most Britons. His abdication was seen as a betrayal of the country, particularly as he was marrying a twice-divorced,

American woman. This didn't go down well in socially conservative Britain and it was regarded as an ugly chapter in the country's history which was best forgotten.

"I knew nothing about any kidnap plots. Has he got any support in Britain?" Roger asked.

"There was a secret organisation called 'The Right Club'. It was founded in 1939 by Scottish Member of Parliament, Archibald Ramsay. It was a far-right, anti-Semitic and pro-Nazi organisation that included MPs, Lords of the realm and writers. There such members as William Joyce, A.K. Chesterton, the Marquis of Graham and the Earl of Galloway. Unbeknownst to Ramsay, MI5 had infiltrated the group and had got hold of his secret list of members through a German spy in the American embassy in London. We were so concerned with the possibility of espionage on Ramsay's part that the British Government interned him in 1940 and he sits in Brixton Prison today. The club was disbanded soon after this and its members went their different ways.

"I tell you this because one of those members, Brian Thomas, came to our attention recently. He was a minor member of 'The Right Club' and is a retired businessman from Manchester. What sent up red flags was that he and his wife, Vivian, moved to the Bahamas a year ago and have been seeing the Windsors at dinner parties. He plays golf with the Duke on a fairly regular basis.

"Another of the Duke's contacts is a Swede by the name of Axel Wenner-Gren. He is probably one of the richest men in the world having made his fortune with the invention of the vacuum cleaner and the solid state refrigerator. You may have heard of his company, Electrolux. Well, we believe that this man is a German agent and is possibly a channel for messages from the

Duke to the Nazis and vice versa. Wenner-Gren now is nomadic and spends time on his enormous yacht the *Southern Cross*. It is equipped with the most up-to-date and sophisticated wireless system so he can keep up with his business operations worldwide and make contact with the Nazis."

Simon stopped talking as the waiters brought their meal of two of biggest, most succulent steaks Roger had ever seen. When they had gone Simon continued.

"Wenner-Gren had been a resident of the Bahamas. He bought Hog Island in 1939 which is close to Nassau, the colony's capital. He built a luxury estate there and called it Shangri-La. After the attack on Pearl Harbour last year, the United States' State Department banned him from America or doing business with Americans and this was shortly followed by the British. This meant he couldn't visit any of the British colonies, like the Bahamas.

"I'm sharing all this background to explain the nefarious activities of the Duke of Windsor. The US State Department have let us know that they believe he and Sir Harry Oakes, another millionaire in the Bahamas, were suspected of laundering money through a Mexican bank and the Bank of the Bahamas, both of which Wenner-Gren owns.

"It seems from recent intercepts that the Germans have shown a renewed interest in the Duke and his Duchess. We want to find out whether there is any danger to him as they are desperate to ease the pressure on their eastern forces. Our guess is that maybe, just maybe, they plan to kidnap the Duke and use him as a pawn with British Government and the royal family to stop or delay the invasion. We have no evidence yet of this although our instincts say that the Nazis could take action against the Duke."

The mention of intercepts went over Roger's head as he listened to Simon intently. The British codebreakers at their headquarters in Bletchley Park, north-west of London, had cracked the intercepted coded military messages the Germans had sent out on their Enigma cipher machine. The allies had been reading German military messages for about two years at this time and several of these had been about the Duke of Windsor. The Germans were completely unaware that this had been done because they believed this machine's system was unbreakable.

It was only in the 1980s that the secrets of Bletchley Park were revealed as the staff at the centre were sworn to secrecy by signing the Official Secrets Act. Most of the staff there were young and kept their secret even after the war had long ended. They didn't tell their parents, spouses or friends even as they grew into old age. The miracle was that the Nazis were totally unaware of the site's existence and this was partly down to the success of MI5 in preventing Nazi agents from working in Britain.

Simon Cookson continued: "We know that when Mr. Thomas was in Cuba supposedly gambling, he had dinner with a Gestapo officer from the German embassy in Buenos Aires, a Major Kurt Bergman. But there is someone else in the colony pulling the strings, so to speak. We can't put our finger on this, but certain events have led us to believe this.

"Also added to this mix of events is the fact that we know the Duke was in communication with his Nazi contacts in Lisbon when he first came to the Bahamas offering to broker a peace between Germany and Britain. We believe he still has ambitions to do this.

"We need someone on the ground in the Bahamas to keep an eye on things and to warn us if the Germans try anything. Unfortunately, our last agent there was found dead. It turns out that he had been killed by a combination of heroin and alcohol in his system, which was used to make it appear that his death was an accident. It turns out that he was a homosexual and his propensities probably led to his downfall since he had a boyfriend but we never found out who it was. So I'm warning you it could be dangerous but your cover as an RAF doctor should help to shield you from suspicion. Do you think you could do this?"

Roger took a long time before he answered because he was feasting on the biggest steak he had ever eaten. This proposition seemed to him to be what he needed to take his mind off his problems. Also, he could serve his country in an important capacity.

"I suppose it would be more interesting than giving penicillin shots to men with VD. Alright I'll do it," he said.

"Good," said Simon laughing. "We need to teach you a little bit about codes and ciphers. It won't be that complicated but you can only contact us by cable. In your communication from now on we will not refer to the Duke of Windsor by name but by a code name: Mandrake. We need you to spend two weeks with us at the Rockefeller Centre where we can fully brief you. I've cleared this with the powers that be at the RAF.

"There is one other thing; you will be contacted by a Tom Wilson who is working undercover for the FBI. His role is to keep an eye on the Duke and Duchess. The Americans have become very concerned about the couple and their potential espionage threat to the allies. Cooperate with Tom who has our blessing, but don't divulge too much to him."

Roger's two weeks in New York went by too quickly. Simon took him to parties and theatres on

Broadway and they enjoyed the company of some women he knew. His time at SIS in New York equipped him with some knowledge of simple codes and he was given a one-time pad to use when sending messages to Simon. He also received letters of assignment should the authorities in the Bahamas become suspicious of him and he was to use them as a last resort. In addition, he had to sign the Official Secrets Act, which was standard practice for anyone working for the British Government on sensitive information mainly related to national security. Any breach of this and you could wind up in jail.

A week later, Roger boarded a troop train at Pennsylvania Station in New York for the three-day journey to Miami in Florida. Although he napped in his seat during this time, he was glad to reach Miami and get to his hotel and sleep. The next day he boarded a small Canadian freighter the *SS Jean Brillant* with other RAF personnel for their overnight voyage to Nassau. Because of the danger of U-Boat attacks, the passengers sat up most the night wearing our life jackets.

Roger was sitting on one of the deckchairs in the stern of the ship and had closed his eyes to try to get some sleep on that hot night when he became aware of someone sitting down in the chair next to him. There was no one else around and he wondered why someone had chosen to sit next to him. He opened one eye and saw a slimly built young man, maybe in his late twenties, who was smartly dressed in a lightweight, khaki suit. He had wire-rimmed glasses and, when he took off his straw boater, Roger could see that his blond hair was short and brushed back with a parting in the middle. Even at his young age he had a bald patch on the back of his head which was probably a hereditary trait. He wore brown and white two-tone shoes and had a watch chain and fob attached to his waistcoat. What startled Roger was the gun he saw in a holster attached to his belt as he sat down.

"Hi there. I see from your badge on your shoulder you are a medical man. You aren't Dr. Lawson by any chance?" said the loud American voice.

Roger didn't know what to say. He wondered if he was being targeted already as he hadn't set foot on to the Bahamas yet.

"Who wants to know?" he cautiously replied.

"Oh, I'm Thomas Horatio Wilson, at your service. Everybody calls me Tom. Simon asked me to look you up when I got to the Bahamas, but here you are."

Roger was startled and looked around but there was no one in sight.

"You must keep your voice down Mr. Wilson. If we are overheard our covers will be blown. Loose lips sink ships," he said quoting a famous poster he had seen in London.

"Call me Tom," he said in a stage whisper.

"Is this the first time you've been to the Bahamas?"

"Nah. My parents used to take my sister and me there when they had a house on New Providence Island. We used to go there in the winter away from the cold and snow of Chicago. So I know Nassau and the Bahamian people pretty well. That's why I was chosen for this assignment by the FBI, which is my first undercover mission. I am the new deputy manager of the British Colonial Hotel in Nassau as my cover and I will be staying at our family house at Creek Point."

"What is your assignment exactly?"

"Well I'm going to keep an eye on the Duchess of Windsor because our people believe she is still in touch with von Ribbentrop, the Nazi foreign minister. She was his mistress before she met the Duke. We know she passed information on to them when they were in France in 1939 and 1940. Wenner-Gren was her messenger boy when she came out here passing information to his contact in the German Embassy in Bueno Aires. She has exclusive access to her husband's private correspondence and cables with your government and we think she has been passing information gleaned from his files to the Nazis. Now that Wenner-Gren is safely tucked away in his house in Mexico because of his blacklisting by us and your government, we need to find out who her conduit to the Nazis is now."

"What makes you think she is still in contact with them?"

"We have evidence that I can't divulge," he said. "What are your plans?"

"Like you, I have to keep an eye on the Windsors," Roger said simply, not wanting to tell him too much. He had a sense that he was not a reliable confidential source.

They arranged to meet regularly so they could swop notes on any developments. Roger suggested that it was not a good idea if they were seen together as they didn't want to alert anyone to presence. Tom got up and left.

The Windsors' St. Helena

Chapter 8

When you met the Duke of Windsor for the first time, you were struck by how small and effeminate-looking he was. His voice was high pitched and whiny and when he lost his temper, it was raised several decibels higher. He was a bitter man. He had a high belief in his self-worth and had a narcissistic ego. This had been bred into him by his royal parents from the day he was born.

When he abdicated as king from the British throne in December 1936 to marry Wallis Simpson, he was shunned by his family as well as courtiers and the British establishment who had previously fawned over him when he was the Prince of Wales and then king. His brother George VI, who succeeded him, was a sick man and his reign took its toll on his health. Queen Elizabeth, the new king's wife, and Queen Mary, his mother, never forgave the Duke of Windsor for deserting his responsibilities as king and burdening his brother with that sacred duty. His banishment came as a shock and rankled the Duke of Windsor until the day he died.

A very relieved British government was glad to see him go and was determined to marginalise him as much as possible. When he had come to the throne, he infuriated Prime Minister Stanley Baldwin by interfering in matters of state. According to the British constitution, the role of a monarch is as a non-political head of state leaving the formulation and the conduct of policy to an elected parliament. This schism between King Edward VIII and government ministers was particularly seen in his private dealings with the German government when he would often call the German ambassador on the telephone and discuss his point of view on the issues with which he personally disagreed with his ministers. These conversations were immediately reported to Adolf Hitler, the German Chancellor, who saw the Duke as a possible puppet king when he had successfully invaded Britain.

The Duke's ancestry was German and it was often thought that he saw himself as a German first. In fact his father, George V, had changed the name of the British royal house during the First World War from the German House of Saxe-Coburg and Gotha to the House of Windsor so that they would be seen as more British than they were.

And then there was the twice divorced Duchess of Windsor, who had very clear pro-Nazi leanings. It was claimed, and it was probably true, that she had been the mistress of Joachim von Ribbentrop, the Reich Minister Ambassador-Plenipotentiary, at large at the time, and then the German Ambassador to Britain between 1936 and 1938. Britain's MI5 internal intelligence service suspected that she was passing on secret information to von Ribbentrop long after their affair had ended, particularly when she became Edward VIII's mistress.

After his abdication and marriage to Wallis Simpson in France, where they were exiled, the Duke of Windsor outraged the British government by visiting Germany in 1937 and meeting Hitler and other Nazi leaders. The Duke held pro-Nazi views which he expressed publicly and had made many unfortunate statements which embarrassed the British government. This was made worse by the views and subterfuge of the Duchess.

When the Second World War was declared in 1939, the Duke of Windsor was made a major-general and attached to the British Military Mission in France. This was mainly a ceremonial position and his time was spent inspecting various military units and installations. It was strongly believed that he relayed information about these inspections to the Duchess who passed them onto von Ribbentrop who at this time had become the German Foreign Minister. In addition, the Duke's inability to keep confidential information secret meant that much of it reached the Germans. Most of the leaked information was passed on by the Duchess and through the Duke's friendship with Charles Bedaux, an American-French millionaire businessman who had substantial contacts with the Nazis. In 1937, the couple had been married at Bedaux's French Château de Candé.

According to a damning secret report by the United States Federal Bureau of Investigation, the Duchess was sending information to von Ribbentrop. One conclusion in the report stated: "Because of their high official position, the Duchess was obtaining a variety of information concerning the British and French official activities that she was passing on to the Germans."

When Hitler's armies were poised to invade France, the allies learned of his plans to attack through the Low Countries of Belgium, Luxembourg and Holland. By chance the German plans had fallen into the hands of the allies because of the crash of a plane carrying a German staff officer with Hitler's intentions in his briefcase. The Germans learnt of this, very likely through the Duchess of Windsor, and changed their plans to attack through the densely wooded and less-well defended Ardennes region. This was a complete surprise to the British and the French whose armies were expecting the attack to occur through the Low Countries. This espionage coup enabled the Germans to easily invade France with disastrous consequences for Europe. Was this a German ploy to divert the allied armies to cover a putsch through the Low Countries? Many people have wondered about this.

When the Germans invaded France, the Windsors retreated first to their villa, La Croë, in the south of France. As the Germans advanced south they were forced to escape to Spain where they were again in contact with von Ribbentrop and the Italian ambassador in Madrid. It was there that they had arranged for their home on the Boulevard Suchet in Paris to be guarded by the German army, their villa, La Croë, safeguarded by the Italian army and their bank accounts at Banque de France carefully protected. At the end of the Second World War, when they returned to France, their properties and assets were in place for them to resume where they had left off in 1940.

Winston Churchill, the British Prime Minister, had wanted the Windsors to return to Britain by boat through Marseilles as he was concerned that they might fall into the hands of the Germans. However, they went to Spain much to Churchill's chagrin. He knew of the close relationship the Nazis' had with Francisco Franco, the Spanish dictator and winner – with German and Italian help – of the recent Spanish Civil War.

A major concern of the British government was that the Windsors had walked into the proverbial lion's den, as Spain was a hotbed of Nazi supporters and intrigues. The Spanish Government made overtures to the Windsors to stay in Spain until the end of the war with many inducements, such as rent-free accommodation. The British expected Spain to join the Axis powers of

Germany, Italy and Japan so the last thing they wanted was for the Duke to remain in Spain.

Events had come to a head between Winston Churchill and the Duke. Word had got back to the Prime Minister that the Duke had been voicing his views, especially amongst American diplomats in Madrid that the war should be resolved by peaceful negotiations and should not continue because of the potential of losing a great number of lives. These indiscreet remarks were regarded as defeatist talk as Britain was on her own and was getting ready to survive the onslaught of the German Luftwaffe in the Battle of Britain. An angry Churchill sent a telegram on July 1st, 1940, to the Duke reminding him that he was still a serving officer in the British Army and threatened to court-martial him if he didn't return to Britain immediately.

This threat had its desired effect and the Windsors moved to Lisbon, Portugal, the next day. Portugal was very much a pro-British, although neutral, country. While in Lisbon, last-minute negotiations were continuing between Winston Churchill and the Duke about the conditions for his return to Britain and top of the Duke's mind was that the Duchess be received by George VI. The court was adamantly against any such meeting despite Churchill's efforts to broker a deal. The Duke soon realised that if he went back to Britain his activities would be very restricted as he wanted to serve his country in some diplomatic capacity, particularly in the British Dominions.

Meanwhile the Germans had been hatching a plan to entice the Windsors back into Spain and into their sphere of influence. SS-Sturmbannführer Walter Schellenberg was tasked with running "Operation Willi" and he was told that if the Duke would not move he was to kidnap the couple and forcibly take them to Spain or to Vichy

France. The British Secret Service got wind of this plan and London scrambled to find a suitable post for the Duke of Windsor.

In a telegram from Winston Churchill on July 4th, 1940, the Duke of Windsor was offered the post of Governor of the Bahamas, which he reluctantly agreed to take. The purpose of this appointment was clear – to keep the Duke as far away as possible so that his pacifist views would not affect the moral of Britons at this dark period in their history. Also, it would keep him out of the reach of the Nazis. Knowing that the royal family were adamantly opposed to his returning to Britain, he reluctantly accepted the post.

The Duke and Duchess of Windsor regarded their banishment to the nether regions of the British Empire and to its smallest colony as very humiliating. They called the Bahamas their St. Helena, which was a reference to Napoleon's exile to the Atlantic island after he lost the battle of Waterloo in 1815 and where he died. They realised they really had no option since they took Winston Churchill's threat to court martial the Duke very seriously and they knew the prime minister had reach the end of his patience with them.

The FBI's report on the Duke succinctly summoned up Churchill's strategy: "The British were and are always fearful that the Duchess will do or say something which will indicate her Nazi sympathies and support, and consequently it was considered absolutely essential that the Windsors be removed to a point where they would do absolutely no harm."

Before the Duke of Windsor left Portugal he arranged with his host, the pro-Nazi banker Ricardo Espirito Santo Silva, a code they could use that would indicate his willingness to return to Britain if the British should require him to take part in peace negotiations with the Nazis. He had all along led the Germans to believe that he had ambitions of returning to Britain as king and replacing what he saw as his weak brother.

The Duke and Duchess of Windsor set sail from Lisbon on an American ship, the *SS Excalibur*, on August 1st which took them to Bermuda. They then boarded the *Lady Somers* and arrived in Nassau on August 17th, 1940.

In taking up this appointment, the Duke was heading into a maelstrom of political and social problems that had been festering in the colony for many years. The intrigues that were niggling the inhabitants of the Bahamas were substantial. About eighty-five percent of the Bahamian population at this time were black but all the wealth and power lay in the hands of the fifteen percent white inhabitants, who were mainly traders, hoteliers and shopkeepers.

From the outset of his governorship, the Duke of Windsor had an ongoing confrontation with the colony's legislature. This body was controlled, Mafia-like, by a white minority group of merchants called 'the Bay Street Boys.' Nothing was done without their agreement and much of the legislation passed was for their financial benefit. Many of these men had made their fortunes as rum runners during the prohibition years in the United States of America between 1920 and 1933. They were now focused on enriching themselves further by developing hotels and resorts for the burgeoning tourist industry on New Providence, the main island of the Bahamas with its capital, Nassau.

Apart from New Providence Island, the Bahamas is made up of about seven hundred islands and cays, some very small, and these are referred to as the 'Out Islands.' When the Duke arrived in 1940 there was a serious unemployment problem on these islands which had been badly neglected by the legislature in Nassau and the Duke was determined to attack this problem head on. Economic development had been focused on New Providence Island and nothing was planned to help the 'Out Islands.' In fact, the legislators in Nassau very deliberately kept the islanders dependant on them by restricting the supply of goods and other services to an absolute minimum. Some of the Bay Street Boys were 'elected' as representatives of the islands. They would only visit their poor, uneducated, black constituents at election time and would bribe them for their votes with money and liquor.

To his credit, the Duke was very resolute about improving the economy of the 'Out Islands' and solving the chronic unemployment on these islands. He recognised that he faced opposition from the legislature but pressed on with his plans.

With America joining the Second World War in 1941 tourism ground to a virtual halt and the economy of the Bahamas was in a nose-dive as a result. But the Duke had been working hard behind the scenes with both British and American governments to help the colony. Through the lend-lease programme with America an agreement was brokered to expand and operate an RAF flight crew training base on New Providence Island at Oakes Field, which up until then had been a small airport serving the tourist business.

A second base was to be constructed in the west of the island, to be called Windsor Field, for RAF Ferry Command to transport bombers built in America to war theatres in Europe, Asia and the Middle East. Key to these projects, and a godsend to the Bahamian economy, was that local unskilled labour would be used, although some men had to be brought in from America because of their expertise. Many of the Bahamian workers recruited for the projects were from the 'Out Islands' and the work was seen as a blessing to their lives for the six months that it took to construct the bases starting in May 1942.

The Duke and the Duchess departed the Bahamas for a month-long trip to America on May 28th 1942. The Duke left Leslie Heape, the colonial secretary, in charge of the colony as acting governor. This getaway, which they regarded as a much-needed holiday, was soon disturbed by news of demonstrations by Bahamian labourers on June 1st.

The black Bahamians hired to help in the construction of the RAF bases were protesting against what they correctly saw as the wide disparately in the hourly wages paid to them compared to the American workers brought in to also work on the projects. They quite rightly pointed out that the wages they received were not enough to lift them above the poverty level. The legislature had not changed the standard rate for unskilled workers (or what we call today a minimum wage) of four shillings a day since it was set in 1936 and had not taken into account inflation over the six-year period.

Social unrest among the colony's black population had been at a boiling point for some time and the pay issue was the catalyst for what happened that June. The riot left six people dead, a half-dozen wounded as well as severe damage to Bay Street, the main business district of Nassau, and in the city's black neighbourhood of Grant's Town.

The demonstration, which was at first peaceful, was not handled properly by the acting governor, the police commissioner or the acting colonial secretary. They were not equipped or experienced enough to quell a mob whose size at one point was more than two thousand angry people strong, some armed with machetes and clubs. The number of demonstrators had increased as they had marched from Oakes Field through black communities, such as Grant's Town, to Rawson Square in the heart of downtown Nassau. The initial protesters were joined by black residents uninvolved in the construction of the RAF bases who saw an opportunity to protest against the injustices spawned by their ruthless and prejudiced white rulers.

Rawson Square consisted of the colony's house of assembly, the colonial secretariat building, the police headquarters and the courthouse. The aim of the marchers was to present their grievances to the colonial secretary but no one from the colonial secretariat was willing to address the demonstrators. Finally Eric Hallinan, the colony's attorney general, spoke to them and had some success at first in quelling the mob's anger. However in his speech, he rashly pointed out that, although the American construction company was pleased with its Bahamian workers, they wouldn't hesitate to replace them with Americans if the Bahamians continued with their demand for increased wages. He urged the crowd not to ruin the opportunity for work that they had. This didn't go down well with the protesters. When Hallinan had finished speaking and had left Rawson Square, armed police suddenly appeared and agitators in the crowd stirred up the ugly mood again.

The mob ran from the square into Bay Street where they smashed cars and store windows, and caused extensive property damage. It is debatable whether the original demonstrators were the perpetrators of this attack or whether the culprits were other hangers-on who took advantage of the chaos. The damaged stores were looted mainly by women who had nothing to do with the protest. With the help of a company of Cameron

Highlanders, the police eventually drove the rioters back into Grant's Town by about noon.

Trouble did not end there. Some of the mob broke into bars in Grant's Town and, as time passed, many became intoxicated. With Dutch courage from the liquor and again their anger being whipped up by agitators, they began to march towards the centre of Nassau again. This time the police and Cameron Highlanders were ready for them and a small number of troublemakers reached the Cotton Tree Inn on Blue Hill Road before they were stopped. A magistrate read the British Government's Riot Act, which allowed the authorities in a community to declare any group of twelve or more people to be unlawfully assembled, and thus they must disperse or face punitive action.

The reading of the act was met with of stones thrown by the rioters as they surged towards the authorities. The soldiers and police opened fire and the rioters retreated leaving two dead and many wounded. A curfew in Grant's Town was announced but not imposed that day because the police were fearful of patrolling the area. The next twenty-four hours saw continued trouble and looting in Grant's Town where the police station there came under siege. Word of the return of the Duke of Windsor to the colony spread on the evening of June 2nd and eventually the following day the tide of violence turned and quiet was restored.

Needless to say, the merchants of Bay Street were furious with the colonial government and, paradoxically, blamed them for the riot. In their howl of anger they had urged Leslie Heape, the acting governor, to use lethal force to stop the riot. This was not done and, as a result, more deaths and serious injuries were avoided. The riot was a shock to merchants of Bay Street who feared further unrest from the colony's usually compliant black population.

The Duke of Windsor began the thankless task of reconciling both sides, which proved to be a monumental undertaking. Returning to America, the Duke was able to negotiate an extra shilling a day and a free lunch for the Bahamian workers from the U.S. Government, which was met with delight in the Bahamas and was viewed with grave concern by the Colonial Office in London.

The Duke's mood changed significantly at the end of an extremely humid and hot August that year with the news of the untimely death of his younger brother, George, in a plane crash. They had been particularly close and the Duke, as the elder, helped to curb the rash behaviour of the young Duke of Kent. His brother's death threw him into a deep depression which turned into resentment at his post in the Bahamas and it was from this time onwards that he kept intensifying his push for the Colonial Office in London and Winston Churchill to find him another post.

The colony's legislature by September were baying for blood and, led by the Bay Street Boys, they were determined to hold their own board of enquiry into the riot. They blamed the colonial administrators for the way they handled the riot and wanted to see them punished for their actions. They appointed a seven-member select committee to conduct interviews and write their own biased report. The Duke checkmated this move first by declaring that colonial officials would not be available to take part in any enquiry set up by the legislature and, secondly, announcing the Colonial Office in London had agreed to hold a commission of enquiry to be chaired by someone from outside of the colony, Sir Alison Russell, formerly chief justice of Tanganyika. This move by the

Duke ensured an independent and unbiased report would be made.

The Duke's Machinations

Chapter 9

Government House, the Bahamas, January 7th, 1943

It was four in the afternoon on what had been a very humid and hot day with temperatures hovering around eighty-five degrees Fahrenheit. Despite the humidity, the Duke of Windsor was sitting at his desk wearing a white, lightweight suit and tie which was tied in his signature Windsor knot. There was a fan in the ceiling doing its best to create a cool draft, but its best was not good enough to help the small, sweating figure sitting at his large mahogany desk.

There was a firm knock on the Duke of Windsor's office door and his equerry, Captain James Dugdale, entered without waiting for a response.

"Robert Moore is here to see you with some papers for you to sign, your Royal Highness."

"Send him in James," the Duke responded as he looked up from his desk.

The Duke liked Robert Moore and was inexplicitly attracted to him. He was always smartly dressed and stylish. He liked his air of supreme confidence and could always rely on him to give his sound opinion on an issue when asked. He had known his father Lord Moore who had often been at his parties at his home, Fort Belvedere, near Windsor, before he had become king. He had taken young Moore under his wing when he had been posted to the Bahamas and the two had become quite close. The Duke was so confident about his loyalty that he had become the Duke's go-to person for various secret assignments he didn't want his staff to know about.

Robert Moore had just returned from one of these missions. He had worked with Axel Wenner-Gren, who was now in Mexico and was the Duke's close friend, to make available much needed funds that were paid into the Duke's bank account in the Bahamas. The British war time currency restrictions had prevented the Duke from directly accessing his fortune tied up in his bank in German-occupied Paris. Through his Nazi contacts he had arranged that his bank account at the Banque de France had not been seized and he was able to retrieve some of his money through Wenner-Gren. This helped the Duke and Duchess to live their opulent and expensive lifestyle in the Bahamas while others had rationing and were living in poverty.

In addition, Robert Moore was the conduit for the Duke and Duchess to the Nazis and his Portuguese pro-Nazi friends. He still had dreams of being the catalyst for peace negotiations between the Germans and the British.

"Come in, Robert, and take a pew," he said warmly.

"I have some documents for you to sign, your Royal Highness," he said, handing the Duke a file.

He took the file and began reviewing and signing various papers. Without looking up he said: "That will be all for now James. Make sure I'm out of here by five." His equerry half bowed and left, giving Robert Moore a withering look of disapproval.

When he had closed the door, the Duke asked: "How's dear Axel?

"Very well sir. He misses seeing you and sends warm greetings."

"I miss him too. I wish the Americans and, for that matter, the British would lift their blacklisting of him. I've told Winston what I think on several occasions, but I can't change his mind. The Americans have really got a bee in their bonnet about him. I suspect that that little queer, Hoover, has a lot to do with it," he said venomously aiming his anger at the FBI Director.

Robert handed the Duke a sealed envelope which he opened and read.

"Well, well," said the Duke, looking delighted. "Axel has deposited some much needed funds into my account at the Bank of the Bahamas from Banco Continental in Mexico City. Did you know he owns both banks? Thank goodness. Wallis will be pleased.

"What's the news from Axel and other people in Mexico City?"

"The Germans are very concerned with their Russian front. Their Sixth Army is surrounded in Stalingrad and in fact the Russians are pushing them back elsewhere. Coupled with this, Rommel is losing in North Africa and it looks like he will be defeated. Their other major worry is the Western Front and whether they have enough army divisions to stop an allied invasion. Hitler has sent most of military resources to the Eastern Front to bolster his operations there against the Russians. Stalin is pressuring the allies to start their invasion in the west to relieve his troops. The Russian front could turn into 1812 all over again," Robert mused.

1812 was the year when Napoleon retreated in the frigid cold of the Russian winter having been thwarted in his attack on Moscow. He lost some 380,000 men or about half his army to not only battlefield deaths, but mainly from cold, starvation.

"Sounds like the Germans have serious problem on their hands. Why on earth did they attack Russia? The Wehrmacht are the only army that can stop the communist hordes from taking over Europe and they are being pushed back. They need our help in thwarting the communist advances. It's a pity I can't intervene and stop this madness. If I had been still king this would never have happened," said the exasperated Duke.

"After Hess's failed attempt to seek a peace deal with the allies last year, my contacts seem to think that discussions are now possible with events going against the Nazis," said Robert Moore.

"They asked me to sound you out as to whether you might intervene with Prime Minister Churchill and suggest a meeting in say Switzerland to try and negotiate a peace treaty. They think there is still time to do this but the window is closing fast."

Rudolf Hess was the deputy Fuhrer but had lost the confidence in Hitler. He decided to try peace negotiations directly by going to Britain himself to seek meetings with the British government. He secretly flew to Scotland, parachuting into South Lanarkshire and was captured. He was treated as a prisoner of war and never achieved his goal. Hitler was furious as he never sanctioned such a move and felt that Hess had a mental breakdown. Meanwhile Hess was imprisoned in the Tower of London and would be tried at the Nuremburg Trials of major war criminals in 1946.

The Duke didn't reply at first, but began to think about the ramifications of trying to bring the warring parties together.

"I want to but Churchill, who I thought was a close friend, would never entertain such a plan from me. Let me think about it more. I would certainly like to intervene and be part of the plan to bring this idiotic war to a close," he said. He was intrigued at the suggestion and his insatiable ego was awakened at the possibility of proving his detractors wrong.

Robert Moore, who knew not to press the Duke, changed the subject. "Sir, I've been approached by an American, Frank Marshall. He has been talking with the lawyer Stafford Sands and with Harold Christie, a Bahamian property developer, about getting a license to open a casino here."

"Christy, there's a shifty character if ever there was one. Be careful of him as he'll have his own agenda. He would shop his own mother for a deal. I know that Sands has been pushing for this to happen since the thirties, but he is corrupt and will also look to see how he can enrich himself."

"Right, sir. As you know, to build casinos here in the Bahamas the law banning them has to change to allow them to do that. So he's lobbying Christie, Sands, Sir Harry Oakes and yourself to get this changed. I am meeting with them in a few days to hear the preliminary details. I have done some checking and Marshall is a front for elements of the American Mafia namely Meyer Lansky. I don't know whether we should get involved with them."

"That is a concern, but better the devil you know than the devil you don't. They are dangerous men I know, but if we say 'no' they could put pressure on us and build elsewhere in the Caribbean and thus ruin our tourism trade. We shall have to proceed cautiously. What accommodations are they likely to make for our cooperation?"

It was just like the Duke of Windsor to wonder what's in it for him personally.

"I don't know yet. Christie is all for it whereas Oakes is firmly against it. But it really needs your agreement, sir."

"I thought that might be the case. Oakes doesn't realise that we need jobs here. He just wants nothing to change his Shangri-La life here," the Duke said.

After a few moments of thought he added: "Let's continue to consider the matter. Be careful, we don't want the FBI to find out about any planned deal. I have enough trouble getting the American Government to allow the Duchess and I to go there for some quiet time.

"Now changing the subject back to more mundane issues. It seems that Sir Alison Russell, head the commission of enquiry into the June's riots, has come out with a very favourable report to the colonial office in London. How do you think this will be taken by the legislature?" asked the Duke.

"I met him briefly when he was here. He has a reputation as a fair man and not easily fooled and he obviously wasn't fooled by the antics of the Bay Street Boys. I think they will be as mad as hell when it's made public and it should spike their own enquiry," Robert Moore said.

"Good. I agree with you. I had to appoint two representatives from the colony to sit with him on the commission. Eric Solomon, the leader of government in the legislature, turned me down, thank goodness, so I choose two men who are not in the legislature." the Duke said.

Just then the office door swung open and in walked the Duchess of Windsor, looking annoyed.

"David, it is time for you take your bath!" she ordered like a fearsome nanny to a wayward child. "We haven't got much time before our guests arrive and you know how you don't like to rush getting dressed. Mr. Moore, I am sure, is about to leave."

"Yes, Wallis, we were just finishing up," said the cowering Duke.

An hour later the Duke joined the Duchess in their private drawing room and was handed a martini by his butler, Sydney Johnson.

"So how was your day, Wallis?" he asked in a friendly tone.

"Bloody awful if you must know," she answered crossly and took a large swig of her drink. "I spent my day working at the Red Cross office and then at my canteen. You know, the women there are so parochial it's difficult to have an intelligent conversation with any of them. God, I hate this place! When are we going to get out of here, David?"

"I've been sending cables to Winston but he has not yet replied. It's damnable that he doesn't help us out so we'll just have to wait." It never dawned on them that the prime minister was attending to more important matters such as fighting a war. It just showed their narcissistic focus on themselves.

A report by the Colonial Office Commission of Enquiry into the June 1942 riots headed by Sir Alison Russell was made public in January 1943. Although it censured the police commissioner for his handling of events, it was highly critical of colony's legislature citing its actions or inactions over the years as the root cause of the riot. It was very complimentary of the Duke's efforts to help the 'Out Islands.' As a result, criticism of the colony's administration from the Bay Street merchants was restrained and their own report on the riot was much muted.

A concern the Duke had was still the unemployment in the colony, particularly as the airfield projects were drawing to a close. He had heard from a number of his contacts in Florida that the farmers there were faced with a shortage of labour as many of the men had joined the armed services. In discussions with the American State Department in October and November of 1942 an agreement, known as the Bahamas Labour Scheme, was set up so that eight thousand labourers could work on Florida farms. An important part of this plan was that a quarter of each man's wages were to be sent home to his family in the Bahamas. This scheme was met with strong opposition from the Colonial Office in London, but in the end they agreed to the arrangement and it was eventually signed in March 1943.

As 1943 dawned, the Bahamian economy was beginning to hum with the influx of GIs and RAF personnel which would number at its peak over three thousand. The Bay Street Boys had been temporally beaten back, although they were plotting their next moves to frustrate the Duke and his administration. The black Bahamians on New Providence were mostly content with the work recent developments had provided.

Intrigues

Chapter 10

Nassau, New Providence, the Bahamas, January 12th, 1943

Nothing had prepared Dr. Roger Lawson for the sight he saw as he stepped onto Prince George Wharf in Nassau from the *SS Jean Brillant* after his overnight journey from Miami. The scene before him was a culture shock, especially after he had spent time in a modern-day city such as New York just a week before. It was as if he had travelled back in time to the British colonial days at the beginning of the twentieth century. The sight was straight out of Sir Rider Haggard's *King Solomon's Mines* or *Jock of the Bushveld* by Percy Fitzpatrick. He had read both books as a youngster and they depicted life in British colonial Africa in the nineteenth and early twentieth centuries.

The quay was full of poor, black Bahamians, many of whom were in bare feet and dressed in dirty clothing made out of a coarse material. They had come to meet the ship, as they did with all ships, and were attempting to sell their wares to the disembarking passengers. Their merchandise was anything from straw hats, fish, and bananas to melons. There were even young men willing to dive for coins thrown for them into the harbour by the mostly white travellers.

Roger was the last to climb down the gangway from the ship and he did not see Tom Wilson, the FBI agent he had met the previous night. He could see to his right the native fishing fleet, which was a ramshackle array of boats that didn't look very seaworthy and were sorely in need of repair. Overlooking the harbour in the same direction but about half a mile away was the imperious-looking British Colonial Hotel.

There was a long shed-like building on the wharf that operated as the customs house and storage facility for outgoing and incoming goods. Roger noticed a white man standing in the shade cast by the shed. He was watching the passengers as they disembarked. He was heavy set and wore an ill-fitting suit, which was much crumbled. He had on a pith helmet and carried a black cane, which had a silver bobble on it. By the time Roger reached the quay, the man had disappeared.

Bales of sisal littered the dock area and Roger could see men bringing more of the crop loaded onto two-wheeled carts called drays pulled by sad looking horses or donkeys. The main business of the islands was the growing and exporting of sisal now that the highly profitable sponge industry had died when the sponges were decimated by a fungal infection. There was some small-time boat building and a nascent American tourist business in the winter months.

All the RAF aircrew and others, like Roger, were met at the docks by two military lorries. He walked towards these vehicles and he was the last to arrive because of his painful knee injury, which continued to slow him down. An RAF corporal with a clipboard was checking off each man's name. When he saw Roger struggling, he suggested that he get into the cab of one of the lorries while the others climbed into the back.

As the lorries left the harbour for the brief journey to Oakes Field, they were driven a short distance along Bay Street, which was the main street in Nassau and the home of the power brokers of the islands. This clique of white merchants was known as the Bay Street Boys.

The lorries turned onto Prospect Ridge Road and shortly they entered the gates of Oakes Field, one of the two airfields on the island. This was where Roger had been assigned as a doctor at the nearby RAF hospital.

Oakes Field base was part of the No. 111 Operational Training Unit that the RAF had set up in 1942 to train aircrews for service in the various theatres of war. This base was responsible for the first part of training aircrews on B25 Mitchell and B24 Liberator bombers. Aircrews received more advanced flight training at Windsor Field, which was some four miles away in the west of the island. The training unit at its peak graduated about ten to thirteen air crews a month. In addition, Windsor Field was used by Ferry Command as a reception and departure base for American made B24 Liberators, which were ferried across the Atlantic to Europe, the Middle East and Far East.

A Flight Sergeant at the guardhouse at the main gate checked Roger in and gave him the number of his assigned room. He walked to the officers' quarters and mess which were in some wooden huts that had been hastily constructed. Each trainee officer shared a room with one or two others and those officers like Roger, who were permanently assigned to the base, had their own individual rooms. Senior officers above the rank of flight lieutenant were billeted in rented homes in and around Nassau. Down the hall from Roger's room was a

137

large bathroom with washing facilities and baths for some twenty men. The mess was really one large room with soft furnishings all around it clustered in groups around small coffee tables. At one end of this room was a bar staffed by an orderly. A door led into an equally large dining room that had several tables and chairs to accommodate all the officers stationed at the base.

The officer accommodations were on one side of a small parade ground which had flag poles at one end flying the Union Jack and RAF flag. On the opposite side of the square were the sergeant's accommodations and mess, which had a similar format.

When he had unpacked, Roger went to the hospital with his briefcase that had confidential SIS material in it. He walked to the hospital on Prospect Ridge Road to report to Wing Commander Meyer Rassin, the chief medical officer in charge of hospital. When the wing commander's secretary had shown him into his office, Roger stood to attention and saluted.

"I hope that is the last time you do that Dr. Lawson. Sit down and let's talk," said a friendly but gruff man behind his desk. He was thick-set, thirty-four year old, who didn't like to stand on ceremony and was about five feet six inches tall when he stood up.

"I'm glad to have you on board. I'm sorry about your wounds, which I know must be quite frustrating for you."

"Yes, I'm afraid they are, sir, but I've learned to cope with them in the last few months. It certainly has thrown my medical career for a loop."

"There's nothing much we do about that now. You've got to keep moving forward," he said curtly. "Well let me tell you about what we need here. We require someone to take charge of the clinics we hold not only for RAF personnel who are based here but those

138

from the other air forces as well as the army. Most of it is the type of work covered by family doctors back home. You will be working with Dr. Christopher Woodson and I want you to collaborate with Dr. Andrew Bain our pathologist when he needs help."

After another ten minutes of discussion, Wing Commander Meyer Rassin took Roger on a tour of the hospital. Roger was impressed with the medical facilities the RAF had supplied to the hospital and he was told much of equipment came from the United States. There was an airman's ward with eighteen beds and one for officers with six beds. They had a fully equipped operating theatre and an up-to-date radiography department. He was then taken to the clinic area where the initial examinations and day-to-day triage took place and there he met Dr. Christopher Woodson.

"I'll leave you two to have a chat. Dr. Lawson, I want you to take the evening surgery tonight. You might as well jump in right away. I'll post your schedule on the noticeboard in the staff corridor. Remember, if you have any problems or questions, come and see me if Christopher here can't answer them," said the wing commander as he left.

"Welcome to our hospital, Roger," said Dr. Woodson. "Dr. Rassin is a bit on the crotchety side but he is really an approachable chap. He is not one for small talk and he is a difficult man to understand. He makes up for his hubris by being a first class orthopaedic surgeon, which is essential here with all the training accidents we see. Sometimes we feel like all the king's men putting Humpty Dumpty back together again," he said, laughing at his own joke.

"This area is really like a hospital emergency department. We get all sorts of encounters from those patients that need immediate operations to those with the flu, measles, sunburn or venereal disease. Take your pick, we see it all. With three thousand RAF personnel on the island we are kept busy. At least you won't be bored."

"What about the nursing staff?"

"We have ten staff nurses and three ward sisters and I don't know how many nursing orderlies. Some of these staff are not bad but many of them are bloody awful," he replied cynically. "Let me show you where we keep things so you will know for tonight."

Christopher asked Roger about his wounds and he told him how he got them. He also described how he was treated at the burns unit at Queen Victoria Hospital in East Grinstead and explained the innovative treatment for burns patients that Dr. McIndoe was pioneering. When Roger asked Christopher about his background, he did not answer and changed the subject.

Dr. Christopher Woodson was about the same age as Roger and struck him as an earnest medical practitioner. He had an athletic build and was extremely fit. Roger learnt later that this was maintained though his avid interest in sailing and that Christopher was well known in the Bahamas as an extremely accomplished sailor. Roger wondered why he was especially sarcastic in describing people he worked with, particularly those in authority and even those who were colleagues. Roger wondered why he had this passive aggressive demeanour. He certainly had a chip on his shoulder about something. In the answer to Roger's questions about his family, it seemed as though he was erecting a façade through which no one was allowed to venture. And this grew more evident in the months ahead as Roger began to know him better.

After Christopher reviewed the paperwork the hospital needed for each patient and a tour of the pharmacy, Roger went in search of Dr. Andrew Bain, the base's pathologist. He walked over to a separate building which was the mortuary and found him working on an autopsy of an airman.

Dr. Bain was a serious-minded man in his fifties, he was overweight and was sweating profusely despite a large ceiling fan that was producing a cooling flow of air. He had been on the pathology staff at the Edinburgh Royal Infirmary before he had taken up a staff position at the Bahamas General Hospital in 1939. He had been chosen to work at the RAF Hospital on a part-time basis and performed post-mortems when needed.

"You must be Dr. Lawson," he bellowed over the whir of the fan when he saw Roger. "Come and look at this. This poor fellow was crushed when he seemingly accidentally released an aeroplane engine from its mounting. But was this the cause of death I ask you? Take a look at his heart valves."

Roger looked carefully at the opened heart and at the blood vessels running to and from it. He picked up a scalpel and examined the blood vessels more closely. After a while, he turned Dr. Bain and told him that the man had atherosclerosis disease. "There's a definite narrowing and blockage of the coronary arteries because of the plaque build-up on their inner walls. This likely caused a blockage and probably a heart attack."

"Good, good," Dr. Bain purred. "It seems our friend here had a heart attack which caused him to let go of the release on the engine hoist and resulted in him being crushed to death."

Dr. Bain began to sew up the cadaver and told Roger about the work he would have to do. "The job here is intermittent but when it happens we are pretty busy. Usually, it involves determining the cause a death from flying accidents and often we have to work on very little in the way of body parts. The samples we take of fluids or stomach contents are sent to the pathology lab at the Bahamas General Hospital for analysis."

As they were finishing up, an aircraftsman came in looking for Roger and blanched when he saw the cadaver.

"Sir, Group Captain Waite wants to see you right away," the out-of-breath man announced.

"In trouble already?" said Dr. Bain, laughing.

Roger followed the aircraftsman to the main administration building and waited outside Group Captain R. N. Waite's office to be announced. He was the officer in charge of all RAF operations in the Bahamas.

When Roger had saluted, he was told to take a seat while the group captain read a file, presumably on Roger. This senior officer was in many ways the opposite of Wing Commander Meyer Rassin. He was thin, dark haired, balding and had a toothbrush moustache. He was typical career officer who was a stickler of formality. He would go on after his Bahamas posting to be an air commodore responsible for disarming the Luftwaffe in 1945 and was a key player in running the Berlin Airlift in 1948 and 1949.

He finished reading the file and looked up and smiled.

"Congratulations on your OBE. Well-deserved. I am sorry that you were burnt badly getting those men out. I see they've assigned you to general medical duties here."

"I'm afraid so sir. I can't wield a scalpel any more, at least not with any accuracy," Roger replied, trying to lighten the atmosphere.

"I see at least you have a sense of humour about it," he smiled.

142

"I have to, sir, it stops me feeling sorry for myself. My dream of becoming a surgeon has evaporated, but I don't regret what I did."

"Good man! I was contacted about your dual role here before your arrival by London and SIS in New York. I want you to know you have my complete support. It is unfortunate we have the Duke of Windsor on our patch but I understand London's concern. It is better he is here rather than in Europe where he can cause trouble. Simon Cookson at SIS told me that there is a danger he might be kidnapped. If you get a tickle of anything going on come and see me immediately."

"Yes, sir. Can you tell me a bit about his staff?"

"Not much. He has a new equerry; a Captain James Dugdale, who seems a well organised man, but I don't know much about him. There's Sergeant Holder, his police bodyguard who has been with him for years."

"What about the colonial office staff?"

"The day-to-day operations of the colony are run by Leslie Heape, the Colonial Secretary for the Bahamas. He is a very experienced officer and the Duke relies on him quite a bit especially when he is out of the country. Heape then becomes the temporary governor and the poor chap had to deal race riots six months ago when the Duke was in America. He is helped by Charles Bethel, who is his deputy and he is a weak and reticent man. He is quite happy to be in the background and not thrust into having to make decisions."

"Is there anyone else I should be aware of, sir?"

"No, not really. I've only been here a short while, but these are my first impressions."

"Thank you, sir. I need to keep some confidential information in a safe place. Is it possible to use one of the safes in your office?"

"Of course. My secretary can set you up with one and give you the combination."

They walked out Group Captain Waite's office and he told his secretary to assign one of the three safes to Roger. He put his briefcase containing his code books and letters in it and went back to his room.

Roger reported to the clinic at four that afternoon and began to see men with medical problems. There was nothing serious and he had seen them all by six. What had interested him more were the glimpses he had had in the corridor near the pharmacy of a staff nurse who was on duty on one of the wards. She was tall, slim and had a confident bearing about her that exuded, not sternness, but kindness and efficiency. She noticed him only once when she passed him with a smile and "good evening, Doctor." And that smile, to Roger, was the smile of an angel and he was immediately smitten with that angel.

Reality threw cold water on his ardour though. He realised that she probably had a number of boyfriends and who was he to dream about taking her out with his disfigurement and gammy leg? It wasn't in the cards. He felt it would be better if he was to just concentrate on his medical job and his work for the SIS. And so it was with a heavy and resigned heart that he returned to his room.

When he walked into the officer accommodations, he saw Christopher Woodson who invited him to go out with him and two other RAF Ferry Command Officers, Alan Jones and Michael Sneed, to the Prince George Hotel where, according to him, all the action was. Roger agreed and the four of them were able to pick up a horse drawn taxi outside the gates of the base that took them along Bay Street.

Bay Street at this point was fairly wide with trees on both sides, which gave welcome shade from the sun during the day. The two and three storey buildings along the street were mainly made of wood, although some were of brick. The ground floor was either a shop, office or a bar and the next floor was where the white owners lived. As they rode along Bay Street, Christopher pointed out Government House on a hill in the city. It was surrounded by an electric fence and patrolled by members of the Cameron Highlanders based there as protection for the Duke of Windsor.

Bay Street was full of cars and was obviously the street to be seen on if you were into that type of thing, as some of the young, supercilious, white women seemed to be. This was Roger's second time in the main street of Nassau and he was surprised by the different shops mixed in with gaudy bars with strange names such as Dirty Dick's and Sloppy Joes. The street was full of RAF personnel and a smattering of American GIs and Canadian soldiers there for a night out.

When they arrived at the Prince George Hotel and Roger had successfully negotiated the four high steps into the reception area, Christopher marched off in search of a table on the patio at the back of the hotel which overlooked the harbour. He found one in the corner, which was being vacated by a party on their way to dinner. A black waiter appeared and took their drinks order.

Roger sat down in one of the chairs that faced the patio and took in the scene. There was about a dozen tables and each was occupied by young white people who were laughing, giggling and getting more animated with each drink they consumed. The only black faces were those of the waiters.

Occasionally, one or two of the young men and some of the women came over to greet Christopher and the other two RAF officers. Roger was introduced to them and was surprised to find out most of them were so called 'refugees' from Britain. Apparently their relatives sent them to the Bahamas to avoid call up for the armed services or to get away from the bombing. One of them, Tony Featherstone, told Roger proudly how he failed his service medical deliberately by pretending to have bad eyesight. This made Roger seethe with anger inside because they both knew what privations people in Britain were facing and to these people life was just one long party. But, it was when he said that the RAF doctors also had a cushy number here in the Bahamas, Roger couldn't contain himself any longer and he exploded: "You're an absolute prick! You have no idea what every family in bombed-out Britain is facing right now. See these scars on me, they happened because I was doing my bit to save the lives of an aircrew that had gone out night after night to bomb the Germans and keep us free from a Nazi invasion. What do you do? Probably play tennis or a round of golf each day and then you have to make the hard decision of which restaurant to go to for cocktails and dinner. You don't lift a finger to help your country. You and your type disgust me."

People at the other tables fell silent and looked in their direction. Tony Featherstone went beetroot red and left in a hurry without saying anything.

"I guess I won't be invited to any of his dinner parties," Roger said with weak smile. The others at his table laughed.

"Alan got back from Accra on the Gold Coast yesterday," said Christopher, trying to calm the mood caused by Roger's outburst.

"How do you get planes to these different theatres of war?" Roger asked Alan, as he was fascinated by the sheer logistical problems there must be.

"We fly B24 Liberators and they have a range of three thousand miles. Our route is through Trinidad,

146

Natal in Brazil, Ascension Island in the Atlantic and we end up in Accra, the capital of the Gold Coast. We only take them as far as Accra and they are flown on by other ferry pilots to wherever they are needed. Then we and other crews catch a Liberator that is loaded with cargo for the return trip to Nassau."

They continued to talk about the logistical problems of ferry command. Then the conversation turned to what they were going to do after the war. Christopher and Roger said they would probably end up in general practice somewhere. Alan and Michael planned to go back to university, Alan to study accounting and Michael to study biology so he could teach.

Roger asked Christopher where he was from and he said he was from the Bahamas, which was a surprise. He had gone to medical school at Queens University in Canada and had done his internship at Toronto General. He came back to the Bahamas to work at the Bahamas General Hospital and then had been assigned to work as a civilian doctor at the RAF Hospital.

Then Roger asked him about his family. At this, Christopher suddenly got up and a change in demeanour had come over him as he crossly left the group to find a waiter for more drinks. Alan Jones leant over and said to Roger: "Christopher doesn't like talking about his family, particularly his old man. He had been a GP in Nassau and his mother had left home soon after Christopher was born. After she divorced his father, she remarried and now lives in New Orleans. His father had been struck off the register of doctors by the General Medical Council in London for performing an abortion on a mentally sick fourteen-year old black girl. As result, he drank himself into oblivion and eventually committed suicide in 1933 by taking some pills. If I were you, I wouldn't mention his family again as it's a very sore subject with him."

Christopher came back with a waiter and they ordered another round of drinks. When the waiter had left, he turned to Roger and looked at him intensely. Then he asked him why he had spent time in New York on his way to the Bahamas. Roger explained that he had some friends there and wanted to see them.

"It was great to see them in a city that is not blacked out and there were no ration cards," He responded, trying to make light of his reply. He was puzzled by the sudden aggressive questioning.

"How was Group Captain Waite, Roger? Another friend of yours?" Christopher asked sarcastically. Roger didn't like his suggested accusation, which seemed almost menacing.

"Oh, he was interested in my medal and how I got it, no more no less," he said ignoring his cynicism. Both Alan Jones and Michael Sneed looked embarrassed.

"Come on Christopher, why the third degree?" Michael asked.

Christopher looked at Roger for a moment and then laughed. "Oh, I'm a tease who likes to pull people's legs. I am frankly jealous of him for spending time away from the war. Here's to you Roger. Welcome to our island." He raised his glass and so did the others as they toasted Roger.

Christopher's sudden change from a friendly, outgoing manner to a hostile attitude after he had been asked questions about his family puzzled Roger. However, he just wrote it off to him wanting to keep a guard on his privacy. He thought he probably felt challenged and had reacted irrationally. He had obviously touched a nerve and he was getting back at him rather ungraciously.

Their conversation was interrupted by the guffaws at a table on the other side of the patio. Roger looked over and there was a young man, who was impeccably dressed, sanctimoniously holding forth to a group of four equally young men who either were in civilian clothes or RAF uniforms. One of the civilian men was looking at him, starry eyed. There was only one woman in the group who was egging the man on to say more outlandish things.

"Who is that?" Roger asked Christopher, trying to seem unfazed by their earlier conversation.

"He is Robert Moore, who is assistant colonial secretary and a career officer at the Colonial Office. His daddy is Lord Moore who had him shipped out here because of some scandal in London some two or three years ago."

"If I were you I'd have nothing to do with him," said Alan. "He's trouble. He'll try and worm his way into your esteem asking all sorts of impertinent questions."

"Sounds as though you've had personal experience of him."

"When I first came out here a couple of years ago, I was friendly with him but I lost favour when he tried to become too friendly, if you know what I mean. I rejected his advances and, as a result, he spread vicious gossip about me, especially to the girl I was dating at the time."

"Thanks for the warning. He's not my type anyway," Roger said and they all laughed. Roger decided to keep a watch on Robert Moore because he just had a feeling he was not what he seemed.

Just then, one of the civilians in Robert Moore's group stood up and grasped his throat and fell onto the floor.

"Oh Michael, Michael!!" Screamed the woman in the group. "Someone do something!"

The men stood up and just stared at the prostrate figure gasping for breath not knowing what to do.

Roger hobbled over to take a look and instructed the men to lift him onto the table so he could examine him. He loosened his tie and shirt buttons. He put his ear to his chest and listened to the rasping sound his lungs were making. In the meantime, his breathing had grown laboured and his face had turned a dangerously bluish colour. Roger looked into the man's mouth he saw that in his throat was a large fishbone which was blocking his windpipe. Try as he might, he was unable to get to it to pull it out.

"Oh boy, we have someone badly choking," said Christopher looking over Roger's shoulder. "I'll go and call an ambulance to get him to the hospital because we can't do anything for him here. See what you can do to help him breath."

Roger knew the man needed was a tracheotomy to open his airways, but he had no instruments or tubing to use to relieve his breathing problem. Then a plan came to him.

"Bring me two drinking straws and a small sharp knife like a kitchen knife as quickly as you can," he shouted at a waiter who was standing around watching. "This man's life depends on how quick you are."

The waiter ran off and soon came back with what Roger needed. Using the knife carefully, he made an incision in the man's windpipe and stuck the two straws into the opening. Almost immediately, his breathing became less and less laboured until it was almost normal and his face pallor lost its blue colour.

Christopher returned and was surprised at the improvement in the patient.

"Where did you learn to do that?" he asked incredulously.

"I learnt to improvise when I was the medical officer at RAF Brooksbery. We often had to ad-lib because we didn't have the right equipment to do the job properly."

Robert Moore's group of friends gathered around the patient deep in nervous conversation. Roger ignored them and walked back to his table and finished his drink with Alan and Michael.

The ambulance arrived soon after that and Christopher went with the patient to the hospital.

***

After this incident, life for Roger at the RAF hospital settled into a predictable routine, when all of a sudden his old nemesis – fear – arrived to give his psyche a jolt. He had been in Nassau about three weeks when a major accident occurred on the aerodrome. Past memories of his catastrophe at RAF Brooksbery flooded into his mind as he fought to keep from having flashbacks and a nervous breakdown. This episode showed that his mind was still raw from his past dance with death.

It happened at about eleven in the evening when an aircrew in a Liberator were doing what was called 'circuits and bumps'. This was an exercise when a trainee pilot lands an aircraft and immediately takes off again and repeats the process a number of times so he can become efficient in landing an aircraft. For some reason the undercarriage on one of these approaches was not deployed properly causing the aircraft to belly land and end up on the scrub next to the runway.

Roger was in his room reading in bed at the time. He heard the crash and the alarm bells ringing on the fire engines and ambulances going to the accident scene. He got dressed as fast as he could and went to the hospital, expecting to treat the casualties. Wing Commander

Rassin arrived at the same time followed by Christopher Woodson. The nurses also arrived and began setting up equipment in their triage areas so that assessment could be made of each patients' needs.

There were only four aircrew on board the bomber when it crashed and the RAF rescue services were able to pull all of them out alive. However, three of them were badly hurt and were unconscious. When they were wheeled in to the hospital, Wing Commander Rassin took a quick look at them and gave his orders.

"I'll take this one and Christopher you deal with that man over there. Roger, look after this man. He's not as badly hurt as the rest of them but he has some trouble breathing and I don't like the look of that cut on his head."

Roger froze for a moment imagining himself fighting through the flames to the burning cockpit to rescue JJ from his Wellington Bomber back at RAF Brooksbery. Then he heard a gentle voice of one of the nurses: "Would you like me to take off his flying suit, sir, so we can examine him properly?"

Roger turned to see Staff Nurse Helen Masters and he woke from his trance-like state.

"Yes. Let's hook him up to an IV when we've done that and then take a look at that cut on his head. I think we need to x-ray his skull to make sure there is no fracture under the swelling pressing down on his brain."

They worked on their patient for about an hour. He came round as Roger was stitching up the six-inch cut on his head. They couldn't see from the x-ray any fracture to his skull but he was running a high fever and Roger was concerned about his prognosis. Staff Nurse Masters wheeled him away to a ward and Roger started to clean up the area.

A ward orderly stuck his head out of what was their small communal office.

"I've just put the kettle on, sir. Would you like some Rosy Lee?"

"Yes, I'm dying for a cup of tea."

They sat down around the table and Roger took a sip of the strong, sweetened tea. Staff Nurse Masters joined them and poured herself a cup.

"I've briefed the night staff so we'll see how he does by the morning," she reported. "Dr. Woodson's patient died before they could do anything for him and Dr. Rassin is still in the operating theatre. I think we were lucky with our patient."

"We certainly were. Thank you for your hard work tonight," Roger said to Staff Nurse Masters. "I think our man will survive to fly again once we get his fever down. It looks like he will have a sore head for some days, but he was lucky."

"Well I'm on an early shift tomorrow so if there's nothing else, I'll take my leave," she said. "I was on my way home when this accident happened. I'll see you tomorrow."

Roger walked to the operating theatre and met Dr. Rassin coming out.

"I think we've been able to stop the bleeding so we'll see. How did you do with your patient?"

Roger briefed him and told him what he knew about Christopher's patient. Dr. Rassin grunted and told Roger to go and get some sleep.

As he walked back to his room, Roger started to fantasise about what it would be like to take Helen Masters out. She seemed to him to be a no-nonsense woman who was not like some of the frivolous and hollow women he had met at the clubs and bars in town. This had been the first really close encounter he had had with her and he was aware of her looking at him when he was focussed on the patient. He decided it was just wishful thinking on his part, but thought to himself that you can't fault a man for dreaming.

However, Roger was about to find out the hard way that his presence in official circles in the colony was 'persona non grata,' or unwelcome.

Persona Non Grata

Chapter 11

A week after the accident, the annual officers' mess cocktail party was held with the Duke and Duchess of Windsor as the guests of honour. Roger was looking forward to this event as it was the first chance for him to observe the movers and shakers in the colony at first hand.

Because Roger was the most junior doctor, he was on duty at the hospital until seven so it was about eight before he appeared in the mess. By then the party was well and truly underway.

As he walked through the door, a woman grabbed his arm and Roger recognised her from the Prince George Hotel incident some weeks before.

"I'm Pamela Jackson and I want to thank you for saving Michael," she gushed as she guided him to her group of friends, which included Robert Moore.

"Let me introduced you to your patient; Michael Barnes." The man shook hands and thanked Roger for what he had done.

"That will do with the 'thank yous,' people," interrupted Robert Moore. "I want to know more about our hero and where he got his awful looking wounds." Roger gave the short version of his story. Robert Moore was obviously not impressed because he soon changed the subject back to himself, which he seemed to like to talk about.

"Robert, what do you do here in the Bahamas?" Roger asked, trying to get some idea of the man's opinions and prejudices.

"I try to keep the colonial office here functioning. It's a very tiresome task as I have a boss who is very demanding and keeps me on my toes, so to speak. You'll find that most people on this arid backwater are boring and haven't got much sophistication worth anything. Take that man of there," he said indicating with a nod a small man in a rumpled suit talking to someone in the uniform of a lieutenant colonel in Bahamian Police.

"That, would you believe, is one of the richest men in the world; Sir Harry Oakes. He owns a gold mine in Canada and moved here to the Bahamas to avoid paying taxes. His conversation is boring and he has as much grace as a charging bull elephant. Over there is an equally tedious man, Harold Christie, who is a property developer and one of the Bay Street Boys. He made his money as a smuggler during prohibition in the United States and has used it to develop hotels and other properties for the tourists. He's talking to another one of the group, a grocer's son by the name of Stafford Sands who is a lawyer and a leading critic of the governor in the legislature," he said with disgust.

"Is there anyone you like?" Roger blurted out without thinking.

"The people you see here make up my little group of friends. Occasionally, one of the trainee pilot boys joins us and we have some fun," he said without taking offence at the question.

Then the conversation turned to other topics and after a while Roger excused himself saying that he must circulate.

Group Captain Waite was conducting the Duke and Duchess around the room to the different groups of people and was introducing various people to them. They were closely followed by the Duke's equerry, Captain James Dugdale and his assistant.

Roger was struck by how small and petite the Duke and Duchess were. The Duke was only five feet seven and the Duchess was smaller at five feet two inches. They were smartly dressed, the Duke in a well-tailored lightweight summer suit and the Duchess in what was obviously an haute couture print dress. They had this insipid smile on their faces, which never changed and clearly hid the boredom they both probably felt at having to attend this official function. Roger thoughts were bitter and prejudiced against them at the recollection of the national trauma the Duke had put Britain through leading up to his abdication as Edward VIII. But he was not prepared for what would happen next.

Group Captain Waite beckoned Roger over to him and he began to introduce him to the Duke and Duchess.

"Sir, let me introduce you to Dr. Roger Lawson who is the latest addition to our staff at the RAF hospital. He was badly wounded helping an aircrew escape from a burning Wellington. In fact, His Majesty awarded him an OBE for his bravery."

"Congratulations, Lawson," the Duke said as he held out his hand to shake Roger's but when he saw its scars, he withdrew it quickly without making contact.

They were clearly shocked to see the scars on Roger's hands and on his burnt face. The Duchess particularly stared distastefully at him and they both moved on quickly without saying another word. Roger turned to another group of guests and he was waiting to join in the conversation when he overheard two of the Duke's equerries talking, sotto voce.

"His Royal Highness wants us to make sure he and the Duchess never see that doctor chappie again. Her grace was very upset at his appearance and wonders why he was allowed to be here."

Their conversation made Roger seethe with anger. He had never heard anything quite like the contemptuousness shown by the couple. They would probably say the same thing about the men who he knew at the East Grinstead Hospital who had risked their lives to save their country.

Squadron Leader Barry Adams, one of the instructors at Windsor Field, was in the group Roger had joined and had heard the conversation and saw his reaction.

"Try not to let it bother you too much, Roger. Maybe it was a blessing that he met Mrs. Simpson when he did and abdicated. Perhaps she did the country a favour. I'm thankful he is no longer our King because I remember what happened to an arrogant ancestor of his in 1645," he said sarcastically.

Roger smiled and calmed down, remembering the execution of Charles I. "You're right, sir, but it hurts all the same."

"Of course it does, but focus on your work and forget they even exist. Now, tell me how you got your OBE."

At about half past eight, the Duke and Duchess left. The party continued and there was an unmistakeable sign of relaxation among everyone in the room. Laughter and conversations were louder. It was if constraints had suddenly been lifted and everyone was free to be themselves again.

Roger circulated around the various groups until he found his quarry, Vivian and Brian Thomas. This was the couple Simon Cookson wanted him to keep an eye on because of the man's former affiliation with the pro-Nazi 'Right Club' in Britain. Brian Thomas must have been in his late fifties, very rotund and with grey hair and beard. His personality, when Roger introduced himself, was that of a loud know-it-all that would not let you get a word in edgeways. Roger thought he was the spitting image of Mr. Bounderby in Charles Dickens's book, *Hard Times*.

Brian Thomas liked his drink. The more he drank the more vociferous and vicious he became. According to the file Roger had read on him, he had insatiable sexual appetite when he was drunk and he was well known among the black women who sold themselves in Grant's Town.

His wife, Vivian, was the opposite. How she put up with him Roger didn't know. She was a quiet, elegant forty-eight year old brunette who had a very attractive, welcoming smile. She was dressed in a green cocktail dress that flaunted her fulsome figure and her high heels showed off her beautiful long legs. She hadn't much to say and seemed to be overawed by her bombastic husband, but Roger suspected she had a resolute streak to her character.

As Roger joined the group, Brian Thomas was railing against the Churchill government in London and the fact that they were just prolonging the war unnecessarily in his view. Roger had decided that the best strategy he should adopt would be a negative one, which would ally him with this man's views and maybe he could get to know him better.

"Now here's a young man who has just come over from Britain who can fill us in on the situation over there," he said as Roger introduced himself to the group. "So, Roger, what's the latest from the home front?"

"Life is tough with rationing and the daily bombing threat. It's not as bad as the Blitz, but people are despondent and morale is low. Many people wonder why Churchill doesn't make peace with Hitler. The longer we go on the weaker our negotiating position with him would be. Everyone is fed up with the continuing turmoil the war has caused and I think it was a shame the British government didn't sue for peace after the Dunkirk debacle," Roger said, without believing a word he was saying.

"My thoughts exactly," said Brian Thomas. "Viv and I moved here from Manchester in 1940 because of the bombing. I sold my company in Britain before the war, so I got my money out just in time and I was able to buy a metal-foundry business in Cleveland in America. We are doing quite well, thank you very much, Mr. Roosevelt! We live here because there are no taxes."

As they were leaving, Brian Thomas asked Roger to be their guest at a dinner party that Saturday that they were holding for an American businessman who was visiting the island. He accepted and was pleased because this was his chance to get closer to Brian Thomas and find out what was happening.

That coming Saturday Roger took a horse drawn taxi to the Thomas's house on West Bay Street. It was a large Victorian, three-story house of typical Bahamian design. It was wood framed with a large balcony going around the second floor. Big windows enabled the sea breeze to blow through the house and cool it efficiently from the humid, searing temperatures outside during the day. It was brightly coloured in typical Bahamian light pink with white trim that emphasised the window frames, doors and the balcony.

Roger pulled the front door bell handle and he heard a ring somewhere in the house. The door was opened by a black butler who was dressed in a white jacket, black trousers and a black bow tie.

"The family is in the lounge, sir. Please follow me."

Mrs. Thomas got up from her chair when she saw Roger walk through the door and greeted him. She introduced him to two Americans; Evelyn and Raymond Goodchild, and, to his surprise, to Helen Masters. He couldn't believe his good fortune to socially meet this beautiful woman who had so entranced him. He thought to himself, what luck, as it seemed that this dinner party would not be boring after all. Helen was dressed in white frock and a short sleeved blouse, which showed her soft, rounded breasts between the buttons of her top. Her hair was short and she wore little make-up, which she didn't need.

"Helen was the daughter of a close friend of mine in Plymouth," said Mrs. Thomas. "She moved here two years ago when both her parents were killed in the bombing there and is now living with us here."

"Yes, we have met briefly at the hospital," he said.

Raymond Goodchild was a non-descript man in his late fifties. He was the arch-type of a backroom engineer who didn't care for social pleasantries and would be more comfortable pouring over engineering drawings or constructing a product prototype. He was as thin as a rake and his clothes hung untidily on his five foot five inch frame, giving him that farmer's scarecrow look. He was a very nervous man, looking around as if he was expecting trouble when he was asked a question. However, he became very vociferous when he talked about his work though or the just-elected-again US President Roosevelt.

His wife, Evelyn, struck Roger as the person who ran the activities of her timid husband and he always seemed to agree with her, doing what he was told. She was very opinionated and had something to say just about everything. She was a large woman not only in her height, which was more than five feet ten inches, but in girth she was almost as enormous as she was tall. When other people were speaking she would stare at them, unsmiling, as if what they were saying was very repugnant. You had the feeling you wouldn't want to get on her bad side.

The butler took Roger's order for a drink and he sat down next to Helen. The long cocktail hour began to loosen tongues.

Roger asked Raymond Goodchild what business he was in. Raymond quietly explained that he owned a machine parts company in Chicago, Illinois, and his main market had been Germany. He expounded angrily that because of the United States entry into the war this profitable market dried up virtually overnight. He had been forced to lay off workers and cut his production schedules.

"But, aren't you able to get business from the US government to replace your loss?" Roger asked innocently.

"I backed the wrong horse in 1940. I was one of the backers of Wendell Willkie who was Roosevelt's Republican opponent in that year's presidential election. As a result, my firm has been ostracised by the government. Mind you they haven't openly admitted it, but contracts we should have won were never awarded to us.

"I think this war could have been avoided if your King Edward was still on the throne. I'm positive he would have made sure the Brits sued for peace."

"Raymond, I think you're dead right there," commented Brian Thomas. "The Duke of Windsor said as much to me on the golf course yesterday. He said he would have fired Churchill, dissolved parliament and had talks with Hitler. I know he's been in touch with some contacts in Portugal to see whether even now he could be of help."

"It's a bit late for that now," Roger interjected, deliberately stirring the pot.

"Rubbish, it's not late to do something about it," said an angry Evelyn Goodchild. "I think you limeys were wrong to force the Duke's abdication. This led us into the war because Churchill eventually conned that weakling Roosevelt into giving aid and now troops. We were proud member of America First Committee until it was dissolved when we declared war on the Japanese. We still believe we should never have gotten involved in another European war."

The America First Committee was an organisation formed to stop America's involvement in another European war. The organisation grew quickly from one started by some Yale University students to one of national importance. One of the leading promoters of its views was Charles Lindbergh, the famous US aviator who was the first to fly across the Atlantic in 1927.

Thankfully, just then, the butler announced dinner.

At dinner Roger sat next Helen. He found out that she had qualified as a registered nurse at the St. Thomas' Hospital in London and then moved home to Plymouth. She had lived with her parents in the city, but one night during the blitz her parents were both killed in an air-raid shelter so she decided to move to the Bahamas at the invitation of Vivian Thomas.

"I was on duty in the casualty department at the Plymouth General Hospital on the night they were killed and the next morning a policeman told me they had died. After their funeral, I took up Vivian's offer about finding a job here. There was an opening for a staff nurse at the

Bahamas General Hospital, which I applied and here I am. I was transferred to the RAF Hospital to help out with the influx of airman. Now, tell me about you."

Roger explained what he had been doing since medical school and about his wounds. Helen listened very intently as his story unfolded and peppered him with questions, especially about the treatments they were doing at the East Grinstead burns unit.

They had a hilarious conversation about some of the antics they'd seen by patients at the hospital. Roger asked her what she did in her time off and was surprised when she told him she was part of sailing crew who were going to take part in King's Cup race that coming Saturday. This was a big event in Nassau and one of the biggest occasions on the social calendar.

"The Governor is holding a reception at government house for the Royal Nassau Yacht Club after the race. Will you be there?" Helen asked.

"Yes. The whole officers' mess has been invited," Roger responded.

After dinner, the men went onto the balcony with their brandies and cigars. Roger was disappointed that he couldn't talk to Helen any further, but he knew he had to find out more about Brian Thomas.

"Roger, for the benefit here of Raymond tell him what you told me of conditions in Blighty," suggested Brian.

Roger then told him about the appalling conditions most people in Britain were under and that morale was rock bottom.

"Following up on my comments before dinner, there is a group of us who would like to see Edward restored to the throne," said Brian Thomas. "If this happened this war would be over, except with the Japs of course. Our real enemy is communism. If Stalin beats the Germans, we're next in line for communism after France and the Low Countries."

"Isn't that treasonous talk?" Roger countered. "Anyway the Americans are building up their strength ready for an invasion, so they will help us stymie the advance of communism."

"Treason be damned! We are just discussing possibilities among ourselves."

Then Raymond Goodchild interjected, "Why should our American boys be unnecessarily killed when it can be prevented?

"We can't make peace with Hitler!" Roger remonstrated.

"We shall see. I believe that moves are being made to resolve the situation," slurred Brian Thomas, who was worse for wear with the drink.

When Roger got back into his room that evening, he was pleased with himself. He had had a wonderful evening finding out about the prejudices of Brian Thomas, but what was really on his mind was the beautiful Helen Masters. He felt more confident that he could make inroads with her and ask her out.

Roger was humming to himself as he got undressed when he noticed that his papers, which were normally stacked in neat piles, were untidy. Also, he saw that a drawer on his clothes cupboard wasn't properly closed. Someone had been in his room. He was thankful that he had managed to arrange for the use of a safe for his sensitive papers. The question was who had searched his room? He had obviously made someone suspicious of him and he realised he had to be on his guard from now on.

The following morning Roger sent his first report to Simon Cookson in New York telling him about his conversation with Brian Thomas and his seeming closeness to the Duke of Windsor. He also reported the search of his room. Simon replied wanting more details, but warned him to be very careful and vigilant.

***

Roger was looking forward to the reception at Government House because Helen would be there. Saturday couldn't come any quicker as far as he was concerned. He was like a child dying of anticipation of Christmas and the presents it brings.

When Saturday finally arrived, the officers who were going to the reception all climbed in to a RAF lorry at the base's guardhouse. After a short journey they were dropped off at the gates of Government House. Roger was helped by the driver to climb down from the cab. He told the other officers not to wait for him because he would only slow them down. By the time he began his slow ascent up the winding path to the front door, the others had entered the building.

Eventually Roger reached the front door and gradually climbed the steps to a reception area where there was one of the Duke's equerries who stopped him and looked at a list he was carrying.

"Name?"

He told him.

"I'm sorry, you can't come in here."

"But all of us at the RAF officers' mess has been invited."

"You're not on my list."

"Are any of the other officers who have just gone in in front of me on your little list? Oh, I know why. The Duke and Duchess don't like my handsome features. I remember overhearing the Duke tell one of you flunkies not to invite me here. It reminds them that a war is on and some people get hurt."

"Are you going leave or have I got to call security?" said the crimsoned equerry.

"You know it would be nice to be arrested and at my court martial reveal the prejudice of the Duke against a wounded serviceman."

Just then, a staff sergeant of the Cameron Highlanders appeared beside the equerry.

"I think it's time you went," said the equerry.

Roger laughed at the man, although inside he was seething. "I'm going. I know when I'm not wanted."

As he began his painful descent back down the stairs, he turned to the equerry and said, "Tell me, why you aren't serving with your regiment instead of running around wiping the arse of that royal remnant?"

Without waiting for an answer he continued his laborious climb down the steps.

Roger was white with anger and decided to go to the Prince George Hotel for a drink and to calm down. It took him forever to slowly make his way to Bay Street and enter the bar at the hotel where there were a number of locals happily in conversation. He ordered a beer and a whisky chaser and sat at the bar a tried to compose myself.

Meanwhile Helen was busily talking to some of the other guests when she saw a group of RAF officers arrive. She walked over to them looking for Roger and asked one of the officers where he was.

"He's following up in the rear. It takes the poor chap some time to negotiate the stairs," she was told.

After a few minutes' waiting, Helen went looking for Roger and asked the staff sergeant at the door whether he had seen him.

"Aye. There was a wounded RAF officer talking to Captain Stanwell, one of the Duke's equerries. The captain wouldn't let him in and so he left after a few angry words. I remember him because of his scarred face and his painful limp. Poor devil," said the sergeant.

"Have you any idea which direction he was heading?"

"Towards Bay Street, I think."

Helen started to walk to Bay Street and began to look into the various bars and eventually found Roger on the terrace overlooking the harbour at the back of the Prince George Hotel beginning his second beer with a chaser. Helen ordered a drink from a waiter and then asked Roger what happened. He told her.

"Look, I agree with you about your treatment tonight, but you can't develop a chip on your shoulder about this. It will only gnaw at you," Helen told him and he knew she was right.

"How could you be interested in me? I'm destined to be a GP in some forlorn place in Britain. Why don't you go back to the party and enjoy yourself with your sailing friends?" Roger slurred as the drink took effect and his self-loathing deepened.

"Oh stop it! Come on, Roger, you're better than that."

After some thought she had come to a decision. "You're not alone, you know. I want to help you get back some of your mobility. Let's plan to walk and cycle so you exercise those wounded muscles of yours."

True to her word, Helen encouraged him to exercise and they went on long bicycle rides and walks together. She introduced him to a group of her sailing friends and they often sailed to one of the outlying islands and picnicked. Together they would go out to the casino at the Bahamian Club or dance at the Silver Slipper nightclub in the 'over the hill' black district of Nassau.

Roger began to fall deeply in love with Helen, but he still thought in his messed up mind that their relationship was useless. He wondered why she should want to go out with someone so disfigured. He hadn't realised that it didn't matter to her.

A Desperate Conspiracy is Born

Chapter 12

8 Prinz Albrecht Strasse, Berlin, Germany, March 25th, 1943

A black Mercedes-Benz 770 pulled up in front of the Gestapo headquarters on Prinz-Albrecht-Strasse in Berlin at six o'clock on a rain-soaked March evening. A diminutive, bespectacled, and moustachioed figure in a black hat and raincoat impatiently opened the back passenger door and had started to climb the stone steps of the building before the Gestapo chauffeur could come around to open the door. Heinrich Himmler, Reichsführer-SS minister of the interior and head of the Gestapo, was in a hurry and didn't care for the niceties of having a chauffeur open car doors for him.

His appearance was deceiving in that this owlish looking man was in fact the most notorious Nazi murderer and the evil genius of the regime. If you saw him in civilian clothes walking along the street you might mistake him for a teacher or a humble bank clerk. He wasn't much of a conversationalist although his staring grey eyes never left the face of the person to whom he was talking.

A guard came to attention and saluted as Himmler bounded up the steps and went through the building's front door. The Gestapo headquarters was formerly Berlin's School of Industrial Arts and Crafts. This vast cavernous place struck awe and fear into visitors who came through its front door and as they passed through its corridors to meet with senior officers of the Gestapo. That's why it was chosen by Herman Göring in 1933 when he formed and ran the Gestapo. It struck a different kind of fear into those who entered through the back and were dragged into the building's underground cellars.

Heinrich Himmler had just come from a meeting with Adolf Hitler when they had discussed the worsening situation on the Russian front where Field Marshall Frederick Paulus had surrendered his Sixth Army to the Russians against Hitler's direct orders. Hitler was livid and beside himself even two months after the surrender. Stalingrad had been relieved by the Russians who were now putting pressure on the remaining German army groups.

In addition, Field Marshall Erwin Rommel was in retreat in North Africa with his Afrika Corp. and he fought his last battle at Medenine in Tunisia. The British had by then broken the German Enigma codes at Bletchley Park and this was of value to the allies in their defeat of Rommel's army.

Compounding Hitler's problems was the start of the build-up of allied forces in Britain ready for an invasion of Western Europe. This was something Russia's leader, Stalin, had been demanding and was furious that the allies hadn't yet invaded. Although the invasion was seventeen months away, Hitler knew it was likely coming now that the United States had entered the war.

This ominous development would mean that his armies would have to fight on two fronts. He thought it would be better to thwart these plans so he could divert some of his western divisions to fight the Russians in the East. Himmler had come up with an ingenious scheme that, if executed properly, would stop the allied build up in its tracks. Hitler had, that evening, given the go ahead for Operation Vixen.

Himmler reached his office on the fourth floor.

"Get Kaltenbrunner and Jüttner here right now," he barked at his assistant, SS-Major Amsel, as he entered his office suite and then disappeared into his inner sanctum.

Himmler's office was like his demeanour; dark and sombre. There were two large twelve foot windows, which reached up to the ceiling, and their curtains were permanently closed. The only light in his office was a single desk lamp and table light on a credenza on one of the walls. When he looked at visitors he created a sinister profile especially when the light was reflected in his glasses. He was no longer the scrawny, twenty-three year old who had joined the Nazi party in 1923, but the most powerful man in Nazi Germany after Hitler.

Ernst Kaltenbrunner was an Obergruppenführer, or general, in the SS and had just been appointed chief of the RSHA department reporting to Himmler. This was the Reich's main security office responsible for finding and eliminating so-called 'enemies' of the Third Reich, which included Jews, Communists, Gypsies, Freemasons, pacifists and Christian activists. Kaltenbrunner was a handsome Austrian who stood at six feet seven inches tall and was very athletic. He had scars on his face which he claimed were from duelling in his youth.

Also an Obergruppenführer, Hans Jüttner had been Chief of Staff for the Waffen-SS since 1940 and was very different in appearance and character than Kaltenbrunner. The forty-eight year old general was heavy set, be-spectacled and much shorter than his colleague. He was well known for his organisational skills, not for his athletic prowess. In 1942, Jüttner had formed a special forces unit called the Sonderlehrgang z. b. V. The unit was made up of a hundred experienced volunteers from the Waffen-SS under the command of SS-Hauptsturmfuhrer van Vessem.

The Waffen-SS was the private army of the Nazi Party run by Himmler. It was formed in 1933 with just eight hundred men because of the growing intense distrust between Hitler and German army commanders. At its height in 1944, the Waffen-SS had expanded to thirty-eight divisions strong with nearly a million men serving in it made up mainly of infantry and tanks. They had a ruthless, cruel reputation and were responsible during the Second World War for many atrocities and massacres particularly in Russia and Poland as well as elsewhere in occupied Europe. They exterminated some six million European Jews and about five million others in concentration camps or in massacres in occupied countries.

Fifteen minutes later, Major Amsel rang him on the intercom to tell him that both men were in Himmler's private meeting room. When Himmler entered the room both generals stood up and gave the Nazi salute and growled "Heil Hitler."

"Sit down gentlemen," the Reichsführer ordered.

"The Führer has tonight agreed to my plan to kidnap the Duke of Windsor," Himmler said simply. "The British and Americans have started to build up their troop levels ready for an invasion of Europe at some

173

time in the future and we have continuing pressure from the Russians. We want to pre-empt this by kidnapping Duke of Windsor and holding him hostage to force Britain to back out or delay the invasion. When this has been successfully accomplished, the Führer plans to launch a major offensive in Russia using some of our divisions tied up in Western Europe. This will push the Russians back and they will want to sue for peace. Now Hans, tell us how Operation Vixen will be successfully completed."

"The operation is really quite straight forward, gentlemen," said General Jüttner. "We plan to land six men of our Sonderlehrgang z. b. V. commando unit from a U-Boat. The Duke is being very lightly guarded by a company of Cameron Highlanders and some Canadian soldiers. We don't intend to take on these soldiers. Our plan is to take him stealthily and get away before anyone has realised he is missing.

"According to our people on the island his security is lax. He has one bodyguard who follows him around and is armed. He plays a lot of golf and is known to go on bicycle rides. SS-Major Kurt Bergman from our Bueno Aires Embassy is making contact with our agents there and will be meeting them to make the final plans and manage the operation. Fortunately there are some pro-Nazi sympathisers on the island who will help us with our scheme to snatch him."

Jüttner then laid out a large map of the Bahamas' New Providence Island on the table.

"Here's what we plan to do."

A week later U-106, an IXB type U-Boat, slipped out at seven o'clock at night from its protected concrete pen at Keroman, a suburb of the Atlantic coastal city of Lorient. Keroman was the major U-boat base in occupied France where large, eleven-foot thick concrete bunkers had been built to protect U-boats from the constant bombing of the RAF and the American air force. The allies were never able to destroy the bunkers, although the city of Lorient was reduced to rubble by the end of the war.

U-106 was captained by Hermann Rasch who had been a particularly successful U-boat skipper in the Battle of the Atlantic, which was an attempt by the Germans between 1939 and 1945 to isolate Britain from needed food, oil and armaments. Over three thousand six hundred ships were sunk in this battle and some thirty-six thousand sailors lost. Despite this enormous hammering, supplies got through to the beleaguered country.

Captain Rasch had been chosen because of his experience and he was regarded as the most successful U-boat commander. He was called to Berlin and briefed on Operation Vixen and his role in the secret mission. He was instructed to land six German commandos at a particular beach on New Providence Island in the Bahamas. He was to take them and a VIP back to Hamburg in Germany. He was not to engage any shipping during his passage to and from the Bahamas as this could jeopardise the operation. To accommodate his passengers, he reduced the number of torpedoes to fifteen from the twenty-two his submarine usually carried.

The 1XB submarine had a range of fourteen thousand miles and Captain Rasch calculated that it would take his U-boat just over two weeks to reach the Bahamas. He planned to have the submarine sail as much as possible on the surface, even during the day, where his speed would be twelve miles an hour compared with four and a half submerged. Usually U-boats spent their nights on the surface to recharge the batteries used to power the engines when submerged. He planned to sail on the surface during the day once he was out of range of coastal aircraft and enemy ships. He knew it was a risk but worth taking.

Once U-106 cleared the estuary at Port-Louis, the submarine entered the Atlantic Ocean and submerged so that it could avoided the prying eyes of search planes. When U-106 was one hundred miles from the French coast, Captain Rasch surfaced and continued his voyage to the Bahamas.

Smuggling

Chapter 13

Nassau, the Bahamas, April 4th 1943

Lazy Jake's Bar on East Bay Street was the archetypical definition of a 'hole in the wall' or sleazy dive. It was a place where only serious drinkers drank and a place where you didn't often see a woman unless she was looking for business. It was sparsely decorated with a few tables and chairs and spittoons conveniently located around the bar. Its customers were white men and mainly the less well-healed merchants or junior managers of Nassau businesses. Nobody wanted to know your business and you certainly didn't want to know theirs.

At the back of the bar was an alcove where three RAF men sat huddled over beers and one of them was laying down the law, although in a muted but harsh tone.

"I don't give a damn what the man wants. We aren't going to do it," said Pilot Sergeant Fred Stapleton. "It's our caper and he's not honing in on it. Mr. Falk has his own contacts in Miami to offload the goods."

Pilot Sergeant Fred Stapleton was a twenty-five year old muscular man who could have been a boxer and was far from his home in Bermondsey in South London. He sported several tattoos on his arms particularly a prominent one of a skull and crossbones. Back home in Bermondsey, he had been the leader in a small gang of petty criminals, which was known for its cruelty of anyone who got in its way.

But Fred Stapleton was very bright and, if he had grown up in a wealthier environment where educational opportunities abounded, he would have been a university graduate and probably the founder of a successful small business. As it was, he had grown up on the streets of Bermondsey where he had to become 'street smart' to survive. Fred had joined the RAF at the beginning of the war out of the need he felt to better himself and his natural intelligence had enable him to become a bomber pilot. He was able to get a posting to Ferry Command and was happy when he was sent to the Bahamas.

The other two men were about the same age as their leader and also from London. Pilot Sergeant Ken Williams was a much smaller, nervous man and Sergeant Navigator Victor Raymond was the most gregarious and had to be stopped from raising his voice so that the whole bar could not hear him. A casual observer would determine from his demeanour that Fred Stapleton was obviously the leader of the group.

All three of them were in the same aircrew with RAF Ferry Command which was responsible for delivering Liberator Bombers to Accra on the Gold Coast of Africa for onward delivery to major theatres of war. They had organised a very successful diamond smuggling business. They would buy diamonds in Accra cheaply and would sell them at a large profit through a third party in Nassau to diamond merchants in Miami, Florida.

Victor Raymond had told the others that he had been approached by a Mark Laramie, one of the Bay Street merchants, who was acting for the Trafficante mafia gang in Miami. Laramie was an old rum runner from the U.S. prohibition days and ran a restaurant on Bay Street.

Raymond told the others that the long and short of their conversation was that he threatened to report their activities to the RAF police unless they conducted their business through him.

"Vic, tell him no." said Fred Stapleton.

"He won't like it. What if he does report us?"

"Then we'll tell the MPs he approached us to smuggle diamonds for him. It's our word against his. I wonder how he got wind of our caper."

"The Trafficante mafia gang in Miami probably found out about Falk's business through one of the diamond dealers," commented Ken Williams.

"Well they're not going to hone in. Now, back to the other business. I'll talk to Bernt about getting a loan to cover our business in Accra next week," continued Stapleton.

Their silent partner who financed their operations was Bernt Falk. He would pay them a percentage of the value of the diamonds when he sold them in Miami. It was a very simple operation that they had been conducting for the past two months. The diamonds were easily available from a dealer in Accra and no one ever suspected the returning ferry crews from Africa of smuggling contraband. Falk needed them and they needed Falk for them all to be successful.

Bernt Falk was a Swedish national and a banker by profession. He was in his sixties and a bachelor. He was overweight and had a very unkempt look about him. He was badly in need a haircut and his greasy, grey hair often fell over his bespectacled face. One of his mannerisms was to constantly flick his long locks backwards towards the back his head to keep them from covering his eyes. He always wore an extremely rumpled, light-tan summer suit and it hadn't been cleaned for a long time. When he was out in the Bahamian heat, he wore a pith helmet and carried a walking stick with a silver bobble, which hid a short sword for his protection. He gave a lubberly impression to the casual observer but his mind was quick and perceptive in its reptilian-like clarity.

Of course, Bernt Falk was not his real name. It was Sven Larson and he had spent many years in Mexico after being released from prison in Stockholm where he had embezzled money from a rich client. The authorities there had never been able to trace the money, although they had been following him in the hope of recovering it. After being released from prison, he had just disappeared much to the distress of the police.

He reappeared as Bernt Falk in the Mexico City and became a successful real estate developer during the building and development boom there in the 1930s. By 1940, the Mexican authorities were investigating him again for embezzlement and he fled to the Bahamas. He had been able transfer large amounts of cash to the Royal Bank of Canada in Nassau many years before Mexican authorities started their investigations. He knew he had to have somewhere to hide.

Falk had a large, walled house opposite Love Beach where he lived a solitary life and he often was very much the worst for liquor. Occasionally he would be visited by a woman from the black neighbourhood of Grant's Town but she was the only person who visited, except for an old cleaning lady who cleaned his house once a month.

At two in the morning on the following day, Victor Raymond reluctantly went to his prearranged meeting with Mark Laramie behind some sheds in the dock area on Prince George Wharf. This area was not lit by lamp lights and was completely deserted until the early morning market at five. The prostitutes who were looking for business and who entertained their clients there had gone and so there was no one to witness their meeting.

Victor told Laramie about the group's decision, which didn't go down well with him.

"It seems you boys need a lesson on how we do business here in the Bahamas," he said callously.

As Laramie walked away, a large black man appeared from the shadows of the warehouse carrying a wooden baseball bat. Raymond tried to run but his path was blocked by another man. As they closed in they began to beat him unmercifully. The last thing Raymond remembered before he lost consciousness was Laramie saying the same treatment would be meted out to the others unless they cooperated with him.

Raymond was hurt very badly and left in the gutter a bloodied mess. When he gained consciousness two hours later he crawled towards Bay Street. Eventually, he was able to stand and began to stagger painfully, as if he was very drunk, but soon he collapsed again. In the end, he was found wandering along the dockside by a Bahamian police patrol who handed him over to the RAF police. He was taken to the RAF Hospital where Roger was on duty.

When Roger examined him, he saw he had a broken arm and his face was a bloody mess. He was able to stitch him up and set his arm but he was barely conscious. Roger was concerned that he might have a severe concussion so he admitted him to the aircraftsmen's ward as a precaution. He tried to get him to tell him what happened but he wouldn't say anything.

Not long after Roger had admitted Raymond to the hospital, he was visited by Pilot Sergeant Ken Williams. They had a quiet conversation for about fifteen minutes with Williams, constantly looking over his shoulder to make sure no one was listening. And then he left.

Roger was in a small office off the main corridor filling out various reports when he heard an intense discussion between Fred Stapleton and Ken Williams about what they should do next following the beating of their friend. They had decided to lay low and not carry out any smuggling operations until they had talked to Bernt Falk. As they started to walk along the corridor, Fred Stapleton noticed Roger in his small office and he pretended to concentrate on his work as if he hadn't heard anything.

Roger finished his shift at the hospital and he began to walk back to the base. He was unaware of being followed as he approached the guardhouse at the main gate. Flight Sergeant Owens of the RAF police was on duty and checking everyone's passes. As there was no one else around, Roger stopped to talk to him to ask how the cut on his arm was doing which he stitched up the previous week.

Roger then began to walk to the officers' accommodations. When he had reached a corner someone grabbed him and pushed him into an alley between two buildings.

"Right, doc, what did you hear of my private conversation back in the hospital?" Fred Stapleton demanded as he pushed his forearm across Roger's throat.

"What are you talking about?" he said, gagging.

"Don't give me that. I saw you talking to that MP just now. What did you tell him?"

"Nothing. He was a patient of mine and I wanted to see how he was doing."

"I am only going to give you one warning. If I find out that you grassed on us I'll arrange to have you topped. Do I make myself clear?"

"Perfectly, but I don't know what you're talking about."

"Good. Keep it that way."

And then he was gone.

Of course Roger had heard bits of the conversation especially the name of Falk and their need to talk to him. He wrote it off as some scheme these men were into but it didn't amount to much, although attacking and threatening an officer like that must mean it was something pretty important. He put the incident into the back of his mind.

***

Dusk was turning to dark the next day as Berndt Falk finished his dinner and was washing up his few dishes. He planned to visit Dirty Dick's, his usual watering hole, and watch the comings and goings at this bar, particularly of the RAF personnel. He had been working for the Germans ever since he had arrived in the Bahamas in 1940 and had been recruited by them in Mexico City.

Over the years he had been able to feed them with low level intelligence first on the Duke of Windsor and then his usefulness had increased when the RAF had set up its bases on the Providence Island beginning in 1942. His role had not been dangerous because he was able to pick-up useful information about the state of bomber

183

pilot training and ferry command from the conversations he overheard. These evenings always became more informative as the night wore on and people became more vociferous fuelled by their drinks.

His biggest coup for the Germans was the uncovering of a British SIS agent, Brian Griffin. Silly man had tried to recruit him because he knew of Falk's frequent visits to Havana, Cuba, to gamble and his friendship there with a number of ex-patriot Swedes. Havana was a haven of spies from many nations including Germany. When he had reported Griffin's approach to the Germans, the man suddenly died under very suspicious circumstances. He had nothing to do with his death, but he always suspected someone else on the island had taken care of the problem. He had become more and more certain that he wasn't the only German agent in the Bahamas.

There was a loud thumping on his front door which startled him. He took his nine millimetre Browning from his desk drawer and cautiously opened the front door. Standing there was Major Kurt Bergman, his Gestapo handler in Mexico. Bergman pushed his way past Falk, ignoring the pistol, closed the door behind him and went into Falk's living room without saying anything. He was carrying a small suitcase which he put down on the coffee table.

Major Kurt Bergman was the son of a school teacher and was born in southern German city of Mosbach in 1910. He graduated with a law degree from Heidelberg University in 1933 and briefly practised law in various district courts there. He joined the Gestapo in 1935 and was posted to Stuttgart where he gradually rose in the ranks and was recognised principally for his harsh interrogation techniques, especially among the communist and Jewish prisoners. In 1938, he took part in

Kristallnacht in Stuttgart when Jewish businesses, synagogues and homes across Germany were destroyed by fire by the Nazis. During this orgy of destruction, he was responsible for rounding up Jews to be sent to concentration camps like Dachau, near Munich in Bavaria. This was the first of the death camps, originally set up to hold political prisoners in what was a converted ammunition factory.

His interrogation successes and cruelty brought him to the attention of Major Walther Schellenberg who was a senior officer in the counter intelligence department. The department's role was to protect the Third Reich form espionage against it by foreign powers. In 1940, Kurt Bergman was serving as an SS-Hauptsturmfuhrer (captain) when he and Major Schellenberg were tasked with kidnapping the Duke of Windsor in Portugal. Although this operation failed, Kurt Bergman was a natural choice by Heinrich Himmler to head up 'Operation Vixen' because he knew his quarry very well indeed. At this time, he had been promoted to major and had been sent to the German Embassy in Buenos Aries, Argentina, in February 1942. He was responsible for recruiting and running agents to spy on the enemies of the Reich in the Caribbean and the Americas, especially the United States of America.

"Sven Larson your reports have been very valuable to us on the RAF movements here," Bergman said, using Falk's real Swedish name. Falk blanched and wondered how he knew this.

"You see we know all about your past, particularly your recent activities in Mexico. I'm sure you don't want us to tip off the Mexican authorities to where you are, now do you? I remind you that the Gestapo doesn't like agents who let them down."

"Of course I would never do that," was all Falk could stutter in reply.

"Now that I have your full attention, we have something else for you to help us with. You and I will be conducting an important operation here in a few weeks' time and I want your complete cooperation or else you know what will happen.

"You will know me as Boris Dahlin, your nephew from Gothenburg. I came here on the Pan Am flight from Miami today and I am staying at the Prince George Hotel. I am a salesman for a sail boat company in Gothenburg. In this small case is a short-wave radio which we will set up here in your house," Bergman said.

He opened the case and took out its false bottom cover to reveal the radio. "Our colleagues will be coming from the sea and we will contact them with this radio. I will tell you more later."

Suddenly, there is a muffled sound outside the open living room window.

"What's that noise? Who are you expecting?"

"No one. It's probably one of the neighbourhood dogs or cats. They are always rummaging around the dustbins for food," Falk replied nervously.

Bergman drew a gun from his waistband. "I'm going to check. Turn off the lights and wait here."

Cautiously he looked out of the window and saw nothing. He then quickly and silently went through the back door into the garden. He searched the gazebo. Nothing. He then returned to the house.

He didn't see a figure running towards the road into Nassau.

"I think you were right. It must have been a dog or cat," he told a relieved Falk.

After another half hour briefing Falk, Bergman left the house. He walked down the driveway with Falk giving him last minute instructions. As he got into his car he saw an RAF uniform cap on the ground and picked it up. Examining it, he discovered the name Stapleton written on the band.

"It wasn't a dog after all. Is this someone you know?" he said turning to Falk showing him the cap.

"Yes, he's someone I do business with."

"Fine, get rid of him permanently as soon as possible. I don't want our plans ruined."

Falk turned ashen, because he knew what Bergman meant by permanently.

Contact is Made

Chapter 14

Bernt Falk was sick about what he was going to do, but he had no choice in the matter. He had liked young Fred Stapleton who had always been honest in his dealings with the Swede but Kurt Bergman had been very adamant that he should take care of the problem, and this only meant one thing. Bergman had a very threatening demeanour when he told Falk to deal with this menace to the German operation's success and this dark side of his temperament had frightened Falk.

Another aggravation was that it looked as though he would have to close down his diamond smuggling operation for the time being, just when it was making good money.

Bernt Falk was at his usual table in Dirty Dick's saloon on Bay Street when Pilot Sergeant Stapleton came in by himself. He looked around the bar and spotted the big man and made a beeline for him.

"Hello Mr. Falk."

"Fred, my boy, come and sit down. Want a beer?"

"I'll get one."

Fred Stapleton went to the bar and got a beer and sat down opposite Bernt Falk.

"What did you want to see me about last night Fred?"

"I didn't go to your house last night."

"That's funny because you left this behind," Falk said as he took out the cap which was hidden on his lap.

Fred Stapleton reddened. "All right, I was there to talk to you about our next trip to Accra tomorrow. We need some cash to buy diamonds since we leave first thing in the morning. When I saw you had company, I left."

"What did you hear of our conversation?" Falk pressed.

"Nothing. Honest Mr. Falk. All I saw was you talking to a man then I left."

"All right Fred. Let us talk about your trip and how I can finance it. You can come and pick up the money at my house tonight, say ten."

"There was one thing I have to tell you. We've had an approach from someone working for the Trafficante gang in Miami. We told him we weren't interested but they badly beat up one of our guys and he's in hospital as a result."

"Hmm. Who was the contact?"

"A restaurant owner here in Nassau called Mark Laramie."

"Leave it with me. I'll sort this problem out."

After a while Falk left to walk back to his home and Stapleton got up to go to the lavatory at the back of the bar. He was followed into the bathroom by two men who had been sitting at the bar.

None of them saw Helen and Roger at another table partly hidden by a potted plant. Roger had seen them though because he recognised Stapleton, but he was not able to overhear their conversation. So that was Falk, he thought to himself. He looked like the mysterious man Roger had seen at the docks when he arrived.

***

Three days later, sponge fisherman Roland Perry, his brother Daniel and his sixteen-year old son Harry were searching for sponges on the west side of Andros Island, which is one of the largest of the 700 islands and cays that make up the Bahamas. The Perrys were the last in a line of sponge fishermen who searched the ocean floor for its ever elusive sponges.

The sponge industry had been an important part the economy of the islands, but this was no longer the case. Over harvesting and, in 1938, a microscopic fungus disease, wiped out virtually all of the sponges. Sponging had been the backbone of the Bahamian economy for seventy-five years, so thousands were thrown out of work when this happened. Very few sponge fishermen were left except some diehards such as the Perrys.

The Perrys were looking for sponges with the naked eye in the clear water of the Caribbean at depth of about eight feet. They were using grapnels on poles and by this method they were limited to about twelve feet whereas divers could reach down to about forty feet.

As they rowed a small wooden, shallow drafted boat called a dory, slowly above the coral beds on the lookout for sponges, they spotted a large canvas bag snagged on an outcrop of the coral reef about ten feet down. Using their poles with grappling hooks they untangled the bag from the reef and slowly began to raise it to the surface. They were surprised how heavy their discovery was and after a long struggle, they were able to lift their find onto the dory.

Young Harry Perry excitedly began to unlace the bag with great expectations of finding something of great value, so that they could sell it in Nassau. Life was hard enough as it was and maybe, just maybe, they had found

190

something significant. As he untied the knots and loosened the rope bindings, he jumped back and crashed into his father as a bloodied hand of a white man flopped out of the bag. He screamed and was violently sick over the side of the dory. His uncle Daniel took over and started to loosen the bindings further until he saw the bloodied corpse of a man in an RAF uniform. They raised the dory's sail and set out for Nassau.

Dr. Bain and Roger first examined the corpse on the quay when they were called in by the RAF police. It was obvious at first sight that the corpse had been bludgeoned very viciously over the head and, by the look of the progress of decomposition, it had been in the water less than a week. Because the corpse was in the canvas bag it hadn't suffered from feeding fish so it was in relatively good shape.

The canvas bag was one used to store sails in and could be seen anywhere or bought in any shop on the island. It was the same with the two small anchors that were used as weights to sink the body. The body had been tied to the anchors with rope which was commonly used by sailors.

The doctors were able to preliminarily identify the body as that of Pilot Sergeant Fred Stapleton by the papers he was carrying and by his dog tags. Also, Roger recognised his large distinctive skull and crossbones tattoo on his arm. He would have to be formally identified by one of his friends.

Dr. Bain and Roger took the body back to mortuary and carried out a post-mortem examination, which did not reveal anything untoward except for the wound on his head and that his lungs were full of sea water. As they were finishing up, Flight Lt. David Andrews and Flt. Sgt Thomas Jenkins of the RAF military police walked in to the mortuary.

David Andrews was a solidly built man in his forties. He had joined the RAF police at the outbreak of the war from Manchester Police where he had been a detective sergeant. He was well over six feet and he towered above most people. He had a reputation of being a no-nonsense, streetwise cop whose experience was honed on the streets of Moss Side, an extremely rough area in Manchester.

"Well Doc, can you fill us in on what you have found out?" Flight Lt. Andrews asked Dr. Bain.

"Sergeant Stapleton was hit over the head several times with what looks like a common hammer because the wounds are very symmetrical and about the same size. But that didn't kill him and it's a shame it didn't. The cause of death was drowning when he was thrown overboard from a boat. We know this because sea water was in his lungs; a froth, called the champagne de mousse, covered his mouth and was inside the lungs themselves, which were extremely swollen. In addition, there was sea water in his stomach indicating that he inhaled sea water through his mouth. Water in the lungs indicates that the victim was still alive at the point of submersion. If he was killed before he was thrown into the sea, there would be no water in the lungs or stomach.

"Unfortunately, this young man died an awful death as he struggled for air. You can see the abrasions on his hands and arms as he probably tried to open the tied sailing bag he was in from the inside. We estimate that his body had been in the water at least two or three days judging by its decomposition, which is beginning to take place."

"What a way to go," said Flight Lt. Andrews. "We know he was last seen on Friday because he didn't turn up for duty the next morning. Several of his mates saw him on Bay Street that night."

"I can confirm that," Roger said. "I saw him in Dirty Dicks at about nine that night. He was with a large heavy-set man. Let me see if I can remember the name he greeted him by. Was it Fawkes, Fork or Falk? It was Falk. The man spoke with a thick foreign accent. Strangely enough I first came across Sergeant Stapleton a few weeks back when he was visiting a friend here in the hospital. The man had been beaten up pretty badly and Stapleton seemed very angry and agitated about something."

"Thanks, doc. Bernt Falk has been on our radar for some time but we've not been able to pin anything on him. We've been working with the Bahamian police and they tell us he is a retired Swedish businessman who came here in 1940. We think he finances a diamond smuggling ring. It seems he keeps at arm's length relationship from the ring but we have suspected he has organised one for some time among some of the RAF ferry pilots. His meeting with Stapleton was probably to talk about their next operation," he said.

Roger was curious about the circumstances of Stapleton's death and his relationship to Falk. It seemed strange to him that he would kill one of his sources of his diamond smuggling operation. Although he didn't hear their conversation, they didn't look as though they were having an argument. He decided to look more closely at the Swede. That night he sent a message to Simon Cookson in New York asking about Bernt Falk and what was known about him.

Two days later, Roger was handed a large envelope by a military policeman. Inside it was a thick file and a letter from Simon Cookson instructing him to send daily reports from now on about what he had found out. The file was very revealing about Falk, who was a suspected German agent. It detailed his past in Sweden and Mexico and gave details of the various trips he had made to Cuba and to Miami.

Roger arranged to see Group Captain Waite and the following morning he was ushered in to the group captain's office.

"Sir, I would like to be with Fl. Lt. Andrews when he interviews Sergeant Stapleton's colleagues because I believe his murder has something to do with the Duke of Windsor and a possible plot. The Germans are in contact with this Swede called Bernt Falk who we know is a low level Nazi spy."

"We'd have to let Andrews in on your role," he responded.

"That's fine sir. Just say I'm working for the War Office."

Late that evening Helen cycled home from work at the hospital. The usual daily heat had enveloped the island with its searing day-time temperatures and a stifling blanket of humidity. When she reached home and her room, her uniform was wet with perspiration and she was glad to take it off. She lay in a bath of cold water to get some comfort from the oppressive heat before she lay naked on her bed and tried to sleep. But she couldn't sleep and was soon perspiring again.

Downstairs there was a knock at the front door. This was answered by the butler.

"Is Mr. Thomas in?"

"Who should I say is calling sir?"

"My name is Dahlin and you can give him this card."

Major Bergman had written two names, Thomas Hunter and Samuel Chapman, two former members of the Right Club in London.

The butler returned and ushered him into Brian Thomas's study.

"Kurt, what are you doing here?" Brian Thomas said after the butler had left.

"Please, sit down."

"I'm going under the name of Boris Dahlin at the moment. I'm a Swedish salesman for a sail maker."

"Fine, I understand. How do you know these two gentlemen?" Brian Thomas asked as he looked at the card again.

"We met before the war in Stockholm. You remember our conversation in Havana?"

"Yes, very much so. How might I help?"

"What I'm going to tell you is very sensitive and must be held in confidence. Your life might depend on your secrecy."

"That sounds ominous. You know my feelings about the war. You have my word it won't go any further," said Brian Thomas, noting the other man's cold staring eyes, which disturbed him a little.

"I have been tasked by the Führer to contact the Duke of Windsor."

A surprised look crossed Brian Thomas's face. "I think we'll go outside on the veranda to discuss this. The walls might have ears."

Brian Thomas rang a small bell. "Would you like a drink?"

"A beer would be fine."

The butler appeared and the drinks were ordered.

Once they had settled down outside in two comfortable chairs, the butler appeared with their drinks. When he had gone, Kurt Bergman continued.

"The Führer is interested in negotiating peace with Britain but it is difficult with Churchill in charge. He will not listen to any proposals even if we made them to him. He is demanding unconditional surrender which is unacceptable. We know the Duke is interested in peace between our two countries and he might be able to influence his brother King George VI. To this end the Führer would like to meet him again to discuss his proposal."

"How can he do that? He's stuck out here in the middle of nowhere."

"We plan to take him by U-Boat to Germany to meet the Führer."

"You mean kidnap him?"

"No, we have no intention of doing that. He will go only if he wants to after hearing our proposal and reading a letter I have for him from the Führer. We understand that you are friends with the Duke."

"Yes I play golf with him and my wife and I often have dinner with him and the Duchess."

"How about inviting him to dinner here so we can discuss this plan with him?"

Brian Thomas thought for a bit.

"What you are asking me to do is treasonous. If I was caught they would hang me."

"We can arrange for you to come with us to Germany and if peace was arranged you could return to your country having done it a great service."

Silence. Both men puffed on their cigars and took a sip of their drinks.

"I'll help you so long as I can go to Germany with you."

"What about your wife?"

"We'll leave her here to face the music."

"Why?"

"I'm tired of her and want a change. I can't stand being in the same room with her anymore. She's intolerable!" he said with surprising venom. "She must know nothing of my involvement otherwise she could spill the beans. That's the only thing that will save her from the rope. Perhaps I can leave a letter to that effect where the authorities will find it."

"I'll leave you to make dinner arrangements. Let me know when this is complete."

"I'm playing golf with the Duke later this week so I'll broach the subject of dinner then."

Helen's room overlooked the veranda where the men were discussing their plans and she overheard part of the conversation through her open window. Their tête-à-tête had woken her up. Groggy, she only heard the last part of their exchange about arranging a dinner party and Brian Thomas's plans to go to Germany without his wife. She wondered to herself what he was up to. She thought about telling Vivian but decided for the moment to hold off until she was sure about what she had heard.

Three days later Brian Thomas was playing a round of golf with the Duke of Windsor. He waited until the Duke had a particularly good hole before he put his proposal to him.

"Sir, next week a Swedish friend of mine is coming to stay and I thought I might have a private, men-only dinner party for him. We could play bridge or snooker. It would be a good opportunity for you to hear the latest news of the war in Europe because he gets into Germany quite a bit."

The Duke took a drag of his ever-present cigarette and thought about the proposal.

"Yes. I would be interested to hear the latest news, particularly Mr. Hitler's fight with Russia. It could be very informative for the British government. I'll have to check with the Duchess to make sure we haven't got anything on. I think she has a Red Cross committee meeting one evening next week. I'll get Dugdale to let you know."

"I could ask Robert Moore to make up the bridge foursome and he can hear what this man has to say and then relay it to the Colonial Office," Brian Thomas continued.

"That's a good idea. I always enjoy Moore's company. Now, you better improve your play on the last few holes if you expect to beat me today."

They continued golfing.

The Plot Thickens

Chapter 15

In a smoke-filled meeting room on the fourth floor at the British Colonial Hotel in Nassau, four men were in deep conversation about bringing casinos to the Bahamas. Bespectacled and heavily set Stafford Sands was a thirty-year old lawyer and one of the Bay Street Boys. As a member of the colony's legislature, he was leading a campaign to legalise casinos in the Bahamas in the hope of making a lot of money on any deals that were made.

Sitting opposite him was the forty-seven year old real estate businessman, Harold Christie, who was a thin, balding man. He was a former rum-runner during prohibition in the United States in the 1920s and had made a fortune for himself. He was now the leading property developer in the colony and was looking to further enrich himself with the expected property boom after the war had ended. He was known for his hustle and salesmanship, especially among wealthy Americans in Florida.

Pacing around the room was forty-five year old Frank Marshall, a native of New York, who represented a syndicate of American businessmen who wanted to open at least two casinos in the Bahamas. This syndicate was made up of mafia heavyweights Meyer Lansky and Charles "Lucky" Luciano who already operated casinos in Miami, New Orleans and Havana, Cuba. Frank Marshall was a man of action who felt the pressure from his bosses to get their casino plan agreed and was irritated and frustrated with slowness of discussions with the powers that be in this Caribbean backwater. He was also very hot and sweated profusely even with his jacket off and his sleeves rolled up.

Unofficially representing the Duke of Windsor was Robert Moore. He was explaining for the umpteenth time to Frank Marshall that gambling had been illegal in the Bahamas since 1901. In 1940, an amendment was added to the law that allowed in exceptional circumstances a Certificate of Exemption to be issued, but the one drawback was that the colony's legislature had to approve such a move first. At that time, the Bahamas had two legal casinos that operated under such an exemption – the Bahamian Club in Nassau and one on Cat Cay, which was some forty miles north-west of Providence Island.

"So what you are saying is that we have to pay off the powers in the legislature to get this thing passed," Frank Marshall bluntly responded. "How much do they want?"

"It's not that easy, Frank. The Duke is interested in agreeing to our plan because he sees employment opportunities for Bahamians. However, we face really stiff opposition from Sir Harry Oakes who has number of friends in the legislature as well as the Duke himself who can be influenced by him. After the Duke, he is probably the most influential man in the colony," replied Robert Moore.

"We have to get him on our side," said Stafford Sands. "The colony is ready for post war expansion when it comes and I have been lobbying influential members of the legislature. But it's going to take time."

"Well, my people don't understand what is holding us up," fretted Frank Marshall. "We had a casino up and running in New Orleans in one year. Why are you limeys taking so long?"

"Things are very different here, Frank," said Harold Christie soothingly. "You are dealing with a tightly controlled British colony compared with local authorities in New Orleans who you could easily coax along with bribes."

Frank Marshall continued to pace around the room as they talked. He looked under the meeting table, picked up ashtrays and peered behind a credenza on the other side of the room. As well as listening to the discussion he was concerned about security taken for the meeting. He had an innate fear of being spied on. This was borne from life in his tough neighbourhood in Brooklyn where you always watched your back and assumed in deals that the other person was going to double-cross you. The higher he climbed in the mafia pecking order over the years, the more paranoid he had become, especially dealing with law enforcement. He had had a number of close calls with authorities and didn't want to go back to prison.

He suddenly stopped pacing in front of a picture on one wall and looked behind it. "Aha!" he exclaimed and tore down a picture from the wall. When he turned it over it revealed a microphone and a wire ran from it through a hole drilled in the wall.

"Son-of-a bitch, we are being spied on!" he shouted.

Everyone in the room leapt up and came over to examine the microphone.

"Do any of you smartasses know anything about this?" he snapped. They all shook their heads and Robert Moore assured him that they were as surprised as he was by the find.

Frank Marshall wanted to know what was behind the wall.

"It's probably the service kitchen for the meeting rooms on this floor," answered Stafford Sands as he left the meeting room and entered the small kitchen from the hall. On the counter nearest one wall was a tape recorder which was missing its large tape spools. The door which led to the staff stairs was ajar and they could hear running footsteps going down. Robert Moore was the first into the stairwell and he saw a figure disappearing through the ground floor door. All he really saw was the man's balding crown and his blond hair.

All four men returned to the meeting room and were berated by a livid Frank Marshall. "Call yourselves leaders of these islands? You can't even organise a simple meeting without being spied on. You couldn't organise an orgy in a brothel. It's unbelievable. We are not going any further in our talks until you have found out and dealt with the person responsible for the listening device. Also, you won't see us again until we have your assurance that this Oakes guy will go along with our plan. I'm on the next Pan Am flight out of here!"

Without another word, Frank Marshall grabbed his briefcase and stormed out of the room.

"Well, I've never been talked to like that before. Who does he think he is, bloody man?" said a fuming Stafford Sands.

"Unfortunately he's got the capital we need," commented Robert Moore. "Let me get to the bottom of this."

After the others had left, Robert Moore went down the hotel management offices looking for Tom Wilson, the manager through whom he had arranged the room booking. He entered the manager's office and was at once greeted cheerily by Tom Wilson.

"Was everything to your liking Mr. Moore?" he purred in his best customer relations manner.

"No it wasn't, you jackass. Someone put a listening device in our room and was recording what we were saying."

"I assure you no one from this hotel was responsible for that, sir. They must have come in from the outside without us knowing. We are having some refurbishing work being done in some of the rooms by workmen from a contractor. Maybe it was one of them. I'll look into situation and let you know what I find out."

"You do that, and pronto."

When he had left and was walking back to his office, Robert Moore began to think about his conversation with Tom Wilson and wasn't convinced that he knew nothing. He seemed to be very evasive. He wondered if the balding head he had seen was in fact the complaisant assistant manager of the hotel. He decided to do some checking with someone he knew on the U.S. mainland.

A week later Robert Moore visited Major Bergman in his room at the Prince George Hotel. They had known each other in Havana, Cuba, where Robert went to gamble and indulge his sexual appetite with the male prostitutes in the brothels of Central Havana. He was an angry young man who had never forgiven his father for arranging his posting to the Bahamas. In 1938, Lord Moore had heard through his contacts at the British Home Office that his son was likely going to face charges of gross indecency following a police drug raid on a party in fashionable Belgravia in London where he was found in bed with another man.

At that time Robert Moore was a junior officer in the British Foreign Office after getting a modern languages degree at the University of Cambridge. By calling in favours from friends, he was able to arrange an urgent posting for his son and get him out of the country before he was arrested. But Robert was an angry man, first at his father and then at the British establishment in general. He was looking to take his revenge. This was despite the fact he had avoided a possible jail term because homosexuality was a crime at that time in Britain.

Major Bergman, who had been just a casual acquaintance of Robert Moore at the gambling tables in Havana, had recognised his usefulness to the Nazi cause when the Duke of Windsor became Governor General of the Bahamas in 1940. When they met in Havana for one of their gambling trips, the major had arranged a number of gay dates for him in Havana for which Robert Moore was extremely grateful. Just in case they were needed, he had photographs taken with which he could blackmail the young man.

They weren't necessary as Robert Moore had poured out his heart at one of their drunken orgies. The major also knew of the young man's sadistic side in his assignations with male prostitutes. In fact, word had gotten around the Havana brothels that he was vicious and got pleasure in physically hurting and humiliating his conquests. He should be avoided at all costs. This reputation had led to difficulties in finding male partners for him at any price Major Berman was willing to offer.

Major Bergman greeted Robert Moore warmly and offered him a drink. When the young man sat down, he admonished him gently for coming to see him.

"It was urgent that I see you right away because I have something that may be of importance to you." He then explained what had happened at the meeting with Frank Marshall and of his suspicions of Tom Wilson.

"My suspicions were well founded. I have found out through my Washington contacts that Tom Wilson is an FBI agent and was likely sent here to keep an eye on the Duke of Windsor."

After a few moments of thought, Major Bergman said: "Hmm. We can't let him ruin our plans. We'll have to find out what he knows and how he contacts his minder. We can't let our operation get fouled up as we are only a few days away from launching Operation Vixen. Robert, deal with him but get as much information as you can out of him."

"Leave it to me. It will be a pleasure."

When Robert Moore left, Major Bergman picked up the phone and dialled a number.

"Can you talk? Right. It seems we have discovered a spy in our operations. We are taking care of it but I need to know from your end if there are any plans to bring in extra men to protect you know who or any unusual activity. Right. Call me back as soon as you can."

Major Bergman felt pleased with himself although he knew complacency was dangerous. Apart from Robert Moore, he had been able to recruit an important agent who was right in the centre of RAF operations on the island. This agent had been feeding him information about the layout of the RAF bases, codes, the deliveries of bombers to Europe and the Middle East, frequency of wireless operations and the procedures of the soldiers that were guarding the Duke.

Tom Wilson's agony began that Friday night. He had taken a bath and was sitting in his living room just wearing a light dressing gown. He had a drink in his hand and, as he relaxed, he wistfully thought about his life. He liked this house because it was secluded in a mixed woodland of pine, palms and sea grapes trees, as well as a dense forest of ground cover growth. The house was well set back and hidden from the main road into Nassau and his nearest neighbours were at least a quarter of a mile away. He mused that perhaps he would leave the agency and just live here. He had his inheritance and he could live comfortably enough.

The front door bell rang and, as he got up to answer it, he wondered who was calling so late at night. As he opened the door, three hooded men burst in, grabbing him by the arms and forcing him into the dining room. They didn't say a word as they gagged him and tied him by his arms and legs spread-eagled on the dining room table.

A fourth masked man, who was obviously their leader, walked in and inspected the work of the others and dismissed them.

"Now you are going to tell me all about your work for the FBI and about your other contacts in the Bahamas," the man said menacingly.

The British voice was familiar but Tom Wilson was so panicked about what was going on he couldn't remember where he had heard it. The man expertly slit his dressing gown with a very sharp knife he had drawn from a scabbard on his belt. Laying there naked and feeling so vulnerable, Tom realised that his death was imminent and somehow found the courage and determination to resist this killer as long as possible.

The masked man lit a cigarette and let it burn until it was red hot.

"You are going to die regardless, so it's a question of how quickly. The quicker you give me the information I want the less likely you are to die in agony."

To illustrate his point he put the burning cigarette on one of Edward's exposed testicles. The pain was unbearable and he passed out as he writhed in agony and uncontrollably urinated. He came to and through a misty haze which had enveloped him, he saw the man start making circular cuts on his chest with his knife. When the man saw that he had come to, he removed the gag in his victim's mouth.

"Now, who is your contact here?"

"Get lost."

His torturer began to cut strips of flesh off his legs and arms. At this stage the pain was less. Funny, he didn't feel the cuts.

"Are you going to talk now?" asked the man looking down at him with a malicious grin on his masked face. Tom shook his head and then spat at the man. Then there was a burning sensation in his left eye as the cigarette was plunged into it. Again, he passed out. When he regained consciousness, he was subjected to another half hour of excruciating cuts on his chest and screamed as his expert torturer continued his grisly work. Then the man forced a broom handle he had brought with him up Tom's rectum. The pain he felt was horrendous and he passed out again.

It became clear to Robert Moore that his victim was not going to give him any information and had reached that point of seeming numbness to the agony he was suffering. For Tom, somehow the pain didn't matter anymore. The constant strain on his tortured body was too much for Tom Wilson's heart and his life mercifully drifted away.

Robert Moore was frustrated because he was not able to extract any information from Tom Wilson. In a sense, he admired the man for his bravery and had been surprised at his tenacity in resisting his interrogation. He spent the next two hours searching the house and was able to find the tapes. But there was nothing that gave any indication that the man had worked for the FBI.

When they found him, Tom Wilson's body was hardly recognizable. The police had been alerted when he hadn't turned up for work at the hotel on the following Monday morning after having the weekend off. A colleague, Richard Todd, had stopped by to see where he was. What he saw was a mangled, bloody mess tied spread-eagled and naked across the dining room table. It was ten in the morning and the flies were ravenously busy with their gruesome feeding frenzy. Richard ran out of the house and immediately vomited.

Dr. Bain, the Bahamian pathologist, urgently contacted Roger and asked him to visit him in the mortuary at the Bahamas General Hospital to help with an important post mortem he was doing. When Roger arrived and saw the corpse, he was horrified and felt extremely nauseous. He had never felt that way before when examining a cadaver because primarily it was someone he didn't know personally. This was different. He couldn't believe the trauma Tom had been through as evidenced by the mutilation of his body. The slow death he had suffered sickened him. He began to worry what information had been extracted from him. Did they, whoever they were, know about him and his work for British Intelligence?

Dr. Bain saw Roger's disgust: "I had the same reaction when I first saw the body. I've been at this game thirty or so years now, but this is the worst case of mutilation I have ever seen, and I've seen many."

They worked on Tom Wilson's remains in silence for some two hours, logging different samples for later examination. When they had finished, they silently changed out of their gowns and went to Dr. Bain's small office. He got out a bottle of scotch and two glasses from a desk drawer. When he had filled them, they both sat there and drank in silence.

On the way back to the RAF station Roger felt panicked and was full of anxiety for his own safety after what he had witnessed in the mortuary. What concerned him was also the fact that someone maybe on to him because his room had been searched. He walked up to the bar in the officers' mess and ordered a large scotch and sat in one of the soft chairs that was in the bar area. Dr. Christopher Woodson came in and, when he had ordered a beer, he sat down beside him.

"A penny for your thoughts, Roger?"

"I have just helped carry out the most appalling post mortem I have ever witnessed and one I'll probably never forget."

Roger then described how Tom Wilson had died and the fact the police were now looking for a very sadistic killer who probably took a great deal of pleasure in killing. Then he blurted out: "The fact that he was an FBI agent will mean we will have the Americans on our backs for answers." He immediately regretted what he had said.

"How did you know he was an FBI agent?"

"Oh, the police found some papers in his house and told us who he was."

"That's strange, because if he was working undercover, he should not have any incriminating documents on him."

"You'd think so wouldn't you? Anyway, it was the most revolting sight I have ever seen," Roger said, trying to close our conversation on this topic.

After a while Roger made his excuses and left. That night he sent an urgent message to Simon Cookson in New York.

Lechery Knows No Bounds

Chapter 16

At midnight that same evening there was a loud banging on Betsy Curry's front door. She was in bed and was woken by the noise. At first she lay there in fear. Perhaps it was the police after her for not paying rent on her three-room shack in Over-the-Hill, one of the native Bahamian neighbourhoods of Nassau. She looked at the old clock on the table beside her bed and saw that it was just past midnight.

Betsy was a seventy-year old emaciated, black woman with unkempt hair, few teeth and a forlorn look about her craggy face. She scraped a living selling straw hats at the Prince George Wharf to the growing number of tourists who had started to visit the colony. Before that she had worked in the sisal fields and before that drying sponges. Tragically, her husband had died of a heart attack twenty years previously and her only daughter had died in childbirth.

Nobody knew who her granddaughter's father was, but Betsy was left to bring up the child. Tameka was now a twenty-five year old women who worked as a maid for a family at Old Fort Bay. She was also a part-time prostitute.

The thumping on her door continued and Betsy decided she had to answer it. She didn't want to disturb the neighbours who would give her a hard time in the morning. She cautiously opened the door and standing there was an angry looking white man.

Brian Thomas had come from dinner with Boris Dahlin, neé Major Kurt Bergman, at the British Colonial Hotel and afterwards they had played snooker. The conversation was light at first but with the brandies in the bar afterwards they began to expound on the current state of affairs in Europe. Brian Thomas was bored and, when he could, he left. What he needed, he told himself, was a woman. His wife was no good. She didn't enjoy or encourage sex anymore so he drove his car to the Over-the-Hill section of town in search of Tameka, his favourite black tart.

"Where's Tameka?" he demanded as soon as Betsy opened the door.

"She's not here," she responded.

"Where is she then, you silly old bitch?'

"Not here!"

Brian Thomas barged past her and searched the shack.

"Well where is she?' he asked Betsy again as he grabbed her arm and twisted it.

"She's working at the Mathews house tonight and staying over there for the night," Betsy said as she cried out in pain.

"I bet she is," he said as he pushed past her, got into his car and left. He did not like any of the other easily available whores in Nassau. Many of them serviced the servicemen on the island and had contracted venereal diseases such as syphilis or gonorrhoea. Frustrated, he drove home. "The sooner I'm out of this place and into Germany the better," he thought as the car weaved along the road.

He reached his house and parked the car haphazardly in the drive. "Time for a little nightcap," he told himself as he tripped over the steps leading to the front door. He walked into the front hall, took off his jacket and shoes and flung them onto the floor. He went to his study, poured himself a large scotch whiskey and sat down heavily in his leather armchair.

As he sat in his chair he began thinking about his agreement to help Kurt Bergman with his plan to take the Duke of Windsor to Germany. It was certainly full of risk but this was minimised given the slow pace of life in the islands and that of the authorities in this forgotten backwater of the British Empire. Once in Germany he would be among fellow travellers and peace would come to Europe once the Duke had negotiated it with his brother, George VI. Communism was the real threat to Europe and everyone's attention could be drawn to fight the genuine menace.

He planned to remarry when he could in Germany to a nice young fräulein, or perhaps he would just make her his mistress. The latter seemed the best idea. God, wasn't he bored with Vivian, with her delicate and graceful ways. He'd only married her for her money, so he could start his engineering firm. They had no children and he realised he should have dumped her a long time ago. She was only a drag on his plans.

Finishing his drink, he decided it was time for bed. He began to climb unsteadily up the stairs. By now he was very drunk and could hardly walk. Then a thought came into his befuddled brain. "I wonder if that little tart needs company. I bet she would be a good fuck," he said to himself, giggling.

He crept along the landing to Helen's door, which was unlocked, and let himself in. There she was, lying on her back, naked and fast asleep. Quietly as possible,

Brian tiptoed up to her bed and took his trousers off. He then leapt on her.

Helen suddenly woke up feeling something heavy on top of her. Then she realised someone was try to rape her. She pushed him off with all strength she could muster and he fell onto the floor with a large thud. Forgetting about her nakedness she grabbed a chair and held it up threatening him with it as he got to his feet.

"Get out of here right now before I scream the house down!" she shouted.

"My, you little vixen, you are playing hard to get are you? I like a woman with a lot spunk. You look delicious and ready for the taking."

Brian stumbled towards her; he easily brushed aside the chair and started to fondle Helen's breasts. As he got closer, she brought a knee up hard into his groin. He buckled with pain and yelled like wounded bull.

Suddenly the bedroom door opened and there was Vivian Thomas standing there with a shocked look on her face. Helen grabbed her dressing gown and covered herself.

Helen was so angry she just blurted out, "He tried to rape me!" And then she began to cry.

Vivian just stared at her husband. Her face was contorted in disgust and hatred for him.

After a few seconds, Helen was able to compose herself and angrily said, "This drunken wretch tried to rape me when I was asleep. Look at him. He's a snivelling excuse for a man! Vivian I'll move out in the morning. I can't stay in the same house as that animal! Go on, you bastard, tell Vivian about your plans to go to Germany without her!"

"Helen, I am so sorry," said a shaken Vivian. "As far as I'm concerned this is the last straw. I've had enough of him and his affairs and his drunkenness. For a long time now I have been planning to leave him. This is the last straw. I'm moving out in the morning also, to my friend Mary's. What's this about Germany?"

"Ask Romeo."

"Well?" said Vivian looking outraged at her husband.

He looked meekly at both women and slurred, "A Swedish businessman dropped by and we had a few drinks. I didn't say anything about actually going to Germany. We were just discussing the war and I mentioned the bombing going on there and I said I'd like to see the devastation for myself. The little tart obviously misheard our private conversation," he snivelled.

And then, gaining some courage, he added menacingly, "I suggest you both mind what you tell other people or else there will be trouble."

"That's not true. You are lying," Helen said, ignoring his threat. "I heard what you were saying; something else quite clearly. Your threats are just empty and mean nothing to myself or, I'm sure, Vivian."

"I know who I believe. I've been married to you too long and I know you. Now get out of here," hissed a fuming Vivian.

Brian picked up his trousers and slinked off to his own room without another word.

The first inkling Roger got of what had transpired the night before was a note from Helen left for him at the hospital asking him to pick her up at the WAAFs accommodations for their date that evening. He thought this was strange; maybe she had visited one of her WAAF friends? When he entered the wooden hut which was the WAAF housing that evening he saw on the noticeboard her name and an assigned room number. He knocked on her door and was met with a frosty smile. They walked to get their bikes in silence.

214

It was Roger's turn to bring the picnic they had planned and he loaded up the hamper onto the back of his bicycle. When they set off, he was acutely aware of a change in her demeanour. He talked about his day and got very little response from Helen. Something was wrong. His first thought was that he had done something wrong and had caused her to be miffed at him. He decided to let the frigid atmosphere continue as they rode their bikes to Love Beach.

When they got to the beach, he didn't say anything, but took out a blanket, spread it on the sand and unpacked the picnic hamper. Helen just sat there looking out to sea and didn't move or say anything. Roger opened a bottle of wine and poured her some into a glass. When he handed it to her she smiled sweetly and took several sips of the wine. This seemed to relax her but then she began to cry, which astonished him because she had always seemed to have such a strong personality and nothing appeared to ruffle her.

Roger didn't know what to do. This was the woman he was in love with and he needed to comfort her. He tentatively placed my arm around her and she responded by putting her head against his shoulder. He squeezed her tightly.

After a while, she spoke in a whisper.

"I suppose you are wondering what an earth is the matter with me; why I have suddenly moved out of the Thomas's house."

"Yes, I was wondering why when I got your note. What's going on?" he responded.

Then the whole story cascaded out of her. He was stunned at what he had heard.

"Helen, I don't know what to say. I'm just appalled. No wonder you're in such a state, my poor darling. I'll go and have it out with him tomorrow."

"No, Roger please don't. Just leave it be. He can't harm me now that I have moved out."

He kissed her gently and she responded. He hugged her really close. They just lay there on the blanket for some time enjoying at close intimate time on that warm evening.

Helen suddenly jumped up, took her shirt and shorts off that covered her swimsuit and said, "Beat you down to the sea!" And she went charging off down the beach to the water.

They swam and splashed each other in the sea and then, after fifteen minutes, they went back to eat their picnic. Roger was intrigued by the overheard conversation Brian Thomas had had with a Swedish man and wondered to himself when he was planning to go Germany.

As they sat on the beach enjoying their meal, Roger turned to Helen and said, "There is something you need to know about me."

"What dark secrets do you have Dr. Lawson?" she asked coquettishly.

He then explained his dual role in the Bahamas and the concerns SIS had for the Duke's safety. He knew he shouldn't have told her, but he needed to get more information from her.

"Tell me all you heard of the conversation however unimportant you think it might be. It could be critical," he said.

"Well, you have to understand that I had been asleep and only heard the last part of the conversation. What I heard was Brian saying that for his taking part in the plan he wanted to go to Germany without his wife. Then he said he was playing golf with the Duke this week and would set up dinner arrangements. That's about all I heard."

At about nine they packed up their belongings and cycled back to Oakes Field. Roger said goodnight to Helen and arranged to see her the following week as she was starting a week of night duty the following day.

That night he wrote a long report about his findings to Simon Cookson in New York and in the morning he sent a long cable to him.

Two days later, Helen walked the short distance to the hospital across a quadrangle from her room deep in thought still about the incident with Brian Thomas. Outwardly she had recovered from her ordeal but inwardly she still was frightened about what he might do to her. She resented him and his implication that she was some easy loose women ready to open her legs for him at the drop of a hat. She realised he was very drunk, but she always thought that he lusted after her even when he was sober. When she looked back she remembered instances of his lecherous nature. It was a look or comment he had made that had made her feel uneasy. He hadn't physically touched her but he always stood close to her when they were in a group of people and she had seen him looking down at her breasts when she was dressed up in a tight cocktail dress. She shivered at the remembrance of that.

The person she felt sorry for was Vivian. She had helped her move out and had seen her several times at her friend's house.

She was deep in these thoughts as she walked through the main gate of the base and turned onto Prospect Ridge Road. She wasn't aware of anyone when suddenly someone grabbed her from behind and dragged her into a nearby alleyway. A damp cloth was held tightly over her mouth and nose. She smelled a sweet scent before she lost consciousness.

Revenge and Escape

Chapter 17

Helen woke up slowly. She had a raging headache and her throat felt dry. It took her eyes some time to get accustomed to the dark so that she could take in her surroundings. Both her wrists and ankles were tied and she was gagged. She was lying on a hard, wooden bed which just had sacking on it.

Although it was dark she could eventually make out the walls of the small wooden hut she was in. There were no windows and a door was at the far end. She listened. There was silence.

At first she tried to free herself from the restraint around her wrists with no luck, as the knots were too tightly tied. She got up from the bed and hopped to the door, hoping this could be easily opened. It was locked. She started banging on the door and screaming through her gag. No one came.

She looked around her prison and spotted a large nail protruding high up on one of the walls. She went back to the bed and pushed it over to the wall the nail was on. When she got up on the bed she could just reach the nail when she stood on her tiptoes. She began a sawing motion on the sharpest part of the nail, which was its head. She got easily tired standing as she was on her tiptoes and, because her wrists were above her head, she

218

had to stop many times as blood would drain from her arms causing her to lose strength. It took more than an hour to hack through the rope but finally it gave way.

She took off the gag and restraints and then started to examine the hut for possible escape routes. The door was bolted on the outside and wouldn't yield to any pressure put on it. Frustrated, she pulled the bed back to where it was originally and sat on it, contemplating her position. Who had done this? Why? Someone wanted her out of the way. Who? Maybe it was Brian Thomas's revenge. The thought of that sent a shiver down her spine. If that was the case she was in trouble.

A few hours later, dawn began to come up as the sun shone through the wooden slats of her prison. Peering through a hole where a wooden knot had been, she could make out a large barn with a tractor and other equipment in it.

About an hour after dawn, an old van pulled up by the barn and two large black Bahamians, a man and woman, got out. The woman was carrying a tray with food on it and unlocked the door to the small shed. She almost fell as Helen pushed past her in an attempt to escape. She ran up a path although she didn't know where it led. Anticipating her direction, the driver of the van drove it around the back of the barn and cut off Helen's escape by stopping in front of her.

The man got out of the van and grabbed the back of her blouse. He roughly frog-marched her back to the shed and thrust her inside.

"Now, Miss look what you have done," said the woman picking up the broken plate.

"You made me spill your breakfast."

"Who are you?"

"I's Jessie and that's Daniel."

"Why have you kidnapped me? Where are we?"

"Mr. Thomas will be here shortly to answer your questions," she said as she left.

Helen froze at that man's name.

Daniel closed and locked the door to the shed.

Helen grew angry. So that devil is responsible, she thought. I'll break his neck if I get the chance. What's he going to do to me, she wondered? Finish off raping me.

An hour later a car arrived and came to a stop by the barn. Brian Thomas climbed out of the driver's side and walked towards the barn. Through the slats in the shed walls, Helen saw him talking to Daniel. After a while they walked towards the car and Brian Thomas was about to get in when Helen shouted. "You bastard! I hope you get what's coming to you! They hang traitors!"

Brian Thomas stopped and walked with Daniel to the shed. The door was unlocked and Brian Thomas walked in.

"What do you mean?" he asked.

"The authorities know all about you and it won't be long before they catch up with you," Helen said hoping that what she was saying was true. "You are nothing but sleazy, immoral, lecherous excuse for a man. You are a disgusting, slovenly drunk who takes pleasure in hurting other people."

With that Brian Thomas walked over to her and punched her in the face which knocked her down onto the floor. She was semi-conscious and blood was flowing from her lips.

"You were always an arrogant little bitch and it is about time someone taught you a lesson."

In her groggy state she saw him take off his belt and then he started to whip her with it. The pain was unbearable, especially when he caught her with the buckle end on her head. She mercifully lost consciousness.

She awoke when water was poured over her head and in her dazed state she saw Brian Thomas standing over her and Jessie was behind him.

"I understand you tried to escape and I'm going to make sure you don't until I'm ready to let you go. Take all your clothes off," he demanded with a sneer.

A 'no' was all that Helen could muster between her bloodied lips.

"If you don't, I'll get Daniel to take them off for you."

Reluctantly, Helen began to strip. All the time Brian watched her with a bemused, lascivious grin on his face. She felt both ashamed and angry at the same time. She was in a great deal of pain because of the beating and it took her some time to take all her clothes off. When she stood there naked, Jessie picked up the clothes and she and Brian Thomas left.

Meanwhile, Roger was getting ready for his meeting at Oakes Field with Flight Lieutenant David Andrews of the RAF police. He hadn't expected to see Helen again for some days as she was on a night shift and he was very busy with SIS business.

There was a knock on the meeting room door and David Andrews walked in. Roger explained his role for SIS and the suspicions he had about a possible kidnap attempt on the Duke of Windsor. He showed David Andrews the file he had received from Simon Cookson on Bernt Falk. They discussed the approach they were going to take to the interviews. Roger told him that he was only there as an observer and not an interrogator and it was up to David Andrews to question the airmen.

"I think we should interview Victor Raymond first. From what I've seen of them both he is probably the weaker link. He's still shaken after his beating and we have more of a chance of getting information from him," suggested David Andrews.

"My superiors in New York want to know about the extent of Falk's activities here. He has probably been sending the Germans information about the RAF training activities and he has been probably getting his information partly from this group of diamond smugglers," Roger articulated his needs for information.

"I think we have them on charges of smuggling. Also, I'm interested in them for the murder of Pilot Sergeant Stapleton. They at least know or suspect who did it," Flight Lieutenant Andrews added.

They walked over to the guard house at the main gate where the RAF police had their headquarters and cells. The interview room there was sparse with just a table and three chairs. Because the room had no windows it was hot and clammy.

Sergeant Navigator Victor Raymond was brought in. His arm was in plaster and he eyed them with suspicion. He looked nervously at the Flight Lieutenant who was sitting opposite him across the table. Then he saw Roger in the corner.

"What's he doing here?" he demanded.

"The doc is here in case you need some first aid," said Andrews.

"What do you mean?" he said looking even more frightened than before and his eyes had become saucers.

Ignoring his question, Andrews continued: "We know of your little group's smuggling activities and you're probably going to spend a lot of time at the Fort Dahlen Barracks prison in Chatham in Blighty. I've booked you a place. I hear the MPs there are very nasty."

He paused and let that information sink in.

"Now tell me who beat you up and why," he said looking at him directly. "I'll know when you're lying so don't bother to try," he said with a sigh.

Mustering all the courage and brashness Raymond could, he faced his interrogator: "I was attacked when two black men tried to rob me, that's all."

"I don't believe you."

"It's the truth. Can I go back to my cell now?" he whined.

"No, I've only just begun," said Andrews getting up. He took off his uniform jacket and rolled up his shirt sleeves. Raymond visibly shrank in his chair and put his hands over his head as he rested his elbows on the table.

Flight Lieutenant Andrews brought one of his large fists down on the table with a loud bang, which startled and scared Raymond.

"Why did you and your mates kill Pilot Sergeant Stapleton? We have evidence that says you did and it's going to be easy to prove at your court-marshal. We want to tie a few loose ends so we don't know why you did what you did. Did you have an argument with him that turned violent?"

Silence.

"It seems you and your friends will have a date with the hangman when you get back to Blighty."

Panic showed in Victor Raymond's face for the first time.

"Come on. This is your last chance to avoid the noose. What did you argue about?' Andrews pressed.

"Nothing."

"Did he threaten to have you beaten up again? Or were you the ringleader of this merry band of smugglers and he was threatening you?" Andrews demanded.

There was no response.

"Aw well, it doesn't matter really because we've got you dead to rights. You were seen by a witness loading the body into a boat," Andrews said closing, his file and starting to get up.

"You're just bluffing."

"Try me," Andrews said looking down into his eyes with a sinister expression on his face. Raymond looked away.

"Now I see it. You're the boss of this operation and he was challenging you and you couldn't take it. Isn't that so?" Andrews asked.

"You must be joking. He was the leader of our group and he made all the decisions."

"So why did you kill him?"

"I didn't. I just didn't." Victor Raymond began to sob.

"I wish I hadn't got into this. He wanted a bomber ferry crew to work with him. I needed a bit of extra cash to send home because my missus was expecting our third child," he cried.

"All right, if you expect me to take the capital murder charge off the table, I need a complete explanation from you of what went down," he said in a lower, less harsh voice. He took a cigarette packet and lighter out of his pocket and offered one to Raymond. He took one and lit it.

Then, slowly, Raymond explained how they would buy diamonds in Accra, Ghana, when they stopped off to rest before returning to Nassau. Bernt Falk would sell them to his contacts in Florida and they would get a cut of the profits. He told them he was beaten up because the smugglers refused to throw in their lot with Mark Laramie, a restaurateur on Bay Street.

"How was the smuggling financed?" Andrews asked.

"Falk would pony up the money for our trip. I know the night that Fred went missing he was going to see Falk to finance our next caper. That's all I know."

Andrews brought the interview to an end and Victor Raymond was returned to his cell.

"It seems we have enough on Falk to bring him in. I'll have to brief Major Lancaster, the deputy police commissioner about what's going on," concluded Flight Lieutenant Andrews.

"Before we do I would like to investigate more what Falk is really up to."

"If he gets wind that we know about him, he might do a runner. I'll give you forty-eight hours before I move."

That same evening, at about eleven thirty, Mark Laramie was saying goodnight to two of his regular customers. His restaurant was a high-end steak and seafood restaurant and was a great success. It had a great reputation and was popular with the British ex-pats as well as visiting American tourists. All his fish was local and he imported his beef from America. He had hired a chef from Florida and given him free-rein as far as the menu was concerned.

Mark Laramie was in his late-forties and was very athletic looking man with a trim, muscular body. He was always smartly dressed and took care of his appearance. His English-born wife, Elizabeth, was similarly motivated about her appearance and the two had a reputation as being a sophisticated couple who were always seen at major social events in the colony. She had come out to the Bahamas as a girl when her father was in the Colonial Office. He retired and she stayed on in the Bahamas and married Mark Laramie.

"Goodnight Peter. I'll see you tomorrow," he said to his chef as the man left.

He went inside the restaurant where Elizabeth was sitting at a table counting the night's takings.

"I wish you would talk to Mathew about his lack of attention in serving of customers," she said to her husband in a peevish voice. "I saw him clear away the plates of people who had finished their meal whilst someone at the table was still eating. That's not polite and is bad manners."

"I'll talk to him in the morning, but it's very difficult to change these Bahamians and their ways."

"Well fire him then. God knows there's enough of them who want to work for us."

Elizabeth finished her work with the books and put them in a safe in the small office which was just off the main floor of the restaurant.

"I'm going up to bed. Are you coming?" she asked.

"In a minute. I just want to check the kitchen," he replied. Everything looked fine and he joined his wife in their flat above the restaurant.

About one thirty in the morning a car pulled up outside and two men got out. They were carrying bottles with petrol in them. They threw two bricks through the restaurant's bay window and then lit the cloth wicks stuffed in the neck of the bottles. Once these wicks were properly alight they hurled the bottles through the restaurant's window. There was an almighty loud explosion as the petrol caught fire and almost immediately engulfed the ground floor.

By the time the fire brigade arrived on the scene there was nothing left of the two-story structure except its brick outer layer. There was no sign of the Laramies and speculation was that they had been incinerated by the intense fire.

One person who was not surprised by the incident was Bernt Falk, although he had nothing to do with the arson attack. He had called some of his underworld contacts and had spread the rumour that the Laramies had taken over the diamond smuggling operations for themselves. He suspected the Trafficantes were taking revenge on Mark Laramie for this and, true to form, they obliged.

Escape with Dire Consequences

Chapter 18

Helen had spent a miserable second night on the hard bed in the shed and she had only cat-napped. The temperature was in the low seventy degrees Fahrenheit, dropping from a high in the mid-eighties during the day. The sacks they had given her for sheets helped keep her warm. She was kept awake throughout the night by the sounds of the night. Racoons were scavenging around the barn outside. Occasionally they would get into fights. She wasn't frightened so much of them as she was of the possibility of rats.

Just after dawn, Jessie arrived with a bowl of rice with crab and fish in it. Jessie stared at Helen as she ate. Noticing, Helen asked: "Why are you staring at me?"

"I ain't never seen no white woman naked before."

"Well, here I am in all my glory!"

Helen began to laugh and so did Jessie.

"You must have done something real bad to make Mr. Thomas treat you so,"

"You don't know the half of it." And after a moment she asked: "Jessie, why do you and Daniel work for Mr. Thomas and keep me a prisoner here?"

"He pays us well. We don't have much money. Most of the negroes around here like us try to make it with fishing or growing sisal. The sponges have all gone. We get by, but when we have an opportunity to make some extra cash we take it. Since the air force have come here some of the younger women make extra money off the men. I won't do that. It just leads to sickness and they have to go and see the doctors," she replied, glumly.

"Jessie where do you live?"

"Near here, in Adelaide."

"What's there?"

"Sisal fields mainly, which Daniel and me works on."

Suddenly a man's voice angrily booms: "Jessie, where are you, woman?"

"Coming."

When Jessie had gone, Helen began to work on a plan of escape. She thought to herself that now she had found out from Jessie that she was somewhere near Adelaide, she knew roughly where she was. Adelaide was a small town on the south west side of New Providence Island. At least she reckoned she was on the main island and not on one of the 'Out Islands.' Getting a boat to sail to Nassau would have been near impossible or at least very difficult.

Now she told herself she would have to work out which was east and north so she would know which direction Nassau was. She would have to follow the progression the sun took during the day as it comes up in the east, follows a southerly path and sets in the west. By doing this, she would know which way to head when she escaped.

Now the question was how she was going to get out of the hut. There was a hole in the roof but how would she get up there? She looked around the shed. There was

229

only the bed. Then it came to her. If she tipped the bed on one end and rested the other on the wall she could just reach the hole in the ceiling. She tried this and much to her delight it worked. She put the bed back in its place.

But what about clothes? She could hardly walk up the road to Nassau stark naked. She realised that the sacks on the bed were her best bet. One of them would be long enough to cover her so it would reach about mid-thigh. She would have to make holes in the bottom of the sack so she could pull it over head and then make holes for her arms. She looked around for something to use to cut the sack and make the holes. There was her trusty nail but that would take a long time to make the holes. Then she noticed a jagged piece of china from the plate she had broken on her first day of imprisonment.

She wrapped part of one of the sacks around the blunt end of the piece of china so it gave her a handle of sorts so she could exert pressure on the sharp part. She began to saw the sack to make the holes for her head and arms, but it was slow progress and she cut herself several times. Also, she had to stop when she heard someone in the tractor shed. Making the holes took her most of the day as she carefully picked at the fabric.

When she had finished, she hid all her work and waited for Jessie, who would be bringing her dinner. Eventually she turned up and brought in some food.

"When are you planning to release me?" she asked Jessie as she was eating.

"Mr. Thomas says in two days' time we should let you go."

"What about my clothes?"

"Mr. Thomas got them."

"So how am I going to get back to Nassau? Like this?"

"Mr. Thomas said that was your problem."

"What!" screamed Helen.

"Don't worry, Miss, I'll bring one of my dresses."

"Thank you Jessie, you're a good person."

Inside, Helen was seething with anger. Brian Thomas was determined to demean her as much as possible, but she was equally determined to get her revenge on him, come what may.

When the sun went down in the west at dusk she knew then what her directional bearings were. She waited an hour when things had quietened down and Daniel and Jesse had left for the day. She then put on her sack, leaned the bed against a wall and climbed up it to the ceiling. She could just reach through the hole and pulled herself through.

She sat on the roof of the hut to catch her breath and then looked for a way to get down. There was a nothing. She would have to jump. She slid down the roof and hung onto the eve of the roof and then let herself fall to the ground. She rolled as she hit the ground but twisted her ankle. This gave her pain but it hadn't been broken.

She started walking up a dirt track in her bare feet heading north. She hoped that the track would lead to a paved road. Then she saw a car's lights in the distance and she guessed it must be on a road because it was going fast. After walking about a half mile, she came to a main road she was pretty certain was South West Bay Road. She was concerned about being spotted if her escape was discovered so she decided to walk in the fields parallel to the road and to take cover each time she saw the lights of a car.

She walked for an hour and then sat down to rest. Her bare feet were sore and she had cuts from stones on the uneven surfaces of the fields she was walking in. Her twisted ankle hurt but she was determined to get to the safety of Nassau. She heard a rumble as a Liberator bomber flew overheard and she watched it as it switched on its landing lights and descended to land at Oakes Field. Now she knew she was heading in the right direction. She found Carmichael Road and was just beginning to see the airfield when a car pulled alongside her. She froze.

In the car were two men in RAF uniforms and Helen relaxed at seeing them. The man in the passenger seat rolled down his window.

"Can we give you a lift anywhere, darling?" said a very drunk aircraftsman.

"Yes, to the nearest police station," she replied.

"Fine. Hop in."

Helen opened the back door at sat on the leather back seat of the RAF staff car. She began to relax for the first time in a long time. The man who was the passenger looked her up and down, which made her feel a bit uneasy because his stare seemed to undress her with his eyes. It was clear that both men were very drunk but she was glad of the lift because she was so tired.

"Would you like a swig?" the man slurred as he offered her the bottle.

"Why not?" she said, and took a swig out of the black rum bottled. "I'm glad to see you. I had been kidnapped by someone and held prisoner. I escaped and I'm thankful for the ride."

"Where are you from?"

"I'm a nurse at the RAF hospital at Oakes Field," Helen replied feeling a little woozy from the rum.

"How come you're wearing a sack?"

"It was the only thing I could find because they took my clothes away."

"You mean you have nothing on under that sack?"

"Yes," she said uncomfortably. She began to wonder if it had been a good idea to accept a ride as the two men were obviously the worse for wear. As the car began to bump along the road, she began to doze off. The lack of sleep in the last two days, the let-down after her ordeal and the alcohol made her very sleepy.

The passenger turned to the driver and said: "Bill, I need a pee."

Bill pulled the car off the road and went down a track that led to a sisal field. The passenger got out and went over to some pushes and started to relieve himself. When he had finished, he walked back to the car and, instead of opening the front passenger door, got into the back with a sleepy Helen.

"Now, let's have a look at you," he said pulling the sack up all the way and covering Helen's face and pinning down her arms.

"Very nice," he said as he fondled her breasts.

Helen began to scream and fight, but the man was just too strong for her and she was restricted by the sack over her head and arms. He hit her hard twice in the face and she passed out unconscious from the blows. He pulled down his trousers and raped her. In the meantime Bill had lined up at the back door of the car waiting for his turn.

Helen woke up slowly in the sisal field bloodied and distraught. She saw the two men climb into the car and saw a number on its wing, which was not the license plate but an RAF vehicle identification number.

She could hardly move and her groin ached badly. With a great deal of difficulty, she pulled herself up into sitting position and sat there for a few minutes getting her breath back from her efforts. Then she tugged the sack down to cover her ravaged body and sat there trying to get her mind into some sort of order, but all she could do was sob uncontrollably. A rumble of a plane landing at Oakes Field woke her from her desolation and her inner strengths began to help her regain some of her toughness too.

Finally with a great deal of effort, she managed to stand. When she did so, she lost her balance at first as the world seemed to swirl around her and it was all she could do to stay on her feet. When her dizziness stopped, she began to stumble forward as she staggered to the road and painfully began her walk towards Nassau.

Another car approached as she was caught in its headlights. She hadn't the energy now to take cover. The driver stopped and got out of the car and walked towards her.

"Now, Miss what happened to you?"

The man caught her as she fell into his arms. She looked up at the black face of a Bahamian policeman and then fainted.

Caught in the Act

Chapter 19

Walking back to the RAF hospital after the interrogation of the diamond smugglers, Roger started to wonder how he was going to tackle getting more information on Bernt Falk. After thinking about various alternatives like following him around or searching his home when he wasn't there, he decided that his best course of action would be to stake out Falk's home and see who came and went.

Roger was also concerned that maybe he was being followed by Tom Wilson's killer and he wondered whether the actions of Bernt Falk and the killer were related in any way. Earlier in the day he had retrieved his Colt 32 and two full magazines of eight rounds each from his briefcase in the safe at Group Captain Waite's office. He needed some protection and he wanted the gun around just in case. He had spent some time at the firing range in New York with one of Simon Cookson's men and he found out that he was a 'natural' marksman, as his instructor called him.

Roger changed out of his uniform into his khaki light-weight trousers and a cotton short-sleeved shirt which was not tucked into his waistband. He put the gun in his waistband, made sure it was concealed by his shirt, and the spare magazine went in one of his trouser pockets. He put a pair of binoculars in the basket on the front of his bicycle and a jacket over the top of it so that it would be hidden from prying eyes.

As he was wheeling his bike along the path towards the air base's main gate, he met Christopher Woodson walking back to their accommodations.

"Just off duty, Christopher? Anything interesting happen?" he asked cheerfully.

"Yes to your first question and no to your second, unless you count boils or VD interesting," he replied grumpily. "I'm looking forward to a nice cold bath. Where are you going?"

"Oh, I'm just off for a bicycle ride. My physical therapist insisted I exercise my legs every day. I thought I would take in the sights along West Bay Street to Love Beach where I'm told that there some interesting old houses along that way," Roger said.

"Yes, there are. Oh by the way, your girlfriend didn't turn up for work last night and Matron is hopping mad. Do you know where she is?"

"No. I'll go and check. There's probably a simple explanation," he said, trying not to show his uneasiness, but he was worried at this news.

Roger put his bike back in the bike shed and walked over to the RAF hospital to check whether Helen had eventually turned up, but the staff there hadn't seen her. What was troubling was that one of the ward sisters said that it was very unlike her because she was usually so conscientious and dependable. Now Roger was spooked. He went over to the WAAF's accommodations and was told the same story. The last time they saw her was two evenings before and, when he checked her room, he saw that she hadn't slept in her bed.

Roger began thinking about his conversation with Helen two days before about Brian Thomas and how he tried to rape her. He wondered whether he knew where she was. According to his file, that fat worm had a cruel reputation with women and he was in no mood to take any excuses from him.

Roger cycled as fast as he could to Brian Thomas's house and hammered on his front door. His butler answered the door.

"Is Helen Masters here?" Roger asked.

"No, sir. Miss Helen moved out a few days back. I haven't seen her since."

Just then Brian Thomas appeared, with a whisky glass in his hand, and wanted to know what the ruckus was about.

"What have you done with Helen?" Roger demanded.

"Nothing. Why? Has she walked out on you?" he responded, laughing.

"I know what you did to her, you disgusting wretch! She told me all about it!"

Brian Thomas went red in the face and stammered: "She has a vivid imagination that one."

Then he regained his composure and sneered: "She's clearly not getting any sexual satisfaction from you and has to invent stories to make up for her sad life. Going out with a cripple does have its downside for her when you can't get it up! Maybe she's gone to Miami to see one of her virile boyfriends. She's been there before."

Roger was seething with a white-hot anger at this slander as he charged forward and lunged at him with his walking stick. But he lost his balance and tripped and fell, much to Brian Thomas's delight. He laughed hysterically and then suddenly stopped and turned ashen. In his fall, Roger's shirt had ridden up to reveal the butt of his gun in his waistband.

Brian Thomas slammed closed the front door and screamed from behind it: "Go away or I'll call the police."

Roger realised what he had seen and this gave him some satisfaction. "I'll be back for you," he shouted.

Roger cycled to the police headquarters in Rawson Square and asked the desk sergeant whether he could see Lieutenant John Douglas. He had met him on several occasions and he was a man in his late thirties and thin in build. He came out of his inner office and greeted him with a broad smile.

In his no-nonsense, forthright manner he asked: "Dr. Lawson, how can I help you?" Roger explained about Helen's sudden disappearance and that he was worried about her, particularly after her run-in with Brian Thomas. He didn't say that he tried to rape her but told him about his sexual harassment of her.

Lieutenant Douglas listened carefully to his concerns and asked some questions, especially about her reason for leaving the Thomas house. He asked whether they had had an argument and suggested, if that was the case, she probably didn't want to be found. He was taken aback by this and assured Lieutenant Douglas that they didn't have a row and, even if this were true, she wouldn't have left her colleagues at the hospital in the lurch.

"I'll make some enquiries about her disappearance. We can verify if she went to Miami as Mr. Thomas has suggested by checking the passenger lists both at Pan Am Airways and with ships that ferry people there. If the answer is negative, we can assume she's still on the island. In the meantime, I will ask our police patrols to keep an eye out for her," he said reassuringly.

Roger left the police station and sat on a bench that looked out at the House of Assembly nearby to try and

238

get his thoughts together. He was feeling quite impotent as there was nothing he could do now to find Helen. He could hardly search for her himself because of his physical limitations and he wouldn't know where to start looking. He rationalised that the police would know where to look and there was more of them on the ground. They knew who to question.

Despite his concerns for Helen, Roger knew he had important work to do to find out what plot was being hatched regarding the Duke of Windsor. His loyalty was torn but he decided he had to press on with his task and stake out Falk's house. He decided that it was time to send a critical cable to Simon in New York. He cycled back to Oakes Field and went to Group Captain Waite's office where he encoded a message to Simon that said: "Believe Mandrake in danger. Kidnap attempt likely soon."

When this had been sent by the duty flight sergeant over the RAF telegraph, Roger started to cycle to Love Beach. It was dark when he reached Bernt Falk's house which was set off the road overlooking Old Fort Point and Love Beach. He hid his bicycle in some bushes near the road and cautiously approached the house.

When he was about two hundred yards from the residence, he started to look around for a hiding place. He spotted an outcrop of rocks, which, when he climbed into it, gave him a good view of the house. He scanned the house with his binoculars, nothing. Then he spotted him. There was a guard posted in the shadow of the house's porch. He looked bored and was smoking a cigarette.

Then the front door opened and he could see from the light cast by the open door three armed men with torches who started to search the area around the perimeter of the house. When this was completed, they spread out and began searching bushes and the nearby tree line. They were obviously checking on their security or maybe they had been tipped off to Roger's presence. But how? He had been very careful in his approach. Maybe, he thought, he was becoming paranoid. He got the feeling that they were looking for somebody though. Roger wondered whether someone knew of his plan to be out there. But who knew?

Then the search party started to comb the beach. Roger got his pistol out and was ready to use it as they approached his position. He got as low as he could and tried to meld into the rocks. Then he heard a voice in German say: "I don't think he would be this far away from the house. Our contact must have got some wrong information but it was worth checking. Let's go."

Roger's German was very rusty as he had last spoken it at school and on a vacation in Austria which seemed like ages ago, but he got the gist of what the man was saying. Someone had betrayed him!

The men walked back to the house and left a guard on the porch as before. He was relieved by someone else an hour later. They talked for a few minutes and then the first guard disappeared into the house.

Apart from seeing the search party and the changing guards, Roger was there about three hours before he saw someone come out of the house and walk towards the beach. The man flashed a torch out to sea and must have been doing this for some fifteen minutes when there was an answering flash. Finally, a small boat with an outboard motor came towards the beach and six men armed with rifles and packs climbed out onto the sand and made their way to the house. The boat turned and made its way out to sea again.

As soon as they had disappeared, Roger scrambled off the rocks and went as fast as he could to find his bicycle. He retrieved it and started peddling hard as he could for Nassau. He must have made a noise when he left his hiding place. This had alerted the guard on the porch of the house.

As he peddled furiously, a car approached him from behind and knocked him off his bicycle. Roger jumped up and started to hobble as fast as he could towards some bushes when he felt a sudden, stinging pain in his shoulder. He fell hard on the ground and his head must have hit a rock and he lost consciousness. Another bullet was fired at him which grazed his head. The man who had chased him put away his Luger pistol in his shoulder holster after taking off its silencer. He dragged Roger's body and bike into some bushes and made sure he was well hidden and then drove back to the house.

As dawn came up a few hours later, Stephanie and Pierre Damianos were heading to market with their chickens along West Bay Street. They were sitting on a two wheeled cart pulled by their donkey Dreyfus. As they approached a turn in the road Pierre suddenly stopped the cart.

"Look someone left a bike over there by them rocks. Maybe we can sell it," he said excitedly.

Stephanie rolled her eyes and wondered why Pierre was so interested in the bike because they didn't fetch that much at the market. If they didn't hurry up they won't get a good place to sell their chickens.

"Come on, Pierre we've got to hurry otherwise we'll lose our place. It's only an old bike and not worth bothering about."

"Nonsense, woman. It won't take me that long to pick it up."

And with that, he got down from the cart and walked towards the abandoned bike. He suddenly stopped and shouted for Stephanie to help because he had found a body. They looked at Roger and Stephanie put her ear down on his chest and listened for a heartbeat.

"There it is. I hear it!" she exclaimed excitedly.

They carefully lifted him into the cart and cajoled Dreyfus to at least trot. As they moved slowly along the road, Stephanie rummaged through Roger's pockets and found his wallet. She looked inside for some identification and found his RAF identification card. It was then she spotted his gun which was still in his waistband.

"We need to get this boy back to the air force. He's got a gun. They will know what to do."

After half an hour, they reached the Guardhouse at the entrance to Oakes Field and the sentries there lifted Roger onto the veranda of the building. They called for an ambulance from the RAF hospital.

Roger began slowly to regain consciousness in the RAF Hospital. He did not know where he was at first, but he began to make out the face of a nurse and the other beds in the ward, although everything was out of focus. Gradually he began to see properly but he had a pounding headache and his head was wrapped in a bandage. His shoulder was likewise bandaged and his arm was in a sling. Then he saw he was surrounded by the familiar faces of his colleagues all wanting to know how he was feeling.

Dr. Meyer Rassin stepped forward and told everyone to go back to their work. When everyone had gone, he began to examine Roger. He took the bandage off his head and looked at the wound, cleaned it and put on a clean dressing.

"You are very lucky, Roger. You were grazed by a bullet on the left side of your head and we removed another from your shoulder. You had a gun in your waistband and a magazine in one of your pockets. What have you been up to, young man?"

"I'm afraid I can't say, sir, only it was government business. Group Captain Waite is aware of my dual role here. I was here undercover and now that's been blown."

"I see," said Dr. Rassin, clearly taken aback by this revelation. "It's a pity no one told me," he sniffed and walked out of the ward.

Sister Marlin, the ward sister, came in to check his vitals and write them down on a chart at the end of his bed. She was an austere woman in her late forties, with no sense of humour. Roger knew this to his cost as he had worked with her in the past and had tried to cut the formal atmosphere by cracking, what he thought, was his best jokes.

"Where's Helen? Have they found her yet? I've got to get up and look for her," he said, as he began to get out of bed.

"You're going nowhere, Dr. Lawson. The police found her this morning and she is fine. We'll let her know you're here. Now get some rest." No one argued with Sister Marlin.

Just then the doors to the ward opened and in walked Simon Cookson. He was accompanied by three large, ominous-looking men and Flight Lieutenant David Andrews.

"I thought it was about time we gave you some backup," he said.

"Better late than never, I suppose," Roger jokingly retorted. He was very glad to see them.

"When I got your message we came at once. We have intercepted some interesting wireless traffic in the last couple of days which indicates something is going on. It seems their plans are being put into action tonight so there's not a moment to lose. Now tell me about what you know and how you got into this mess."

Roger briefed Simon on what he knew and what Helen had overheard of Brian Thomas's plans.

"Right. We need to talk to this Falk character. But before that, we need to get together everybody involved in the law enforcement side and the army. We can't have anybody going off half cocked. The pigeons will just scatter."

Simon turned to Flight Lieutenant Andrews: "David can you arrange this, for, say, two this afternoon?"

At this point in time, all Roger knew was that Helen was safe following a coordinated hunt for her by the police. What he didn't know was that she had been savagely raped. After much insistence from him, a ward orderly helped him into a wheelchair and wheeled him in a separate room and to Helen's bedside. When he saw her he was aghast at the sight of the woman he loved looking grey and frightened. She didn't say a word but cried. The ward sister came up to her with a syringe filled with morphine and injected it into her in her arm. Almost immediately, Helen fell asleep.

Sister turned to him: "Dr. Lawson, can I have a word with you."

Roger followed her into her office in his wheelchair and she closed the door. She told him that Helen had been raped by two RAF men when she escaped from her prison and was trying to find her way home. Instead of helping her, they attacked her.

"We have been able to clean her up and extract evidence from inside her and these samples have been sent to the lab for testing to at least find the blood type of her attackers. At the present time we are loathe to call in police as she is mentally traumatised by the horrible experience and is not ready to be interviewed."

"Oh my God. Who could have done this to her?" said a distraught Roger. "Has she said anything about her attackers?"

"She has been mumbling incoherently about a car and a number."

"Do you remember what the number was?"

"She kept on mumbling about William the Conqueror. It didn't make any sense"

Roger was dumbfounded and thought about what this meant. Then he got the answer: "Ah! 1066. She must have remembered the part of the identification number on a car's front wing. Can I use your phone?" Roger asked.

Roger called Flight Lieutenant Andrews office and reached Flight Sergeant Jenkins. He filled him in on the fact that Helen had been raped by RAF men and he had a RAF car identification of the car.

"If we can find the car we can check its log book and find out who used it that night. Every driver has to account for the mileage so it will be straight forward enough. Leave it with me."

Roger went back to Helen's bedside and sat there watching her and praying she would recover.

"Vixen" is Unleashed

Chapter 20

Bernt Falk was sitting at one of the tables at Dirty Dick's having his lunch of a conch salad, which is a traditional fish dish in the Bahamas, and a beer. Being in the bar at this time of day was unusual for him because he never went there before at least six in the evening. However, he needed to get out of his house, which had been taken over by Kurt Bergman, four of his men from Argentina and the German snatch squad who had come from the sea the previous evening.

He had found their company intolerable. They were rude and treated him with utter contempt. There had been a problem when the men had come ashore from the submarine. Apparently, they had discovered that they were being spied on, which had caused them to panic, and search the area around the house. One of Kurt Bergman's men had come back and reported that he had taken care of the problem and had hidden the intruder's body where it wouldn't be discovered.

Bergman had then turned on Falk, demanding to know whether any of his RAF contacts had been spying on them. What frightened Falk the most was his cold, evil stare that seemed to penetrate his psyche and sow terror into his consciousness. Falk had assured him that he had taken care of the problem and he had broken off contact with his RAF smugglers. He could tell Bergman was still suspicious of him.

Falk was so engrossed in his thoughts that he hadn't noticed two men in light-weight suits come into the bar. He was surprised when they sat down next to him, one on either side.

"We're going to take a quiet walk to the back door and you're not going to say anything or I'll blow your balls off," said one of them as he stuck a pistol in the fat man's crotch. The other man took Falk's walking stick with its hidden blade out of his reach.

"You can't do this to me. I don't know who you are but I'm not going with you," said Falk in a loud voice, hoping someone in the bar would intervene on his behalf. The other patrons ignored his protestations. He stopped objecting when the man pushed the barrel of his gun harder into his testicles, which made him wince.

Reluctantly, Falk got up. All three men walked to the back of the bar and into a yard where there was a car waiting. Falk was handcuffed and bundled into the back of it and sat between the two men. A third man drove them away.

"Where are you taking me? You can't do this, I'm a Swedish citizen. I know my rights," he screamed.

"Ah shut up!" said one of the men as he elbowed him hard in the stomach. This took Falk's breath away.

When he had regained his composure he began wondering who these men were. Did they work for Major Bergman and had he decided that he should be eliminated? Oh God what am I going to do to get out of this mess, he thought to himself. He was now sweating profusely and was very distraught. Then he realised that the man that had spoken had a British accent. I must be a prisoner of the British, he concluded.

He hadn't got long to wait to confirm this as the car pulled into Oakes Field. The sentry at the gate waved them through without checking their identification because he had been expecting them. The car drove to the far south end of the aerodrome and stopped outside an empty hanger. One of the men pulled Falk out of the car and dragged him into the hanger. The large doors of the hangar were shut with the loud bang that echoed around the empty building.

Then Falk heard loud footsteps coming towards him.

"Take him to the store room," said a voice.

The men dragged him into a room, which was empty except for a table and two chairs. He was made to sit on one of the chairs and was handcuffed to the back of it.

The men, who had seized him, left and closed the storeroom door. One of them remained outside on guard.

Falk was left sitting at the table for thirty minutes. The silence was disquieting in the cavernous building and this added to Falk's anxiety. Then he heard loud footsteps again echoing around the empty structure. Simon Cookson walked into the storeroom with a folder. He looked threateningly at Falk for a long time without saying anything.

"Why are German soldiers staying in your house?" Simon asked.

Falk was taken aback by the question.

"I don't know what you are talking about. I am a Swedish citizen and I want to talk to my country's consular representative," he replied, finding some courage.

"Bollocks! You are German spy who has been sending them information for at least two years. You have no rights. You are sitting in this empty hanger on the far side of this aerodrome and you can scream as much as you like and you won't be heard. And by the

248

time we finish with you you'll be screaming alright. So again the question is what are the Germans doing in your house?"

"There are no Germans there. I hate the Germans after what they did to my brother in Norway. He was too slow getting out of the country and they shot him as a spy. I don't know who has been telling you any lies about me, but I swear there is no one there."

"Don't lie, you piece of crap. One of our agents saw them come ashore from a submarine and went into your house. Who is Kurt Bergman?"

"I've never heard of him."

"How about Boris Dahlin?" Simon slid over a photograph of the Gestapo officer taken in Havana, Cuba.

"The name is not familiar and I don't recognise him."

"That's funny, you have been seen with the man," said Simon as he pushed another photograph of Falk talking to Major Bergman at a casino in Havana.

Falk blanched but didn't respond.

"Let me explain your situation. The police here in the Bahamas are about to arrest you for the murder of an RAF sergeant who was involved in your diamond smuggling venture and we want you for espionage. Now you know the punishment for both is hanging. I'm told the hangman in the Bahamas is really careless because he doesn't get much practise. Instead of breaking your neck you will die from slow strangulation just as they did in the old days."

He let that sink in before he said: "If you cooperate with me I will see what I can do for you. We've picked up Bergman and maybe he will tell us how involved you are with the Germans. I'll give you some time to think about what I've suggested before we take other measures to get information from you."

Simon Cookson left the storeroom and one of his men took out of his pocket a thumb screw and put it onto the table in front Falk, who just stared at the instrument that could easily break fingers.

Simon didn't return for another half an hour, giving Falk enough time to think through his position. When he entered the room, there was a visible change in the man's demeanour. All colour had drained from his face, he was sweating profusely and his whole body was slumped forward. He was sobbing quietly.

"Right, let us begin," said Simon and one of his men stepped forward and picked up the thumb screw. Falk looked up with eyes that were reddened and were large with fear.

"Please don't hurt me," he whined. "Is your offer still on the table?"

"Yes."

Falk then told them of the plot to kidnap the Duke of Windsor that night.

***

The meeting that Flight Lieutenant David Andrews of the RAF Police had organised convened at two that afternoon in Group Captain Waite's office at Oakes Field. The participants, apart from Flight Lieutenant Andrews, were Lt. Col. Reginald Erskine-Lindop, Commissioner of Bahamian Police, Lt. Col. A.S. Haig of the Cameron Highlanders, who had been tasked with protecting the Duke of Windsor, and Roger in a wheelchair. He had reluctantly left Helen's bedside to be at the meeting in case there were questions.

Lt. Col. Erskine-Lindop was the last of the attendees to arrive and began to grumble about being dragged away from an important meeting.

"I hope this won't be waste of time. I was told the subject of the meeting was a national security. Who called this meeting anyway?"

As if to answer his question, Simon Cookson and Group Captain Waite entered the room.

"Gentlemen, I am Simon Cookson deputy director of SIS operations here in the Americas and the Caribbean. We have had clear indications that there will an attempt to kidnap the Duke of Windsor by a snatch-squad of Germans that infiltrated the island from a U-boat last night," he began.

"Why wasn't I told about this!" demanded a pompous Erskine-Lindop.

"You are being told about it now, colonel. We only found out about the exact details this morning."

"I need to brief the governor," said Erskine-Lindop, as he got up to leave.

"That won't be necessary," Simon said firmly.

"Who are you to tell me what to do? You have no authority."

"I am sure my boss in New York, William Stephenson, would happy to put you right on that matter because he has already briefed the prime minister on our operation."

Canadian William Stephenson was SIS's director responsible for the western hemisphere during World War II and a close confidante of Winston Churchill. The mention of William Stephenson, whose code name was 'Intrepid,' silenced Erskine-Lindop and he sat back down again. Several in the room smiled to themselves. Erskine-Lindop was regarded as a stickler for protocol and difficult to deal with by all around the table and they were glad to see that he was put firmly in his place.

"Here's our plan to thwart this kidnap attempt," continued Simon as if he not been interrupted. "I would like your comments and suggestions. We haven't much time to organise ourselves because the kidnapping of the Duke is planned for tonight."

**

Meanwhile, Brian Thomas was nervously busy with the arrangements for the dinner for the Duke. He had hired three staff who were to work with his butler Nathaniel. In fact it was Nathaniel who had recommended them. He planned that they should have cocktails before dinner in the large living room. When his guests were having dinner a bridge table would be set up in the room.

Brian Thomas had already packed his small bag with some clothes and a few of his personal items ready for his escape that night. Although he was nervous, he was confident that they could carry out their plan. They had a good final meeting that morning in Major Bergman's room at the hotel. One thing he liked about the Germans was their thoroughness in organising an operation.

Major Bergman planned to show the letter from Hitler to the Duke during the after-dinner drink session and discuss with him about going to Germany with them. If he resisted, they were to call in the German commandos who would then escort him to a waiting car and they would leave for Love Beach. The whole operation would take about thirty minutes and they would be clean away in the U-Boat before anyone realised the Duke was missing. As insurance, there was a plan to create a diversion at Oakes Field so that the police and military would be preoccupied by this.

The telephone rang and it was the manager of the caterers who Brian Thomas had arranged to cook the food in his kitchen and were about to leave for his house. They had a few questions concerning some of the equipment they should bring and he was on the telephone with them when suddenly the line went dead. He tried to use it again but it would still not work.

"Nathaniel!" he screamed. "Nathaniel!"

"Yes, sir," said a calm voice behind him.

"The phone doesn't work. Send the boy down to the exchange to get someone to fix it right away," he ordered. He was too busy with the arrangements for the dinner not to wonder why the telephone had suddenly gone dead.

An hour later a telephone repairman rang the bell on the front door. Brian Thomas opened the door.

"I understand you have a problem with your telephone, sir," said the thick set repairman.

"Yes I certainly have. I've got an important guest coming to dinner tonight and I need that phone to work."

"Alright sir. I'll have to check all extensions."

"Just get on with it man!" said an irate Brian Thomas as he marched off to his study.

An hour later there was knock on his study door and the repairman reported that everything was working fine now. He left the house, got onto his bike and began to cycle back to Nassau. As he did so he passed a van parked on a side road opposite the Thomas's house and gave a thumbs up to the driver.

Brian Thomas sat in his study with a scotch in his hand and feeling pretty satisfied with himself. Then the telephone rang. It was Major Bergman.

"Falk has disappeared. Have you seen him?"

"No."

"I checked his usual hang outs. He was in Dirty Dick's late this morning for his lunch but hasn't been seen since. I hope he hasn't been arrested. It would throw a wrench in our plans. He was always the weak link in our operation and I should have taken care of him before now."

"I know he owns a chicken farm on Andros one of the 'Out Islands.' He's probably gone there to hide until our operation is all over."

"You're probably right. He is a coward and has probably run away until it's all over. I still don't like it. I'll check with a contact I have and see whether he has seen him."

"I wouldn't bother. It will be over in the next few hours anyway and he'll be left holding the bag," said a confident Brian Thomas.

The Unravelling

Chapter 21

The Duke of Windsor arrived punctually that evening at seven thirty and was greeted by Brian Thomas who had been waiting for him at the front door of his house. The Duke dismissed his bodyguard and told him to come back for him at ten.

They walked into the front hall and Brian Thomas introduced the Duke to Boris Dahlin (neé Major Kurt Bergman) and Robert Moore.

"Ah, Mr. Dahlin how nice to meet you," the Duke said as they shook hands. "I understand you are Swedish. Where is your home town?"

"Gothenburg, your Royal Highness."

"Ah, I remember the city well. I used to sail there on Lake Vänern."

"Yes sir, it is a very picturesque city on the edge of the lake."

"I am looking forward to hearing from you about the war in Europe. I understand the Germans have serious problems with the Russians. But, first I want your advice on sails because I understand that you are a leading authority on the subject. The Duchess and I are planning to purchase a yacht and I need your thoughts on what rigging we should consider."

The Duke accepted a cocktail from the butler, Nathaniel, and sat down opposite Major Bergman. They talked at some length about sailing and the terrific opportunities there were here in the Bahamas.

Then Bergman asked him about life in the Bahamas and the Duke was very disdainful about the colony. According to him, the so-called leading citizens were small-minded little Englanders and shopkeepers. As such a decent social life was non-existent and that was why he and Duchess went to America whenever they could.

"You know, I have to laugh at my friend Harry Oakes, who is the only person in this colony worth knowing, apart from you Brian," said the Duke to Brian Thomas who acknowledged the compliment by a slight nod of the head. "He had a man called Count Alfred de Marigny pursuing his daughter, Nancy, who was just eighteen and he thirty-two. They married secretly in New York this year. The way Harry goes on about him, he sounds like a real cad and that he is someone after her money. It seems that de Marigny is not much liked by the leading lights of this God-forsaken place and especially by Harry. I've met him a couple of times and I must say I found him to be very arrogant and someone who doesn't know his place. The one good thing about this man is that he is an excellent sailor and he recently won the King's Cup at the Royal Nassau Yacht Club much to the chagrin of the members there.

"Anyway let's change the subject and talk about the war in Europe. We are so far away from the action here, it will be good to hear from someone who has been there recently. Do you think that Hitler has a made a strategic blunder with Operation Barbarossa by invading Russia? It's reminiscent of what Napoleon did in 1812. Also, if I remember my history correctly, German Emperor Frederick Barbarossa was swept away in the strong currents of the Saleph River in Turkey when he was on a Crusade. He was too impatient to cross over on a bridge because it was blocked by his troops, he decided to ford the river and was drowned. Do you think Hitler would be swept away because he has made such a monumental mistake?"

"As I see it, your Royal Highness, it seems, as you British say, that he has bitten off more than he can chew," responded Major Bergman, who was surprised by the Duke's accurate assessment. "Certainly his army is stretched very thin at the moment but if he can come to terms with Britain and now the Americans as well, he could switch his divisions to the east and take on the real enemy of us all: communism."

"That's not very likely," said the Duke. "Winston has the bit between his teeth, so to speak, and won't let up. Britain took a real pounding at Dunkirk and during the blitz so bringing them to the peace table would be an almost impossible task, particularly with Americans now in the war. Hitler was foolish to declare war on America. I wish things were different, Britain I think would have sued for peace before Pearl Harbour but now it's too late."

"Declaring war on America was a mistake but he had treaty obligations with Japan."

"Ah treaties and the havoc they cause! If it wasn't for them in Europe in 1914 we would never have had World War One," replied the Duke.
Just then, Nathaniel the butler announced dinner and the small group got up and went into the dining room.

The conversation at dinner was focussed more on the development work the Duke had been promoting in the Bahamas. The discussion was light and there were jokes about the golfing habits of some of the Duke's golfing partners. Robert Moore was in his element with his disparaging yet funny descriptions of life in the Bahamas. The atmosphere was amiable, as if everyone was avoiding the true purpose behind the meeting.

After dinner, the group returned to the living room and, after Nathaniel had served them after-dinner drinks and cigars, they settled around a card table that had been set up and began to play bridge. Brian Thomas told Nathaniel that he and the other staff could go home and that he would serve further drinks to his guests.

The Duke was partnered by Major Bergman and they played several hands and were well ahead of the other two in scoring. As the Duke was shuffling the cards for another hand, Major Bergman looked at him and said: "Sir, I am afraid I come to you under false pretences. I am really an envoy from Germany and I was hoping we could discuss a delicate matter. Mr. Moore and Mr. Thomas facilitated this meeting so that I may speak for the Führer."

Without looking up from what he was doing, the Duke replied crossly: "I thought you weren't who you said you were. Gothenburg isn't on Lake Vänern but Vänersburg is. I knew you were German by the way you hold your cigar between your thumb and index finger and by the way you partly clicked you heels together when we were being introduced."

Everyone around the table stopped what they were doing and stared at the Duke.

"Now what can I do for Herr Hitler?" asked the Duke looking up angrily at Major Bergman and the others.

For his part, Major Bergman was taken completely by surprise at being caught out by this man who he regarded as nothing but a narcissistic aristocrat. For a moment he was at a loss for words, but eventually pressed on.

"Sir, I have a letter here for you from the Führer inviting you to Berlin to discuss the possibility that you could broker peace terms between us and the allies."

Bergman handed the Duke the letter.

"Why does he contact me rather than the Prime Minister Churchill?" said the Duke as he read the letter.

"Mr. Churchill would not agree to talk about terms."

"What do you think Moore?" the Duke asked.

"I think it might be worthwhile considering, sir, because Britain is economically bankrupt and I'm sure the people are tired of the war," he replied.

"If I agree, how are we going to get there Mr. Dahlin?"

"We have a U-boat offshore ready to take you to Germany."

"I need time to think about your proposal. What about the Duchess? I'm not leaving without her."

"I'm afraid we can't take her since we have to leave tonight."

"In that case, I'm not going," said the Duke firmly and got up to leave.

That part of the conversation was the signal to the SIS agents wanted to hear as they listened through their planted microphones in the house. They began to move stealthy towards the house and were joined by other men who had been hidden nearby.

Meanwhile, Simon Cookson, Group Captain Waite and Roger were in a temporary office at Oakes Field where they were monitoring the activities of both the Cameron Highlanders and the SIS agents. Both RAF airfields were on full alert and air force personnel had been confined to barracks. The guardhouse had been instructed not to let anyone in or out of the base until the curfew had been lifted. Flight Lieutenant Andrews of the RAF Police had organised patrols around the perimeter of the bases in case there was any diversionary attack from the sea.

What they hadn't thought about was an attack from inside the tightly controlled bases. At Oakes Field there were a cluster of fuel tanks that held about 15,000 gallons of aviation fuel which were isolated at the far end of the airfield away from the main hangers and the airmen's accommodations. Two sentries had been posted at the fuel depot.

Aircraftsmen Tommy Fitton and Harry Chapman had been assigned to the guard the fuel tanks. Thirty year old Tommy was a mechanic and twenty-three year old Harry was a cook. They had no idea what guard duty entailed and were sitting on a low concrete wall that surrounded the fuel tanks.

"I don't know what the fuck's going on tonight," moaned Tommy. "But what I know is this is a complete waste of time as usual. I could have been out at Dirty Dicks having a cool beer instead of sitting here sweating and being bitten by bloody flies."

"Flight Sergeant Jevons told us to walk around to make sure no one was here and interfering with the tanks," commented Harry.

"Then what we are to do if we catch them? Well if you want to play soldiers you walk around and catch a Gerry setting fire to those tanks," he laughed contemptuously.

Aircraftsmen Harry Chapman set off on patrol around the fuel farm. Unlike the underground fuel storage that was common on airfields in Britain to protect them from attack, Oakes Field had five large tanks above ground. When he was half way around Harry stopped to relieve himself. Just as he finished, and as he bent down to pick up his rifle, he was felled by a blow to his head from a large hammer.

A dark figure dressed in black and wearing camouflage paint on his face and hands checked to confirm that Harry was dead and then carried on laying his dynamite sticks in tied a cluster of seven against one of the tanks. He put a detonator into the middle the cluster, which had six-foot fuse wire attached to it. He then checked his watch. He had half an hour to go before he was to set off the explosion.

He was looking forward to seeing the effect the explosion had on the fuel and the commotion it caused on the base. He mused to himself that the British pricks were going to get their comeuppance and the Germans would be on their way to winning the war. The plan had panned out just like Major Bergman had told him it would two months ago in Havana. They had chosen Oakes Field because it was the further east of the two airfields and would draw the security forces away from Love Beach area where the submarine was to pick up the Duke and his party.

Aircraftsmen Tommy Fitton was still sitting on the concrete wall wondering where Harry had got to. After a while, he decided to go and search for him. As he rounded a corner he saw a body lying on the ground.

"Silly bugger is taking a nap. Harry it's no time to sleep on the job!" he shouted. That was the last words Tommy Fitton ever uttered as he was floored from behind by the same heavy hammer.

The Nazi agent checked his watch again and saw it was time. He lit the fuse and left. When he had got back to his hiding place between some storage sheds he waited for the fuel tanks to blow. Nothing happened. After waiting fifteen minutes, he decided to go back and see what had happened.

When he started to retrace his route he saw the headlights of a Land Rover approaching the fuel farm.

He ducked behind one of the sheds and saw three RAF men get out and start calling out to the guards. Then one called out that he had found them. The agent decided that it was time to leave.

***

Corporal Angus Bullock of the Cameron Highlanders crawled unseen until he was about three hundred feet from Bernt Falk's house and had settled well hidden in an outcrop of rocks. He then reported on his radio to Lt. Col. Haig that all was quiet although he could see movement in the house. An hour later nothing had changed until the front door suddenly opened and two men dressed in German uniforms and wearing parachute regiment helmets were seen loading equipment into an old lorry which was parked near the building.

When they had finished loading the lorry, Lt. Col. Haig, through a megaphone, ordered them to surrender as they were surrounded. The German commandos immediately opened fire and retreated into the house. They continued firing at the Cameron Highlanders through the windows and the British soldiers returned fire.

Lt. Col. Haig then ordered his two two-inch mortar teams to open fire with their high explosive rounds. Once they had found the range, the mortar shells began to demolish the house. The lorry was hit and exploded into a ball of fire. The firing from the house ceased and the British soldiers cautiously advanced on the ruins of the house and checked for survivors. Of the six German commandos, only one was alive. He was badly wounded and, after he was disarmed and searched, the army medics began working on his wounds.

Back at Brian Thomas's house, Major Bergman drew his Luger pistol and attached a silencer.

"I am sorry you won't cooperate, your Royal Highness, but you will come with us whether you want to or not. Refusal isn't an option. I have some German commandos waiting to escort you to the submarine.

"Now, Brian, tie Robert up to a chair. He is too useful to us as our agent in the colonial office so he'll stay here. Robert, thanks for taking care of that FBI agent. It was a pity he didn't give us any useful information."

Then they heard several explosions.

"Ah, that is our little diversion which will keep the authorities busy. Time to go."

Brian continued tying Robert Moore up and gagging him. When he had finished he turned to Bergman: "All set."

"Thank you for your help, Brian, but we won't need you anymore."

Bergman took aim at an astounded Brian Thomas and shot him twice. He took a torch from his pocket and flashed a light out of one of the windows.

Then there followed a crashing sound as men came running through the front door.

"Ah, there's my back up. Now, your Royal Highness, let us leave."

As he pushed the Duke of Windsor towards the dining room door, it swung open and the Duke and Major Bergman walked into the darkened front hall. They were momentarily sightless in the sudden darkness. Their eyes didn't have a chance to get used to the blackness before a blinding, bright light was shone on their faces. The Duke was grabbed by two strong arms and pushed to one side into the downstairs bathroom. Other men snatched a surprised Bergman and forced him to the ground. His Luger hit the floor and was picked up by one of the SIS men.

The front hall light was switched on to reveal a distraught Bergman with two large men sitting on him. He was dragged to his feet, handcuffed and thoroughly searched. Another hidden gun was found attached to one of his legs and a cyanide capsule was in his pocket. He was led out and pushed into a car and driven away.

Simon Cookson entered the house and knocked on the bathroom door.

"All clear, you can come out now," he said to his man who had been tasked with protecting the Duke. A dishevelled looking Duke of Windsor left the bathroom and looked intently at Simon.

"I was sceptical at first when you told me about their plan but thank you for intervening in the way you did," he said, smiling at Simon.

"Sir, thank you for volunteering to go through with this. It took a lot of courage."

"I knew I was more valuable to them alive so I was happy to play along although I don't know what use I'd have been. They must have been desperate. Do me one favour, Simon."

"Anything, Sir."

"Don't tell the Duchess what happened tonight because she will give me hell." And they both laughed. The Duke of Windsor left escorted by two armed sergeants from the Cameron Highlanders.

Simon went into the living room as one of his men took off the gag from Robert Moore's mouth. The agent then untied him but then put handcuffs on him.

"Robert Moore, you are under arrest for espionage."

"What do you mean?"

"We have recordings of you here tonight and our search of your house turned up incriminating files and code books. We've known for some time that someone on the island has been sending information to the Germans through their Bueno Aires office. When our agent, Brian Griffin, was murdered, we suspected you because of your affair with him. And thanks to this evening's recording, we now know you murdered the FBI agent Tom Wilson in the most gruesome fashion. You and Bergman are going on a cruise in a few weeks, courtesy of His Majesty's Royal Navy to Blighty. Take this scum out."

The Captain of U-106, Hermann Rasch, had submerged his submarine just below the surface about half a mile off Love Beach in shallow water. He had seen, through his U-boat's periscope, the attack on Berndt Falk's house about an hour previously and he had waited for any signals from the shore at which time he would have surfaced and pick up the German commandos. None came and so he had decided to leave.

Captain Rasch gave the order to steam on the surface because it was faster and that the darkness gave him cover. He wanted to leave as soon as possible in case any surface ships or aircraft had been alerted to his presence off New Providence Island. His escape course was set in a North Easterly direction through a channel between Eleuthera and Great Abaco islands, which led to the much deeper Atlantic Ocean where he could just disappear.

Meanwhile, Pilot Officer James Riley and his crew took off from Windsor Field in their B-24 Liberator on a search and destroy mission. They had been alerted to a possible U-boat sighting off the island of Eleuthera. Where this information came from, they didn't know or care. This mission was the culmination of their six-week training and they were ready to go into action. They wanted to impress their instructors before they took up their posting to the RAF Middle East Command.

Their aircraft was fitted with a Leigh Light on one of its wings, which had been successfully used by the RAF in hunts for U-Boats at night. Most U-boats, when they were not attacking ships, came to the surface at night to preserve and recharge batteries and oxygen and this presented an opportunity for an attacking aircraft to sink them. An aircraft would pick up a signal through its air-to-surface-vessel radar and, as they approached the target, the crew would turn on their powerful searchlight at the last moment an illuminate the U-Boat. The aircraft's bombardier would then have enough time to aim and release his bombs as the submarine crashed-dived.

For Pilot Officer James Riley and his crew, the sky was clear and the moon was in its third quarter, which was not as good as a full moon but still gave enough light to spot a U-boat on the surface. Riley and his crew were hopeful as they scanned the sea from four thousand feet. Then their radar picked up a contact on the surface. They dropped down to a thousand feet to investigate, turned on their searchlight and there on the surface they saw an IXB type U-Boat. It was crash diving and in the next pass by the Liberator at two hundred feet the crew released two depth charges set to explode at twenty-five feet under the water. Circling around again, the crew of the bomber could only see debris on the surface of the water. The excited aircrew headed home to report their kill.

Fortunately for the crew of U-106 there was only slight damage to the conning tower because the depth charges had been set to explode at a too shallow a depth by the excited trainee aircrew. Captain Rasch had released through one of the torpedo tubes some clothes and equipment that he had brought from France just in case he needed it for this purpose. The deception worked because the aircraft didn't return to attack again. Captain Rasch set sail for Lorient in France.

Two months later U-106 was sunk off northern Spain by a Sunderland flying boat of the Royal Australian Air Force operating out of North Pembroke in Wales. All her crew were lost.

The Clean Up

Chapter 22

Roger's vigilance of Helen by her bedside was rewarded a day after the rescue of the Duke of Windsor. He had watched her all night and must have fallen asleep in his wheelchair, when he felt a hand on his. He woke up with a start to see Helen's smiling face.

"What are you doing here, you silly boy? Shouldn't you be working?"

"There is nothing more important to me than to be with you, my love. How are you feeling?"

"I feel wretched. I want to get my own back on Brian and those men. I feel dirty and I have had nightmares," she angrily replied.

"Well, Brian is dead and the RAF police are on the trail of the men who attacked you. Would you be able to recognise them again?"

"Not really. It was dark and I was asleep in the car. Roger you've got to get them."

A few days later, Helen was released from hospital and Roger took her in a car to convalesce at Mary Stuart's house where Vivian Thomas was staying. The two women helped her understand that what had happened was not her fault and tried to take her on outings to help her. Physically she mended but mentally she was very fragile and would have nightmares and fits of crying. The doctors put her on anti-depressants.

Roger was back into his hospital routine and he would visit Helen every day after work. Apart from his concerns for Helen, which were lessening, this was the first time he had really relaxed since he came to the Bahamas because he was not living a double life anymore. He was still wearing a sling as his shoulder was slowly healing from the bullet wound he had sustained.

Roger was in the bar at Prince George Hotel late one evening after visiting Helen with Flight Lieutenant Andrews. Christopher Woodson staggered up to them carrying a large glass of whisky and asked whether he could join them. He had obviously been drinking and looked very dishevelled and unshaven, which was unlike him.

"Of course. We were just going over the events of last week. I'm glad you came because it will stop us being bores and reminiscing on the satisfactory outcome of operations against the Nazis. They must be desperate to try such a foolish operation. I think what surprised me most and what was so concerning was the number of British traitors that were willing to help them," Roger said.

Roger saw Christopher bristle slightly at this and he was puzzled by his reaction. He knew he had a chip on his shoulder about his father's unfortunate run-in with the British medical authorities. Roger decided to try something because he sensed that Christopher knew more than what he was letting on. It was one of these feelings you get when you see someone else's body language and sense their hidden anger.

"How's the investigation going? I understand that you were able to put together Bernt Falk's smuggling operation, his spying activities and eventually his connection to Bergman. How did you do it?" Christopher asked.

Roger was curious why he mentioned Falk's smuggling gang as their existence was never revealed. Falk's co-conspirators had been shipped quietly back to England for trial. Their flight back to Britain was immediate after their interrogation. Also, there was never any connection made public between Falk and Bergman. How did he know that? Roger looked at David Andrews and he nodded his head slightly.

"It was a matter of clever deduction and old-fashioned police work," Roger answered.

"Now that the perpetrators have been caught, can we now have our lives back or are we all still under suspicion? You of all people should know having been here under false pretences," he slurred sarcastically.

Roger ignored him: "I was talking to my friend Simon Cookson yesterday and he was saying that they still need to capture the person responsible for placing the dynamite charges on one of the fuel tanks at Oakes Field. After our talk, I got thinking about who had been responsible. I talked to Dr. Bain who carried out the post mortem of both airmen he killed and, whoever it was, knew exactly where to hit each man so that they each died almost instantaneously. Both wounds were in precisely the same place. So he was an expert assassin or knew his anatomy well. But the charges he had set on the fuel tank didn't go off because of his carelessness. It was clear that the idiot must have been a rank amateur in this area," he said, waiting for a response.

"What do you mean?" asked Christopher.

"Well, the connection between the fuse wire and the detonator was not crimped properly so that it fell off the detonator when the dynamite charge was attached to the fuel tank. In the dark our Nazi agent didn't notice or check for the problem as he was probably in too much of a hurry to leave. When the ignited fuse wire reached the end of its burn there was nothing to set off the charges and each wire just fizzled out."

"That was a lucky escape," commented a reddened Christopher. "I would imagine that there would have been an almighty explosion."

"Yes it was lucky," Roger said. "The other good thing was that the police were able to lift finger prints of the murdering bastard who would have set off the charges. Apparently, the fingerprints on the sticks of dynamite were not that of Bergman, Moore or the dead man, Thomas, but that of a fourth man."

"At the moment, we are busy searching through their fingerprint files to find a match," said David Andrews.

"But it will take you forever to find a match, won't it, and the culprit will be long gone? They'll never know who the fourth man was," Christopher said arrogantly, although he looked a bit concerned at this news.

"Well not really. They're checking all the RAF staff first. They have all our fingerprints on our personnel files. They believe the killer works here at the base because everyone was confined to barracks that night and security was very tight. In other words, they believe the sabotage attempt was an inside job," Roger told him.

Christopher fell silent and a worried look came over his face again.

"Can I buy you a drink?" Roger asked.

"Thanks for asking, but I've got a meeting with some people at the British Colonial Hotel." And he got up and left in a hurry, drunkenly weaving as he walked away.

"What's put the wind up his tail?" David Andrews wondered out allowed.

"I think I did. There is more to Christopher than the simple doctor he portrays. From the moment I got here to the Bahamas he has acted strangely towards me. His behaviour is very passive aggressive. From what I understand his father was very demanding and autocratic. I think he learnt to automatically retreat into his shell and have this veneer of cynicism that hides his insecurities.

"In my conversations with him he was always complaining about something, whether it was not being appreciated or resenting the demands of Dr. Rassin. And then there was the fact that my room had been searched soon after I arrived which tells me someone was suspicious of my role. I bet it was him. Anyway, I wanted to put a bee in his bonnet to see how he reacted."

"And did he?"

"Oh yes."

Roger got a handkerchief from his trouser pocket and picked up the glass out of which Christopher had been drinking.

"Let's take this to your office and we'll see whether there are any matches."

Flight Sergeant Jenkins was pouring over a desk full of RAF Personnel files. The office was very humid and full of cigarette smoke as the constant smoker worked. He was in his shirtsleeves and he was using a fingerprint magnifier comparing the fingerprints on file to those taken from the dynamite sticks. He had relieved Corporal Adkins as both policemen took it in shifts to compare the fingerprints. They needed constant breaks because reading each print required detailed concentration and they could only examine a small number each hour. It was a slow, laborious process as they searched through over three thousand fingerprints of RAF personnel and civilian staff.

"Flight Sergeant, could you please lift the prints on this glass. I think we may have a suspect for you," David Andrews said to the exhausted man.

"Sir, anything that will give me a break from this tedious job. I'm going cross eyed. Where did you get this glass from, sir?"

"I don't want to say until we know whether there is a match because I might be completely wrong in my suspicions," he said

Jenkins shrugged and started to dust the glass with a fine black powder and soon several prints appeared. He then put a clear piece of tape over a thumb print he had found and the impression of the print created by the powder stuck to the tape. He took the tape off the glass and attached it to a white card. He then bent over the card with his magnifying glass and compared the print to that which had been taken from the dynamite sticks.

After a few minutes of examining each print back and forth, he looked up and declared: "We have a match. Now sir, whose prints are these?"

"Dr. Christopher Woodson's."

"Right. We need to find him. Come on."

The Flight Sergeant grabbed his jacket and put it on as he ran to the guardhouse at Oakes Field followed by Flight Lieutenant Andrews.

"Put the field on lock-down. You are to detain Dr. Christopher Woodson if you see him. He may be armed and dangerous," he ordered the duty sergeant. "I want two armed guards to follow me."

The RAF police searched Christopher's room. There was no sign of him and all his belongings were gone. An alert was put out to the Bahamian police and they began to search for him. The police spent the next two days searching for him and coming up empty each time. They interviewed people who knew him and searched their homes.

After two weeks there was no sign of him and the police felt that he had left the island somehow. The search was then called off, although contact was made with other Caribbean police forces who were asked to keep a look out for him.

Roger, however, was not convinced that he had left New Providence Island.

Then a major crime occurred in the Bahamas which put the search for Dr. Woodson on hold, never to be resurrected again. To this day the crime has never been solved, although there were many suspects and many theories. On July 8th, the body of Sir Harry Oakes, one of the richest men in the world and a leading resident in the Bahamas, was found brutally murdered in his bed. As he slept, he had been bludgeoned to death and set on fire to cover up the evidence of the crime.

A good friend of his had been the Duke of Windsor who, as governor of the colony, made some fatal decisions, which were to negatively affect the outcome of a botched investigation. First, he immediately imposed a media blackout by closing the island's only telegraph system as well as telephone service to the outside world. Unfortunately for the Duke this didn't work as Etienne Dupuch, the editor and owner of the *Nassau Daily Tribune,* was able to telegram the bare bones of the story to his wire service contacts. So the world knew about the dramatic crime in paradise that had happened on the Duke of Windsor's 'patch'. This story attracted worldwide news coverage as it was mainly a welcome relief for newspaper readers who were bored with the news about the war.

The second and biggest mistake the Duke made, was to bring in two American detectives from Miami to head up the investigation. He believed that the Bahamian police hadn't the skills to handle the enquiry, but other Caribbean police forces certainly had and it is a mystery to this day why he did not enlist their help. This event really miffed the local police force as they were to play a secondary role to the Americans. It turned out that the American detectives manufactured evidence that nearly sent an innocent man to the gallows.

Alfred de Marigny was arrested and put on trial in October 1943 for the killing of Sir Harry Oakes. De Marigny was known as playboy, although he was married to Nancy, Oakes' daughter, and was heartily disliked by the movers and shakers in Bahamian society. The Miami detectives claimed to have found a fingerprint on a Chinese screen in the murdered man's bedroom where his body was found. In fact, they had lifted the fingerprint from a glass of water that de Marigny had drunk from during an interview with one of the detectives.

The murder and trial made sensational headlines all over the world and was the biggest story that had come out of the Bahamas to that date in its history. The presence of the Duke of Windsor as Governor General gave it an enhanced notoriety so that public interest, particularly in the United States, was white hot. The public saw the story in the media as extremely salacious compared to their usual diet of war news.

Thanks to the ability of his defence lawyer, Alfred de Marigny was found not guilty. His lawyer, Godfrey Higgs, proved in court that the detectives had manufactured evidence and, thus, he had completely decimated the prosecution's case.

Needless to say, the hunt for the errant Dr. Christopher Woodson was put very much on the back burner, if not forgotten about, by the Bahamian police in all the excitement of the murder and trial. So Roger was very much on his own. He was sure that Christopher hadn't left the island and was hiding in some bolt hole somewhere. Then, by chance, he got his first clue into his whereabouts from an unexpected source.

Helen, who was still recovering from her ordeal, and Roger had become avid sailors. It had been good to take her mind off her problem even for a short while. She had started back at work and had become absorbed in it, which helped in her recovery.

The two airmen who had assaulted her were found and court martialled. At their court martial, Helen had to give evidence. She had to relive her traumatic experience yet again and her appearance at the trial had set back her recovery. However, she was so determined to give evidence and no one could make her change her mind. The outcome was never in doubt and the two men were sentenced to six years each in a military prison. So that hurdle had been cleared and she was getting better each day, although she still didn't like Roger touching her.

Roger tried as much as possible to take her on activities to take her mind off the trauma she had experienced and sailing was one passion that helped immeasurably. He often wondered whether this sailing bug they had caught had anything to do with the pirate past of the Bahamas and whether the infection was something you caught when you spent some time in the islands. Nassau has been the headquarters of a number of famous pirate captains of the eighteenth and seventeenth centuries including one of the most famous Blackbeard, or, to give him his proper name, Edward Teach. The sailing bug was in the air and during the Second World War as many from the RAF enjoyed their down time in sailing boats of all shapes and sizes.

Helen and Roger were lucky because a mutual friend of hers, a Bahamian called Charles Lightwater, owned a beautiful Pirate Class Sloop named *Beatrice*, which he had purchased in the 1930s. Why the boat was named Beatrice, Roger never knew but he thought it was one of his favourite girlfriends or mistresses. Charles was in his late seventies and didn't sail much anymore so it was like having their own boat. Because of his physical problems, Roger had become an adept coxswain and Helen and some of their friends were the crew.

One evening they were in the bar at the Royal Nassau Sailing Club enjoying their drinks after a day of sailing. The club, which was usually for members only, had welcomed military personnel as temporary members during the conflict. They were talking to two members of the club when in walked in a striking red-headed woman in a close fitting dress that showed off her full figure. She made a beeline for one of the men in their group.

"Hello, Francis darling. How have you been?" she chirped in an American accent as she put her arm around his waist. Their red-faced friend exclaimed with delight: "Molly, darling, you've come back to us! Everyone, this is Molly Taylor."

Helen dug Roger in the ribs as he took in the fullness of this beautiful women and interrupted his carnal thoughts. It turned out that Molly was an annual visitor to the Bahamas and that her father was a leading lawyer in Philadelphia.

"When did you get here?" Francis asked.

"This morning on the Pam Am shuttle from Miami. Daddy has rented a place at Lyford Cay. So how is everyone? Has much changed since I was here last year. I see there are more British fliers here now. That'll make life interesting because you know what flyboys are like!" she squealed with delight.

"Have you seen Dr. Christopher with that wonderful bedside manner of his?" she asked sarcastically.

"Do you mean Dr. Christopher Woodson?" Roger asked.

"Ah yes, sweetie," she answered looking him up and down.

"Well Helen and I worked with him at the RAF Hospital. He's had a run in with people at the hospital and nobody can find him. Are you a close friend of his?"

"You can say that. We had a fling last year and he's never got over our affair when I ended it. I imagine he's sulking at his father's old place."

"His father's old house! Do you know where it is?"

"No, I haven't a clue. I never went there. All I know was that he was very reluctant to sell it after his father's death and I believe he disappeared there when we had one of our rows and he was in one of his moods. At least that's what he told me when he came crawling back."

Roger was on duty at the hospital for the next two days and couldn't do any research to find Christopher's hiding place, but it did give him time to think about how he was going to approach finding him. He decided to first start with Christopher's father's suicide and see if newspaper stories gave a place where he lived. His second choice was to request records from the Registrar General's office for any property deeds under his name. This was a long-shot and would take some time to search through the records.

On his next day off, he visited the Nassau Public Library, which was in an octagonal shaped building located at the southern end of Parliament Square. It was constructed as a jail in 1797, but in 1879 it was converted into a library, reading room and museum.

Roger remembered that Christopher had told him that his father died in 1933 so he started to scan copies of the *Nassau Daily Tribune* for that year.

It wasn't long before he found what he was looking for. There was quite a large section in the paper devoted to Dr. Woodson's death and it detailed his help for the black communities of Grants Town, Bain Town and Over-the-Hill neighbourhoods. The newspaper termed his death as a tragedy and said that the medical authorities in Britain had his blood on their hands. This white Bahamian's obituary said that he split his time between his practice in Bamboo Town, which was on the south side of New Providence Island, and his medical office on Wolfe Road in Grants Town. It said that he was a resident of Malcolm Creek area. It said that he had come from a wealthy family of small ship builders and had decided to take up medicine and serve the poor.

That afternoon Roger wrote a note for Helen to say where he was going and started off on a five-mile bike ride to Malcolm Creek. He took his revolver, which was tucked into the waistband of his trousers, and his binoculars. He cycled south on Market Street with his walking stick draped across the handlebars. The street became Beach Road once he had left Nassau and, after three miles, he turned east on Cowpen Road. This took him into Bamboo Town.

Roger was at once struck by the abject poverty he saw in this black Bahamian community. All along the road there were shanty cabins, some in desperate need of repair. There were ragged children playing in their bare feet in the dusty dirt road watched by their mothers who were doing chores, but when they saw Roger they all stopped and stared. The only men in sight were two old men playing Dominoes in the shade of a straw-roofed, dilapidated cabin.

Roger noticed an elderly woman sitting in the shade of a Gumelern Tree smoking a pipe and braiding a straw basket. He couldn't tell how old she was, but her craggy, worn face told him she was someone who had come through many traumas in her life and managed to survive. She was clearly the matriarch of the community because those people who passed her nodded deferentially as they walked by.

Roger lay his bike on the ground, took up his walking stick and limped over to the woman.

"Excuse me, could you tell me where Dr. Woodson's house is?"

She looked up from her work and studied him with a hard, steady stare. She took the pipe out of her mouth. "Who wants to know?"

"I'm Dr. Lawson and I am a colleague of his son, Dr. Christopher Woodson. I'm looking for him. I know his father died ten years ago and Christopher came down here."

"What do you want him for?"

"The people at the hospital he and I work for want to make sure he's alright and are concerned about him because he has not been at work."

Changing the subject she said, "Have you ever been a doctor to the poor?"

"Yes, when I was a new doctor at a hospital in London."

She laughed a deep laugh and in doing so showed her only three blackened teeth. "That's ain't helping the poor. They're all rich in London," she said, knowingly.

"I'm afraid that's not true. There are some very poor areas, particularly on the east and south sides of the city where people can't pay for a doctor. I helped them by delivering their babies and took care of such things as colds, flu and sometimes chicken pox."

"Hm. You don't seem like a poor doctor to me, not like Dr. Woodson. Now there's a saint of a man. His son comes down here when he has time off to help us. How did you get that limp?" she asked, changing the subject again.

Roger explained what had happened to him and the fact that there was a world war going on. She had no recollection of this but said she had wondered why so many aircraft were flying around the normally quiet island.

"I don't know why you white folk want to fight each other all the time. Seems to me a waste of time and energy."

There was nothing Roger could say to that. He knew that the character of the black Bahamians was such that they were a friendly and happy-go-lucky people despite their poverty and hardships. In many ways he admired this attitude.

After a lengthy silence, the old woman looked him up and down again. "I suppose you're alright." She then gave him directions to Woodson house in Malcolm Creek.

Roger continued to cycle east along Cowpen Road until he saw the large silk cotton tree the old lady had told him about and opposite it was a narrow road. The vegetation at the sides of the road was so overgrown he had some difficulty cycling along the road and had to get off and walk several times. He followed the road until he saw in the distance the sea and below him, snuggled in the side of a hill, was a small cottage on a beach. There was a wooden dock that went out from the beach to the deeper part of the sea. Tied up alongside it was a beautiful two-masted Ketch sailing boat.

Roger left his bike at the side of the road and walked down to the cottage. He knocked on the front door. It was open so he walked in. The front door opened up onto the living room, which was caked in dust but all the belongings of the family who lived there were still in place as if they had gone out to beach and never returned. There was a grandfather clock, two chairs, a newspaper dated April 4th, 1933 and reading glasses on a table next to the sofa. In a small office off the living room was a desk and on it records of patients, an old stethoscope and a blood pressure gauge as well as numerous medical instruments. The shelves were stacked with medical reference books and past copies of *British Medical Journal*.

Everything was blanketed in a thick coating of dust and Roger saw that nothing had changed at the cottage since its owner had committed suicide. The place was now trapped in time and would remain so forever or until Christopher decided to make changes. He had done nothing to alter anything and Roger realised cottage was a sort of shrine to his beloved father he wanted to preserve. Roger then understood Christopher's deep paranoia about his father's death.

Roger walked into the kitchen and there were signs that the owner of the house had left after his last breakfast five years previously and had not bothered to do the washing up. That was the last thing Roger remembered as he crashed to the floor unconscious.

Roger slowly began to come round. At first everything was out of focus and he had a searing headache from the wound at the back of my head. He finally began to get his bearings and realised that he was outside in the unrelenting sun. He was tied to one of the bollards at the end of the wooden dock and opposite him was the sailing boat he had seen from the hill above the cottage. It was then he heard footsteps and, when he looked up, he saw Christopher Woodson walking towards him carrying a box.

"The intruder has finally woken up from his two-hour nap. How did you find me?" he asked as he climbed onto the boat and went below with his box. He then appeared again and climbed back on the dock. "Well?"

"One of your girlfriends, Molly something or other, told me that you were likely at your dad's place so I came looking."

"So Molly's back in town is she? Well I will miss her, as I am leaving here today."

"Where are you going?"

"You don't think I would tell you, you bastard!"

"I don't understand why you would be so evil as to work for the Nazis. What's your motivation for taking such a drastic step?"

"Well let me tell you something about my life, Mr. Clever Dick. My dear father killed himself because he was struck off by the General Medical Council in London and couldn't continue his life's work. He was a good doctor who spent all his time with the poor black people until some white man reported him for performing a necessary abortion on a child who was in a desperate medical position. Also, my father had rankled the powers that be in Nassau by vociferously demanding better health services for the poor through numerous articles in the newspapers and pressed his case with members of the legislature. So they were out to get him one way or another and they did.

"I grew up with many black friends and I know a lot about the deprivation they suffer and how whites grew richer as they grew poorer. It's a form of slavery as black people have to suffer the ignominy of lack of work, very low wages when there is work, dilapidated housing, little

283

or no education. And what do the British do? Nothing. I think the riots last year frightened many whites a bit out of their complacency."

"What about your mother?" Roger asked.

"She skipped town as soon as I was born. I've never talked to her and don't want to. My father brought me up."

"But why is your hatred so visceral? Surely you don't hate the people you have worked with so much?"

"They're all made from the same cloth. They are conceited and look down on people who are different from them. I hate them all for what they did to my father. They assassinated him. Their actions caused him to kill himself. I was also blacklisted by the British medical schools because of my name and association with him. I finally found a medical school in Canada that would take me.

"The British are the world's worst carpetbaggers! They have taken over countries like those in Africa and in India and arrogantly put their own aristocrats in charge to teach the natives the British way to live while milking them for everything they can in the way of resources and wealth. The British ruling class are egotistical and cannot be trusted to keep their word. They allow people such as the 'Bay Street Boys' here in the Bahamas to prosper while subjugating the blacks in this God-forsaken colony."

Roger was taken aback by his vitriol and suspected that he had been harbouring this resentment for many years and that recent events had ignited his venom.

"What are you going to do now?" Roger asked.

"I'm going to sail away from here and find somewhere where I can find peace of mind."

"Will you ever find that considering what you have been through? So you plan abandoning the people your father spent his life helping?"

"I'll keep trying to find somewhere I can help other poor people. I can't here because I'm a wanted man. In the meantime you will remain here, tied up until I'm well clear of these islands."

"But I'll die of dehydration or sunburn if I'm left exposed like this," Roger pleaded.

"Well, a person who works for His Majesty's Secret Service and the British establishment doesn't deserve any mercy. You and the likes of you only facilitate their crimes! No, you are going to die a slow death as punishment because of your interference with my German friends' plan to kidnap the little man."

With that, he untied his boat, jumped in and raised its sails. Roger watched as the boat slowly disappeared over the horizon. He then tried to loosen the ropes that tied him to the bollard with no success at all. Being a seasoned sailor, Christopher knew how to tie someone up successfully. His only hope was that someone would find and free him.

Roger spent a very uncomfortable and long night lashed to the bollard. There was no give in the rope. He was tied in a sitting position and couldn't move to a more comfortable one. He dropped off to sleep several times only to wake with a jolt as the noises of the night woke him. First, it was raccoons fighting, then it was some Capybara, which are large versions of guinea pigs, gnawing on some tree trunks and then several Liberator Bombers practising their bombing runs.

Morning finally came and, with it, the blistering heat from the sun. By mid-morning he was incredibly hot and extremely thirsty. He knew he was becoming dehydrated as sweat was pouring out of him and he had urinated on himself. He watched out for anyone that could help him. There were passing ships and sailboats but they were too far away to see or hear him.

Then finally, night came and, with it, relief from the scorching heat. He knew he had to do something but he was trussed up so tightly. The noises of the night were the same as the night before. Morning came and then a blessed rain storm which cooled down his blistered body and gave him some sustenance. Then as quickly as they had come, the rain clouds disappeared and he was back again roasting in blazing sun.

In the afternoon of his second full day he began to hallucinate. Earlier in the day he had decided that he needed to talk to himself in order to keep from falling asleep in the sizzling heat and from going mad. But talking to himself also made him see people and places he knew. In his delirium, he was taken back to his childhood and saw his mother walking towards him with a lemonade drink in her hand. And then she disappeared. Then he saw his friend Jim and they were running and jumping off a cliff into a lake below. Just before he hit the cool, inviting water, he woke up.

That night he was able to sleep some but when morning came he was unable to open his encrusted eyes. He felt that he was going mad and then he just passed out. In his unconscious state, Roger felt as though he was flying and the great pressure on my body from the ropes had been released. Was he flying to heaven? He came round in a delirious state, babbling to himself again. Then he heard muffled, unintelligible voices. The unbearable burning of his body had stopped and he felt very cold. And then he passed out again.

When Roger woke everything was quiet, but he had a very cold sensation on his body. He was able to open his eyes and he saw that he was lying on a hospital bed surrounded by ice packs in a darkened room. There was an IV drip bottle which was attached to one of his arms and a nurse was taking his blood pressure. When she saw his eyes were open, she left.

A few minutes later Dr. Rassin came in to the room with Helen.

"Roger, you gave us quite a scare. You've been here for a couple of days and at one time we thought we'd lost you," he said.

Roger tried to speak, but the words wouldn't come out of his mouth.

"Now don't try to say anything. Your speech will come back slowly. There is one young lady here to see you and I'll leave you in her good hands. We're glad to have you back." And he left.

"I should be mad with you for going off on your own, but I'm so happy to see you, my love," Helen said as she burst into tears.

When she had stopped crying, she explained how he had been found. A couple of boys from Bamboo Town had come down to the dock to fish and had found him. Some of the men from the town took him to the home of the town's matriarch who then summoned the police.

"What about Woodson?" Roger croaked.

"The police found out from the boys that Christopher had a boat and they had assumed that he had made his escape in it when he tied you up. They asked the RAF to see if they could locate it and they eventually found it on some rocks at Coakley Cay just off the Exuma Island. What was strange was the boat only had its mizzen sail raised and the tiller jammed so that the boat sailed in a southerly direction. There was no sign of Christopher and it's a mystery what happened to him in the open sea between New Providence and Exuma. Maybe he fell

overboard and drowned by accident or he deliberately
killed himself. I suppose we'll never know."

Roger fell asleep.

The Aftermath

Chapter 23

It took Roger at least two weeks to recover from his ordeal. He was confined to a wheelchair but he was determined not to miss a short ceremony that took place on Prince George Wharf.

The Royal Navy frigate *HMS Swale* arrived at the wharf. Helen and Roger watched with Flight Lieutenant Andrews as a RAF lorry arrived. It was raining hard as the chained prisoners were escorted to the ship. The RAF police handed the three men over to two Royal Marines who marched them up a gangway onto the ship and they disappeared below deck. The whole ceremony was over in minutes and the ship immediately set sail.

As they went back towards Bay Street, Helen asked: "What will happen to them?"

"*HMS Swale* is a convoy escort in the North Atlantic and she will probably meet a convoy leaving Halifax, Canada, for Britain," replied Flight Lieutenant Andrews. "The prisoners will be taken there for further interrogation and trial. Bergman and Moore will probably have a date with the hangman and Falk, because of the deal with Simon, will spend the rest of his miserable life on Dartmoor in the prison there.

"However, we have still not caught Dr. Woodson who was responsible for the murders of the two airmen and the failed sabotage of the fuel tanks. We have his fingerprints and we'll get him eventually. I suspect he's long gone from the Bahamas," he added as he left them.

***

Six months later Helen and Roger were married at Christ Church Cathedral in Nassau and, after their wedding reception at Royal Nassau Sailing Club, they spent a week in a small cabin on a beach on Cat Island, one of the major islands in the Bahamas. And they got a big surprise when they got there. On the table in the dining room was a big floral arrangement of plants native to the Bahamas – Hibiscus, Yellow Elder and Allamanda.

Leaning against the bowl of flowers was a telegram and when Roger opened it he was astounded to see who it was from. It read 'All is well. Good luck, Chris W.' He saw that the telegram was from Buenos Aires, Argentina.

"So that's where he ended up. I wonder how he got there," Roger said to Helen as she read the telegram.

"The question is how he found out where we were?" she replied.

"That, my love, is a mystery. He probably still has many friends in Bahamas who keep him up-to-date with things that happen here."

At the beginning of 1946, Roger was demobbed in the Bahamas and Helen and he moved back to Great Britain. He was lucky enough to find a position as a partner in a general medical practice in Engelfield Green, just west of London, and Helen resumed her nursing career at a hospital in nearby Windsor.

***

Helen's English Aunt Cynthia, who had married a German student, Alexander Bader, in 1912, managed to reach Britain in 1946. She had lived in Germany during both the First and Second World Wars. She had survived because her German in-laws had given her shelter in their home in Freiberg, which was some twenty-five miles southwest of Dresden and near the Black Forest.

Cynthia's husband, Alexander, had been arrested in 1939 on trumped-up charges by the Gestapo and had been incarcerated in the Fuhlsbüttel concentration camp, which was near Hamburg. She hadn't heard from him or learnt his fate and, as the years went on, she had come to the realisation that he was probably dead. Added to her grief was the death of her estranged son, Albrecht, who had been a bomber pilot for the Luftwaffe and had been shot down over Britain in 1941.

By 1945, Germany was in desperate straits on all fronts as its population fought for continued existence. Food was in short supply and the beleaguered people began to turn on each other in their frantic quest for survival. The Gestapo and SS troops were summarily executing anyone who they regarded as subverting the Nazi regime in their drive to keep people in line. In February, the British and the Americans firebombed Dresden that caused a horrendous loss of over 130,000 civilian lives and, to this day, the resentment about whether the city was a legitimate military target or not still smoulders among Germans. Cynthia remembered standing outside her in-laws' house in Freiberg and seeing an ominous glow from the direction of Dresden as allied bombers dropped their lethal loads.

By March 1945, the Russians had invaded East Prussia and reached the Oder River, which was close to Berlin, and they were threatening the rest of eastern

Germany as they marched westward facing little resistance from the depleted German military.

Herr Bader called Cynthia into his study one day in March: "My dear, I think it is about time you left us as fast you can before the Russians arrive here. They have a terrible reputation of cruelty, especially towards women, who they regard as nothing but objects of their carnal desires. They are cruel animals and will only destroy our homeland."

"But I couldn't do this without you both coming with me," she protested.

"I'm afraid we are too old to travel now and the Germany we knew for most of our lives has gone forever thanks to Hitler. But you must get away while you can. Think about what I've said overnight and you'll realise it is something you must do in the morning."

The next day, Cynthia was making breakfast in the kitchen. She thought it was odd that she hadn't seen Herr Bader, who was normally an early riser. An hour passed and she still hadn't seen either of them. She knocked on their bedroom door and there was no answer so she opened it and peeked in. The Baders were both lying there still in bed and in their nightwear, looking as if they were still asleep. She realised almost at once that they were both dead and her touch of Herr Bader's cold forehead confirmed this. The discovery of an empty ampule on his side table indicated that they had taken their own lives in a suicide pact. Cynthia sobbed.

Two days later, Cynthia attended the Baders' funeral in the small local church that they attended. There was no one there except the priest and the undertaker, who scurried off as soon as the burial was completed to attend to other clients needing his help to bury their dead.

Cynthia went back to an empty house and packed a small suitcase. As she loaded her suitcase on to a bicycle she had been using during her stay, she heard the distant rumble of artillery from the east and she knew it was time to go. She started peddling west towards Frankfurt and once she was on the main road to the city she joined a tumult of other refugees making their way westward.

Eventually, Cynthia made her way to Britain with help of British representatives she had eventually found in Frankfurt and stayed with Helen and Roger for a short time. She was soon recruited by the British Foreign Office as an interpreter and was based in Bonn, Germany. In 1950, she left the Foreign Office and became a teacher again, teaching English to German students at a school in that city. It was there she met her second husband, Karl Adler, and lived happily with him until her death at eighty-one years old in 1972.

***

The Duke of Windsor finally left the Bahamas on May 3rd 1945, having resigned his post as Governor. The Duke and the Duchess continued to be treated as pariahs by the Royal Family who were determined that they should not return to live in Great Britain. Much of the angst was because of the Duke's abdication in 1936, which left his totally unprepared brother to reign in his place as George VI. The royal family and the British government believed that he had put his own personal needs before his duty to his country in marrying the twice-divorced Wallis Simpson. Also the couple's egocentric behaviour and Nazi affiliations before and publicised beliefs during the Second World War irked the British establishment who regarded him as utterly untrustworthy.

As it turned out, the Duke's abdication in 1936 was a blessing in disguise for the nation because he proved to be very fickle and self-centred. He was a loose cannon who could not be trusted to perform his duties as monarch in the few months that he reigned and afterwards as a former king.

The big question Roger had in the back of his mind was why the Duke agreed to take part in Simon Cookson's plan to foil the Nazi plot to kidnap him. Roger had become very distrustful about the actions of those in power. Was his reason a cynical plan to show the British establishment that he wasn't a Nazi and that he had bravely helped out despite his life being in danger? Roger wondered.

When the Windsors left the Bahamas they lived for a short while in New York. The Duke lobbied the British Government again for a diplomatic role, but his entreaties fell on deaf ears. Eventually the couple moved back to Paris in September, 1945, and resumed their pre-war existence in their properties in Paris and the south of France which had been preserved for them by the Nazis and the Vichy French.

But the Duke had left a whirlwind behind him in the form of near-treasonous, pro-Nazi telegrams and papers that were among the documents recovered from German archives and from his German cousins at the end of the Second World War. The British Government and the royal family spent years locating and suppressing these and their copies so that they would not be made public or fall into the hands of enemies of the state, such as the Soviet Union. Unfortunately, one of MI5's agents tasked with recovering some of these documents was Anthony Blunt, who was also a spy for the Soviets, and it is certain that copies of the Duke's papers fell into their hands soon after they were found. The British were patching up the Duke's mistakes long after he retired to France and only in recent years have his nefarious dealings with the Nazis been made public.

The Duke and Duchess spent most of their time between their homes in France, the high society whirl of New York and Palm Springs where they were for a while hosted as celebrities. The Duke, who died in 1972, never acknowledged his many mistakes. Although he did criticise Hitler as a personality in a memoir, he never conceded that his views of the Nazi regime were wrong. His attempts at rapprochement with the royal family over the years were only on his terms, which was unacceptable to George VI, his mother, Queen Mary, and his arch-critic, Queen Elizabeth. Relations began to thaw in the 1960s when he and the Duchess made a number of visits to Britain. On their deaths, they were both buried at the Royal Burial Ground on the Frogmore Estate in Windsor.

***

The Bahamian economy took off after the Second World War as tourism returned. There was a boom in the building of hotels and resorts, particularly on New Providence and Grand Bahama islands. With a loosening in regulations for casino licenses in 1969 through the Lotteries and Gaming Act, further expansion in the burgeoning tourist industry helped the Bahamian economy. The 1960s also saw an expansion of offshore banking and financial services.

However, the political atmosphere after the war gradually became more caustic. The 'Bay Street Boys' cabal still ran the colony as it had done since the nineteenth century. The Colonial Office in London had forced some changes on the legislature but the over eighty percent majority black Bahamians were not represented properly. The riot on Bay Street in 1942 was the beginning of a movement that would take twenty-five years to eventually see a black majority government in the islands and it marked the end of Bay Street's hegemony.

The Progressive Liberal Party (PLP) led by Lynden Pindling began to voice opposition to Bay Street's white United Bahamian Party (UBP) in the 1950s. Although the PLP was soundly defeated in the 1962 elections, they began to turn the tide of reluctant black voters to their cause and a serious demonstration was held outside the parliament building in 1965, which was known as Black Tuesday. This was the catalyst for political change in the colony and in 1967, Mr. Pindling became the first black premier by a majority in the legislature of one. He then won by a landslide in 1969 and took the colony to independence from Great Britain in 1973.